The Caldey Island Murders

A Pembrokeshire Murder Mystery

Carys Morgan Book 1

M S MORRIS

Margarita Morris and Steve Morris have asserted their right under the Copyright, Designs and Patents Act 1988 to be identified as the authors of this work.

Published by Landmark Media, a division of Landmark Internet Ltd.

M S Morris® and Carys Morgan® are registered trademarks of Landmark Internet Ltd.

msmorrisbooks.com

CHAPTER 1

The bell for Matins rang at three-thirty in the morning.

In the darkness of his cold cell, Father Anselm pushed himself up to standing and straightened his back as far as it would go. His knees throbbed from kneeling on the hard wooden floor. He steadied himself with one hand on the bed frame and reached for his walking stick. Solitary prayer had eluded him this morning despite being awake since three. Now the bell was ringing for Matins, the first of the canonical hours that punctuated the daily lives of the monks of Caldey Island. Father Anselm grasped the door handle with arthritic fingers and stepped into the dimly lit corridor. The bell continued to toll.

The other monks were waiting when he arrived in the cloisters. Their numbers had dwindled in recent years and now only six monks including himself inhabited the large monastery buildings at the heart of the island.

The brothers, as the monks were known, stood apart from each other, not speaking. Ghostly, silent figures in their long white habits. Brother Cadoc, a relatively young man in his fifties, broad-shouldered and strong, acknowledged Father Anselm's arrival with a barely perceptible nod. The abbot felt himself being judged – too old, too slow, too weak. A series of unwelcome thoughts flitted through his mind. Cadoc was a proud man. Cadoc wanted to take over as abbot. Cadoc was waiting for him to die.

As quickly as the idea had arisen, a feeling of guilt rushed in to take its place. Father Anselm chided himself for his uncharitable thought. He sent up a silent prayer. *Forgive me, Lord.* In truth, where would they be without Brother Cadoc? Consigned to the annals of history, no doubt. Of Nigerian descent, the man was able and diligent and did sterling work as the monastery's face of "public relations", a term that Father Anselm understood derived from the secular world of business, although after fifty years in the monastic life he was out of touch with modern linguistic usage. It was thanks to Cadoc's hard work that retreatants continued to enjoy the spiritual benefits of a stay at St Philomena's guest house and that tourists flocked to the island between Easter and October, spending their money in the shop and café, thus ensuring a steady income for the island. The monks – like the other islanders – were of flesh and blood. They couldn't survive on prayer and water alone. No, Brother Cadoc was a good man and they were blessed to have him in their midst.

Still, Father Anselm couldn't quite dispel the feeling of foreboding that had been growing in his heart for weeks. What would happen to the monastery when he was no more? Who would be elected as abbot in his place?

He must have wobbled for a moment because the sturdy figure of Brother Gregory moved to take his arm. A native of North Wales, Gregory was the monastery's chef and healer, feeding their bodies and tending to the sick. It was no secret that he and Cadoc were rivals.

Father Anselm righted himself and put up a hand to ward off Gregory. He was not ready to admit defeat just yet. The brothers lined up behind him and the abbot led his flock toward the monastery church.

The bell ceased as Novice Thomas – the youngest and fittest member of the community – joined the end of the line and for a couple of minutes there was no sound apart from the shuffling of feet and the occasional tap of a rubber-tipped walking stick on the stone-tiled floor of the cloister. Beyond the monastery walls, it was still dark and the islanders were – Father Anselm assumed – sound asleep in their beds. Only the monks were awake at this unearthly hour before dawn on a cold October morning.

Brother Gregory stepped forward to push open the heavy south door of the church, then moved aside in deference to Father Anselm who entered first.

The sight that met his eyes caused him to stop in his tracks and cry out – an inarticulate expression of shock like an unholy mix of prayer and profanity. He staggered and thought his legs would give out beneath him. For once he was grateful for Gregory's strong arm that gripped his own and held him upright. He was only vaguely aware of the other monks crowding in behind him, curious to see what had caused this sudden exclamation from their leader.

Brother Cadoc – inevitably – took charge. 'Come and sit down, Father.' To the rest of the monks he commanded, 'Stay back, all of you. Do not enter.'

No one listened to him.

In too much shock to protest, Father Anselm allowed Gregory and Cadoc to manoeuvre him into the nearest pew. He sank down wearily, his head in his hands. *What dreadful evil has visited this holy place?*

Very slowly, he lifted his gaze.

The body of a young woman lay across the altar. Her arms were folded over her chest like those of a medieval effigy on a tomb. She appeared to have been stabbed multiple times and her blood had run and stained the stone altar with streaks of crimson red.

The abbot's breath caught in his throat and a tear trickled down his lined face. The horror was too much to behold. Anselm sank to his knees and the other monks followed suit. A lone voice started to sing the words of the

Requiem Mass. *Requiem aeternam dona eis, Domine.* Grant them eternal rest, O Lord.

Beyond the monastery walls, a single owl hooted above the moan of the wind.

CHAPTER 2

'You won't forget to pick Billy up from after-school football club at five-thirty, will you, love? Only I promised Mrs Pryce I'd do her roots and a cut and blow-dry at five. She can't get away during the day now she's looking after the grandchildren. Her daughter's gone back to work at that new shop that's opened in the town centre, d'you know the one I mean?'

Rhodri Evans nodded mutely through a mouthful of toast and jam. His wife's instructions were always so full of extraneous detail that he'd long since learned to filter out most of what she said and only retain the bits that were relevant to him. *Billy, football club, five-thirty.* He'd already forgotten the rest.

'Oh, and another thing,' continued Amy, wiping Lila's face and piling dirty dishes into the sink, 'could you pick up more bread on your way home? The one we like, you know? Only I used half a loaf making sandwiches for Mrs Dillon across the road. She can't get out to the shops now she's had her hip operation and if you don't buy another loaf there won't be enough for Billy's sandwiches tomorrow. Go and clean your teeth now, Billy. Hurry up, we're late.'

Billy ran from the room and clattered up the stairs. There was the sound of water gushing in the bathroom.

Loaf of bread. Rhodri mentally added it to his list of instructions. *Billy, five-thirty, bread.* He could manage all that. Just as long as there was nothing else to remember. Three items was his limit. More than that, and there'd be trouble.

'And can you get a pint of milk too?' asked Amy, checking her reflection in the mirror and pushing a stray lock of blonde hair back into position. 'You know how much Billy drinks after football.'

'Mmm,' said Rhodri, washing down his toast with a glass of orange juice. *Billy, bread, milk.* He'd got this.

Billy reappeared in the kitchen, his school sweatshirt splashed with water.

'Right, must dash,' said Amy, wiping a smear of toothpaste from Billy's nose and scooping Lila into her arms. She gathered up Billy's school bag and football kit, and grabbed her car keys from the hallway table. 'You won't forget now, will you, Rod?'

Rhodri shook his head. 'Course not. Billy, bread, milk. No worries.' He smiled and helped Billy into his coat and shoes, ruffling the boy's hair. 'See you later, mate.' He gave Lila a kiss on the forehead. 'And you too, princess.'

'Love you,' said Amy, pecking him on the cheek.

'Love you too,' said Rhodri.

Then Amy and the kids were out of the door in a flurry of coats and bags and he had a moment of blissful peace and quiet to himself. Time for one more piece of toast and a chance to catch up with the sports news before work.

His phone rang.

He frowned at the screen. Detective Chief Inspector Gareth Pritchard. It was rare for Rhodri's boss at Haverfordwest to call him at home, especially at eight o'clock on a Monday morning. Had Rhodri forgotten an important meeting? The *digital forensics awareness* course was next week, he was sure of it.

'Morning, sir?' he answered warily.

'Rhodri, you need to get yourself over to Caldey Island ASAP.' No greeting. No apology for the early call. Just an order. Pritchard wasn't usually such a dragon. The DCI's breathing sounded laboured and Rhodri pictured him pacing his office. What on earth had happened?

'Caldey Island?' Rhodri was bemused. The little island off the coast of Tenby was a haven of tranquillity. Hardly a crime hotspot.

'A suspicious death has been reported. Uniforms and SOCO went over at first light on the lifeboat, but someone from CID needs to take charge.'

Rhodri heard the words and his chest swelled with pride. He was about to be made Senior Investigating Officer in a murder investigation. Finally, Pritchard had recognised his potential. As a recently promoted detective sergeant with Dyfed-Powys Police, this was a golden opportunity. A fast track towards his next promotion. There would be overtime too, and that would help with the family's ever-stretched finances. He couldn't wait to tell Amy. The news would put a stop to her nagging him about money and maybe they could take that holiday he'd been dreaming of...

He realised that Pritchard was still talking and that he'd missed most of what the older man had been saying. That habit of filtering things out of conversations – it should really only apply to his wife.

'...and so the new DI from Cardiff will be leading the investigation,' Pritchard was saying, 'and will meet you at the harbour in Tenby. Eifion James is waiting to take both of you over in his boat.'

'The new DI from Cardiff,' echoed Rhodri. 'Right you are, sir.'

The feeling of excitement he'd enjoyed so briefly rapidly dissipated. He wasn't going to be SIO after all. Yet what he felt wasn't disappointment but relief. Could he really have handled the pressure of running a murder inquiry? *Billy, bread, milk.* Life was frantic enough without more responsibility.

The new DI from Cardiff... he remembered hearing something on the grapevine about a high-flyer transferring to Pembrokeshire from the capital but couldn't recall their name. Had Pritchard mentioned it just now? He couldn't ask or he'd look a fool. 'I'll get down to the harbour now then, sir. Thanks for...'

But Pritchard had already hung up.

Rhodri hastily crammed the breakfast bowls into the dishwasher, resigned himself to checking the football results later, then headed out the door. Usually he drove his VW camper van to work, but today he left it outside his tiny terraced cottage in Trafalgar Road and set off on foot towards the harbour, no more than a four-minute walk at his brisk pace.

Rhodri had lived in Tenby all twenty-eight years of his life and knew its winding streets and alleyways like the back of his hand. He took a couple of shortcuts, striding alongside the old town walls that flanked White Lion Street, and emerged onto Crackwell Street, a narrow, cobbled road that led steeply downhill to the harbour. According to legend, Henry Tudor had escaped through a tunnel beneath these houses when he fled into exile in France, to return later and claim the throne as the first Tudor king of England. An old school friend of Rhodri's, Jon Jenkins, claimed to have seen those tunnels with his own eyes. But Jon Jenkins was a born liar, and Rhodri didn't believe his story for a moment. Nevertheless, the tunnels were real enough – one of many historical features that linked the town with its past.

To Rhodri's right stood the pretty rows of pastel-painted Georgian houses for which Tenby was so famous. Even on a dull day like this, they shone amid the gloom. Their seafront location and period charm were enough to push their prices way beyond anything he and Amy could ever hope to reach, although that didn't stop her from fantasising about living in one, one day. At the bottom of the hill lay the harbour, slowly emerging from the early morning autumn mist. To his left were the sands of the North Beach, tucked beneath the graceful curve of the bay. The town was lucky enough to have three beaches – North, South and Castle – as well as a harbour and a lifeboat station. Tenby had started out as a fortified port in the Middle Ages, complete with a curtain wall, towers and gates, and its Welsh name, *Dinbych-y-Pysgod*, meant "little fortress of the fish", a name that had conjured up comical images in the head of the young Rhodri Evans of sea bass and pollack dressed in suits of armour brandishing spears and shields. These days, the fishing was confined to tourist trips, and the old stone walls served no purpose other than to make the town's traffic even more congested during the peak season of July and August.

A fresh October breeze, heavy with moisture and salt, tugged at Rhodri's hair. The tourist season was well and truly over for another year. Yet the sight of the sea always awakened in him a longing to get back on his surfboard.

Surfing wasn't simply his hobby, it was his passion. In his younger days, he had lived for the rhythm of a rising swell, for the split-second reading of the shifting waters. And when he caught the right wave, when the board lifted him up and he felt that rush, that wild, pure exhilaration of riding a force of nature that nobody could tame, there was nothing in the world that even came close.

The golden sands of Freshwater West had the best surfing around here, but he rarely got a chance to go there these days, and his board stood neglected in the shed at the back of the house. There just wasn't time in between work and home life. He'd married his childhood sweetheart when they were both just twenty-two. Now here he was, six years later, with a five-year-old and a two-year-old. How had that happened? He loved his family to bits – he really did! – but sometimes felt as if he'd been tied down too young. None of his mates had kids yet. None of them were even married.

He arrived at the bottom of Pier Hill and spotted Eifion James on the quayside beside his boat, a thirty-foot open launch. Perfect in sunny weather, not so great when it poured with rain.

The boatman was a familiar figure around Tenby. During the tourist season between Easter and October he ferried visitors out to Caldey Island and back all day long. As a teenager, Rhodri had spent one summer helping Eifion on the boat, jumping ashore with the rope when they landed at Priory Bay on Caldey or returned to Tenby.

'All right there, Eifion?'

'All right, Rhodri?'

Unlike Amy, Eifion was a man of few words. Rhodri didn't mind that. You always knew where you were with him. Eifion understood the sea and Rhodri, as a surfer, respected that.

'What's it like out today?' Rhodri nodded towards the expanse of grey sea churning at the base of the harbour wall.

'There's a swell running up from the west. An Atlantic storm's brewing.'

Rhodri imagined the long, rising waves and wished he was out on his board. Cold weather was never a problem, not if the surf was up.

'It's going to get dirty later this week,' continued Eifion. 'You won't want to be out when the storm hits.'

Rhodri checked his watch. 'Pritchard said you'd be taking me out to the island. We just need to wait for the new DI to arrive.'

Eifion nodded. 'I'll get the engine started. She takes a bit of warming up these days. Getting on a bit, she is, just like her owner.' He stroked his bushy grey beard, then clambered into the boat and started the engine. After a few attempts, it coughed hesitantly into life then settled into a slow, reluctant chug. Diesel fumes filled the air. Eifion was right – that engine was on its last legs.

Rhodri wandered along the pier, looking for anyone who might resemble a hotshot detective inspector from Cardiff. Rhodri pictured someone dressed for the city in a smart suit and tie. He laughed to himself, thinking of the oil-stained ropes that coiled like snakes in the bottom of Eifion's boat, and the damage that salt water spray could wreak on polished leather shoes.

But there was no one on the harbourside that fitted the description.

The town was slowly waking up. A team of builders parked their van in front of one of the terraced houses overlooking the harbour and began unloading and setting up a cement mixer. Rhodri waved to them, recognising them as locals. A pair of elderly off-season tourists in matching navy cagoules hovered expectantly by the ticket kiosk, no doubt hoping for a day trip to Caldey Island. They would be disappointed. The island was off-limits today and the kiosk was closed. They soon changed their minds and set off up the hill in the direction of Tenby Castle and the Prince Albert Memorial.

A woman in a dark green duffel coat and a plum-coloured beret emerged from St Julian's Street, walking briskly. She wore Dr Martens boots and a hand-knitted scarf looped double around her neck. Loose black hair escaped from her beret, and there was a distinct second-hand look to her coat and the thick woollen jumper she wore beneath it. Rhodri attempted to intercept her, but she strode straight past him and headed for Eifion's boat.

With a sigh, Rhodri set off after her. He'd have to tell her there were no public trips to Caldey today. She was already trying to attract Eifion's attention. The old sailor emerged from his cabin and gazed up at her, nonplussed.

'Excuse me,' called Rhodri. 'I'm afraid this boat's reserved for official police business.'

The woman turned to face him, her shoulder-length hair blowing across her face, her coat flapping in the breeze. At close quarters, Rhodri could see that she wasn't much older than him – perhaps mid-thirties. A Celtic cross dangled around her neck on a silver chain. 'Are you DS Rhodri Evans?'

'I am,' said Rhodri, becoming aware that he'd probably just made a howling error.

An amused expression flickered in her green eyes like fire. 'Detective Inspector Carys Morgan.' She turned away and Eifion held out a hand to help her down into the boat. She ignored him, stepping lightly into the boat unaided, like a pro.

Shit! Rhodri knew he'd made a complete idiot of himself. But how was he supposed to know that the new DI would show up looking like she worked in a charity shop?

He climbed down to join her and Eifion clapped him heartily on the shoulder. 'Well done, lad.'

Rhodri grimaced.

Carys had already taken up position in the bow. 'What are you boys waiting for, then?' she asked. 'Shall we get going?'

CHAPTER 3

Rosalind Greaves pushed open the door of St Illtud's church and stepped inside, shivering in the half-light of early morning. The heavy oak door banged shut behind her and she felt herself enclosed within the ancient walls. She paused, breathing in the still, cold air, then made her way cautiously over the pebbled floor, the stones polished smooth by the tread of feet over hundreds of years. A row of wooden seats ran along each wall, facing inwards.

As she approached them, she felt that familiar thrill of history coming alive, and she pictured medieval monks sitting there, heads bowed in silence. One of them would have a dark and sinister secret on his mind. What would he be plotting while his brothers prayed?

In a career spanning twenty years, Rosalind had written and published – with modest success and some critical acclaim – a series of medieval murder mysteries featuring her intrepid protagonist, Brother Aidan. But now, in her sixtieth year, she found herself suffering from writer's block. How to take the series forward? That was the question that kept her awake at night. Her recent sales hadn't been as high as the earlier books, the reviews less glowing. This year, she had not been invited to speak at any of the main literary festivals. Her star was dimming and she feared that her publisher might drop her in favour of some bright new thing with a photogenic smile and an Instagram following – one of the new young voices emerging every day, so it seemed, from the creative writing academies that were springing up like mushrooms on a damp autumnal day. Writing retreats to the islands of Lindisfarne and Iona had resulted in two of her most successful books and she hoped that a few days imbibing the atmosphere of Caldey Island with its medieval monastic history would exert the same magical influence on her creativity.

She approached the Ogham Stone which stood against one wall. Roughly six feet tall and eighteen inches across, it dated from the sixth century and bore inscriptions in Latin and in Ogham script. She reached out a hand, touched the broken stone with the tips of her fingers, closed her eyes, and allowed her mind to wander freely, opening herself up to the possibilities of serendipity.

Here in this thirteenth-century church, breathing the air of centuries past, in communion with the ancient stone, she could clearly picture her rugged hero making the arduous journey from Northumbria on horseback – *how long would that take?* – on a secret mission from the Venerable Bede – *could she weave a reference to the Lindisfarne Gospels into the story?* – then rowing single-handedly across the choppy waters of Carmarthen Bay to arrive at Caldey Island in the dead of night only to find...

The door creaked open, startling her out of her train of thought. She had been on the brink of discovering Aidan's next compelling adventure – he had been so real to her in that instant that she could have reached out and touched the hem of his habit. But now, with the sound of footsteps and the cold gust of wind that blew in with them, her inspiration was gone, like a dream dissolving into nothingness when the alarm clock rang.

She frowned at the intruder. It was Paul Roberts, one of the other guests staying at St Philomena's. Five of them – strangers to each other – had sailed from Tenby harbour on Saturday morning in a boat with a taciturn sailor – *a bearded sea dog who had endured many a winter's storm* – and an engine that sounded as if it was choking on its own fuel. There were two other men and one woman in the group. So far, they hadn't had much to do with each other apart from at mealtimes, which were served by the old, but sprightly Sister Monica. Last night, after dinner, Rosalind had attempted to engage the other woman – Sarah Black – in conversation about her reasons for coming to Caldey, but Sarah had been unwilling to talk. Rosalind wondered if she might be escaping an abusive relationship but hadn't liked to press the matter.

Rosalind had been the first of the group to go to bed and the first down to breakfast this morning. Sister Monica had made her a coffee and then told her to help herself to whatever she fancied because she had been called to the abbey church on an urgent matter of business. Rosalind wondered if one of the monks had been taken ill – or even died. Many of them were getting on in years. She had eaten a light breakfast, then decided to make the most of her early start and explore the island on her own. Solitude was essential to her for discovering the seed of a new story.

But now her contemplation had been rudely interrupted.

The door banged shut and Paul approached her, his rubber-soled shoes making an irritating squeaking sound on the stone floor. 'Great minds think alike,' he said, nodding towards the Ogham Stone.

Don't flatter yourself. In the short time she had known Paul Roberts, she had found him to be overbearing and arrogant. He was a schoolteacher who liked to show off his knowledge of everything – history, geography, wildlife – and had bored them all on the first evening recounting at length the history of the Benedictine Order – a subject that Rosalind had researched extensively before coming to

Caldey. On discovering that she wrote mysteries, he had patronisingly declared that he only read non-fiction. What were his words exactly? *I prefer facts to flights of fancy,* thus dismissing the power of the imagination and her life's work. She had done her best to steer clear of him since then.

'Did you know the Ogham Stone was excavated in the grounds of the priory in the eighteenth century?' he said now, going straight into his teacher mode.

'Yes, I did, actually,' she said curtly. She might write fiction but that didn't mean her stories weren't firmly rooted in historical fact. She was willing to bet she knew more about the island and its monastic history than he did.

He moved closer and she could smell his unpleasant breath. His appearance was shabby and she found his physical presence oppressive. 'But its origins are much earlier than that,' he continued as if she hadn't spoken.

She took a step back. 'Yes, I am perfectly aware of–'

He spoke over her. 'See these markings on the edge of the stone? That's Ogham script. It's an early Irish alphabet used in medieval texts. The stone refers to Bishop Dubricius, who consecrated Samson as the second abbot of Caldey in the sixth-century community.'

'That's right,' she said, seeking to put him in his place. 'Do you know the story? The first abbot died after falling into the monastery well while drunk.'

Paul wrinkled his nose in disapproval. That clearly wasn't the kind of history he liked. She had a sudden vision of pushing him down a well herself. Sometimes her novelist's imagination ran away with her. Was that a bad thing?

She moved away, keen to escape and to return to the safety of St Philomena's, but Paul followed her.

'The stations of the cross,' he announced abruptly.

Against her better judgement, she turned back. 'I'm sorry?'

'See here,' he said, pointing at a series of small wooden carvings fixed to the walls on both sides of the church. 'The fourteen stations of the cross. They depict the Passion of Christ from the moment he was condemned to death to the moment he was laid in the tomb.'

A shiver ran down her spine. This talk of death was making her uncomfortable. What was his point? Did he just want to show off his knowledge? Or was there a hidden meaning behind his words?

And then another thought disturbed her.

Had he followed her all the way across the island to St Illtud's? She had come early in the morning to be alone, and yet of all the places he could have gone, here he was. A coincidence? Or something more sinister? Brother Aidan, her protagonist, didn't believe in coincidences. He would challenge someone like Paul Roberts. She should do the same.

'You said last night you're a teacher. But it's not the school holidays. Are you taking a sabbatical?' She kept her voice light and curious, but her novelist's instinct told her there was a dark story lurking in Paul Roberts's life.

He turned his penetrating stare on her, but his mouth remained firmly closed.

Well, that's one way to shut you up.

'It's time I was heading back,' she said aloud, hurrying towards the door. He didn't follow her.

Outside, she breathed a sigh of relief, then set off in the direction of St Philomena's, keen to be among other people. Real people for once, and not just her fictional creations.

CHAPTER 4

The tide was in, so the boat carrying the detectives took the shortest route to Caldey Island, sailing between the mainland and the small tidal island of St Catherine's with its nineteenth-century fort built in response to the threat of invasion by Napoleon III.

From her position in the bow, Carys watched the receding shoreline – the steep, rough rock faces and the grand houses on the clifftop painted in pastel blues, yellows, pinks and creams. She had been living in Cardiff for the past fifteen years with only occasional trips to Pembrokeshire to visit her sister and grandmother. Now she was back for the foreseeable future and she was trying to get used to the idea that this was her home once more.

She had grown up, and was now living again, in the tiny village of Manorbier, fifteen miles along the coast to the west of Tenby. As a child, Tenby had been the "big town" where you went when you needed new clothes or shoes. It had always seemed busy, full of shops and restaurants and bustling with tourists. Now she saw it with urban eyes. Undoubtedly pretty with its colourful houses, quaint old streets and dramatic clifftop setting. But very small. And

Manorbier was even tinier. Part of her longed to return to the city she had left.

As the boat moved beyond St Catherine's Island and headed into deeper water, the bow rose with the swell of the waves. Rhodri stood in the cabin at the back of the boat with Eifion. He hadn't spoken to her since they'd set sail. She imagined he was feeling quite foolish having mistaken her for a tourist at the harbour. It had been funny really, although she felt a little mean for allowing him to jump to the wrong conclusion. She was aware that she didn't conform to people's expectations of what a detective ought to look like. People labelled her eccentric, unconventional – rebellious even – and she never tried to blend in. Life was too short to live by other people's rules. As for her first impressions of her new sergeant, he seemed likeable enough, although perhaps he shouldn't have allowed his prejudices to get the better of him quite so easily. She would keep an open mind and see how he performed on the job.

A thin drizzle had set in since leaving the harbour. Carys had forgotten how much it rained in this part of the world. On this western tip of Wales, you were closer to Dublin than London, and the weather was shaped by the Atlantic. Locals joked that in Pembrokeshire you could get four seasons in one day, and that wasn't far from the truth.

A wave crashed against the boat, covering her in spray, and she dipped her hand into her coat pocket to find the iron key she kept there. She turned it over in her fingers for reassurance, but knew she'd need more than a good luck charm to keep her dry. If she stayed in the bow, she'd be soaked before she even reached the island. She stood up and made her way towards the stern.

'It's getting a bit wet out there,' she said, ducking into the shelter of the cabin. It was a tight squeeze with three of them in there.

Eifion kept his hands on the wheel and steered the boat head on into another wave. 'I've seen worse.'

'I'm sure you have. How long have you been sailing to

Caldey?'

'Longer than I care to remember. Must be forty years now.'

'You take tourists in the summer?'

Eifion nodded. 'Day trippers mostly. Season runs Easter to October. Folk go to visit the monastery, and also to see the wildlife – birds and seals mainly. Then there are those who stay at St Philomena's on retreat. I also ferry the islanders back and forth when they need to visit the mainland and I bring the post over.' He tapped a grey canvas bag with his foot.

Carys nodded. After life in the city, it was hard to imagine a place so isolated that the post had to be brought across by boat. Food and other supplies also had to be ferried from the mainland. Yet that isolation was the very reason for the monastery's existence. 'Is there any other way to reach the island?'

Eifion shook his head.

Carys smiled. 'What would they do without you?'

Eifion shrugged modestly. 'Mine isn't the only boat that makes the journey, but not all skippers enjoy going out in rough weather.'

As if to prove his point, he skilfully swung the boat to meet an oncoming wave, lifting the stern over the rising swell as it broke across the cabin roof. Neither Eifion nor Rhodri batted an eyelid, but Carys was glad she had chosen to take shelter within the cabin.

Now they were getting closer, she could see the top of the lighthouse on the far side of the island. Immediately ahead of them lay a flat strip of coastline bordered by trees. The entire island measured only one mile by a mile and a half.

They docked at a jetty beside a small beach – Priory Bay, if she remembered correctly. Rhodri jumped ashore with obvious agility. Eifion flung him the rope, and he tied it to a metal bollard with practised skill.

'You look as if you've done this before,' said Carys.

'I had a summer job on the boats as a teenager,' said

Rhodri. 'I learned from the best.' He nodded towards Eifion.

For a moment Carys felt like an outsider. Fifteen years in the Welsh capital must practically make her a foreigner in the eyes of some of the locals. But then Rhodri held out his hand.

She didn't really need help, but she accepted it graciously, clambering ashore. His grip was strong and reassuring after the choppy ride. As she acclimatised herself to dry land, a monk in a white habit emerged from the woodland and came down the path to meet them.

The newcomer cut an imposing figure, tall, muscular and handsome. His skin was a striking black against the plain undyed wool of his habit. His black hair was silvered at the temples. Carys judged him to be in his fifties.

His voice was deep and harmonious. 'Brother Cadoc. May I welcome you to Caldey. I wish you were here under more auspicious circumstances.'

'DI Carys Morgan and DS Rhodri Williams,' said Carys.

If the monk was disconcerted to find a woman in charge of the police operation, he showed no sign of it. On the contrary, his manner was friendly and open, as if he was used to welcoming all kinds of visitors. 'If you would care to follow me, I'll take you directly to the scene of the murder.'

They set off up the path, leaving Eifion checking the engine on his boat. The motor had growled like a grizzly bear on the way over and Carys hoped the boat would get them back at the end of the day.

'You believe it was murder, then?' she said to Brother Cadoc.

'No doubt about that,' said the monk. 'Although who might commit such a dreadful atrocity is beyond my understanding.'

The path wound through the dense woodland up a gentle incline. A man in a dark green waterproof jacket, corduroy trousers and stout boots was chopping logs with an axe in a clearing beside the remains of a smoking bonfire. He was mid- to late-forties, dark-haired and bearded, with skin bronzed and weathered. Brother Cadoc held up a hand in greeting, but the man swung his axe over his shoulder and stomped into the woods without a word.

Unperturbed by this apparent slight, Brother Cadoc said, 'That's Dafydd Rees, the island's gardener and woodsman. He does a fine job keeping this place well-tended.'

They passed a sign pointing to St Philomena's.

'That's our guest house where people come to stay on short retreats,' explained Brother Cadoc.

'How long do people stay?' asked Carys.

'Usually no more than a week.'

'How many retreatants are here now?'

'Five, I believe,' answered Cadoc.

They turned a corner and the monastery rose up in front of them. It wasn't a traditional medieval abbey in the style of Tintern or Tewkesbury, but a magnificent, white-painted building in the Arts and Crafts tradition with a red-tiled roof, arched windows, towers and turrets. It dominated the tiny village below, which consisted of little more than a row of whitewashed cottages, a souvenir shop, a café and a post office with a steeply sloping roof and more arched windows. The buildings were set around an expanse of grass. Picnic tables on the lawn outside the café were deserted. Opposite the café was a fishpond, overgrown with reeds.

'The abbey church is this way,' said their guide, leading them up a long flight of stone steps at the side of the abbey. The steps were bordered on both sides with trees that met in the middle to form a canopy. The island's woodsman, Dafydd Rees, may not have shown much affection for the monk or the visiting detectives, but he clearly loved his plants.

At the threshold of the church, Carys stopped and closed her eyes for a second. It was a habit of hers always to acknowledge when she was stepping from the secular world into a sacred place. She briefly touched the cross she wore around her neck, then switched back into her police persona. This was also the scene of a shocking crime and it was her job to get justice for the victim, whoever she may be.

CHAPTER 5

T he study where Father Anselm performed his practical duties as abbot was modest in size, sparsely furnished and warmed only by a small paraffin heater, but for once he was glad to escape from the holy setting of the abbey church and immerse himself in earthly concerns. The horror of what he had seen at Matins was burned into his memory, and he could hardly shake it from his mind.

What devil has come to stalk this sacred place? And under my watch! Oh Lord, what have I done to deserve this?

'I've prepared a list of everything we need to see us through the winter months, now that the weather is starting to turn and boats from the mainland will be less frequent,' said Brother Gregory, breaking through the abbot's private thoughts and giving him some welcome relief from the vision of the murdered girl, her body draped across the altar like an unholy sacrifice. 'The vegetable harvest was poor this year, the spring too wet and the summer too dry, and so we must stock up on tinned food. We may be holy men, but we must still eat.' Gregory patted his well-rounded stomach and handed the abbot a handwritten shopping list.

Father Anselm cast an eye over the list – tinned beans, tinned fruit, tinned soup – their storeroom would look like a supermarket, not that he had been inside a supermarket in well over half a century. The total came to nine hundred pounds. *Nine hundred pounds!* To feed six monks, two of them so frail that they ate like sparrows and might not live to see another spring?

'Prices have risen,' said Brother Gregory. 'That's the modern world for you.'

'I realise that,' said Father Anselm. 'I'm not completely out of touch.' He knew that people in the outside world were facing all sorts of difficulties due to the cost of living – a reality of life from which the monks were largely immune. Still, money was always a consideration, even when one had taken a vow of poverty.

He removed his reading glasses and regarded his fellow monk. Brother Gregory, the monastery's cook and herbalist, was someone he trusted. Gregory was a practical man, who had been a farmer before becoming a monk. A few years older than Brother Cadoc, Gregory also held ambitions to become abbot when Father Anselm passed away. Whereas Cadoc was the modern outward face of the monastery, Gregory knew its inner workings and traditions better than anyone. Both men were strong contenders to take over the running of the monastery, yet both were limited by their blinkered perspectives and fierce rivalry.

'Between you and me,' Anselm began, 'I'm concerned about how today's tragic discovery will affect our financial position. Our only source of income is from the tourists. I quite understand why the police have closed the island today, but if this goes on too long, and when news of this appalling tragedy is made public...'

Brother Gregory stroked his long beard and nodded his head thoughtfully. 'Not only may we face a drop in income, we risk attracting the wrong sort of visitor when the island reopens.'

Father Anselm gave an involuntary shudder at the

thought of morbid hordes wielding mobile phones, chasing sensation and posting lurid pictures on the internet. Caldey Island was a haven of peace and tranquillity, where monks lived a contemplative life of spiritual harmony, the handful of villagers ensured the island's upkeep, and visitors came to find solace in God and nature. And to spend their money in the café and gift shop.

But evil walked among them and now it seemed to Father Anselm that their very existence was under threat.

A knock at the door roused him from his brooding. 'Come in.'

Novice Thomas stuck his head around the door. The sight of their one and only novice – a young man in his early thirties – gave Father Anselm a feeling of hope. In the years ahead it would be down to men like Thomas to ensure that the monastery had a future when he, Father Anselm – and Cadoc and Gregory too, for that matter – had gone to meet their Maker.

'I beg your pardon for the interruption, Father,' said Thomas, 'but Brother Cadoc sent me to tell you that the detectives have arrived. DI Carys Morgan accompanied by DS Rhodri Evans.'

'A woman is in charge of the investigation?'

'Yes, Father. It would appear so.'

The abbot sighed. He supposed this was the way the world was going, but it wasn't how things had been in his youth, nor still within the Catholic Church. 'Well, that's going to be awkward, isn't it?'

Brother Gregory chuckled into his beard.

*

Rhodri followed Carys into the church, watching as she touched her cross and murmured a few words before crossing the threshold. Rhodri wasn't religious and had no idea what to make of her. She'd barely addressed a word to him on the boat ride over or on the walk up from Priory Bay. He was usually good with people, but how was he going to get along with his new boss if she didn't talk to him? He wished DC Elen Vaughan was here too. Elen wasn't just a colleague – she was a good mate. He could work with Elen. But Carys? The jury was still out.

He turned his attention to his surroundings. He had been expecting something a lot grander but the monastery church was really very plain – stark white walls, a wooden beamed roof, and two rows of choir stalls looking across at each other like in the House of Commons. The scene of crime officers were already at work in their head-to-toe white suits, crawling over the floor on their hands and knees, marking, labelling, photographing. Rhodri recognised the lead SOCO officer and thought he might make himself useful by introducing him to Carys, but Carys was already making her way over to him. Rhodri hurried to catch up.

'Morning,' Carys was saying. 'I'm DI Carys Morgan. I'll be leading the investigation.'

'Pleased to meet you. Anthony Davies.' The head of SOCO gave her one of his glowing smiles.

Rhodri knew the SOCO boss from previous cases he'd worked on. Anthony was tall with fair wavy hair, penetrating blue eyes and movie-star looks. He was also super smart, with a PhD in forensic science. He was modest too, never introducing himself as *Dr Davies*, simply *Anthony*. He had caught the attention of more than one female officer and Rhodri had brooded on the unfairness of life – some guys seemed to have everything women wanted – until Elen had informed him that Anthony was gay and in a longstanding relationship with his partner, Matthew, an artist. After that, Rhodri had felt much more relaxed in Anthony's presence.

Anthony acknowledged Rhodri with a smile of recognition. 'All right, mate? Would you like to see the body?'

Rhodri shrugged. *If I have to.* He never enjoyed this part of the job. Who in their right mind would? He preferred to spend his time in the company of the living, not the dead. But he hid his misgivings and did his best to appear keen.

Anthony led them to the far end of the church, pointing out a safe path for them to follow on stepping plates to avoid contaminating the scene. Carys went right up to the altar, but Rhodri hung back. He could see more than enough from where he was.

The victim lay on the altar, a rectangular block of creamy sandstone, now stained with her blood. She was youngish – in her thirties perhaps – and wore a black leather jacket, a white shirt, skinny jeans and black ankle boots. Her blonde hair – darker at the roots – hung over the side of the altar. Her arms were folded over her chest like a stone effigy.

To her credit, Carys appeared horrified by the sight of the woman's body and the violence that had been perpetrated against her, but she overcame her initial reaction and leaned in closer for a better look. 'Interesting,' she murmured, examining the victim from the top of her head to the tip of her black boots.

'She was struck here, here, and here,' said Anthony pointing out locations near the victim's heart, throat and belly. 'It looks like a frenzied attack. The wounds are more like slashes than thrusts.'

'Frenzied, hmm,' murmured Carys, 'or very deliberate. The body has clearly been carefully staged.'

Rhodri turned away, feeling bile rising. He couldn't be sick, not here, not now.

'You can go outside for some fresh air if you need to, Rhodri?' said Carys without turning around.

'I'll be fine,' he answered, though feeling the opposite.

'If you say so.' Carys turned her attention back to Anthony. 'You've documented the blood spatter, I presume?'

He nodded. 'We've measured everything so it can be modelled later by the blood pattern analyst in the lab. But what I can tell you is that we've got three distinct strikes from a sharp blade of some kind. The trail of droplets towards the west door' – he pointed towards the door through which they'd entered – 'suggests she tried to escape, but she likely fell here.' He indicated a larger pool of blood beside one of the choir stalls. 'This line of drops across the floor suggests the victim was then dragged or carried to the altar where she bled out.'

'Yes,' said Carys, her eyes quickly taking in the details. 'So she may still have been alive when she was moved to the altar. Is there any trace of blood outside the church?'

'None,' said Anthony.

'There are two doors into the church,' said Carys. 'The west door is open to visitors, but what about the south door?' She indicated a second door between the choir stalls and the altar.

'I can answer that,' said Brother Cadoc who had been lurking on the periphery of the scene throughout. 'That door leads directly into the abbey grounds. Members of the public do not have access there, so the victim couldn't have entered that way.'

'The victim, no,' said Carys. 'But what about the killer?'

Cadoc's mouth fell open as if Carys had uttered the most damning blasphemy. 'From the abbey? That's impossible!'

Rhodri was inclined to agree with Brother Cadoc. He understood that Carys was keeping an open mind, but surely she didn't think a monk was capable of this deranged attack?

'This was found lying open on the victim's torso,' said Anthony, handing Carys a clear plastic evidence bag.

Rhodri peered over her shoulder to get a better look. The bag contained a Bible, open on a particular page. It was visibly stained with the victim's blood.

Brother Cadoc gasped. 'That looks like one of the Bibles kept at the back of the church. They're provided for use by the congregation during services. Members of the public are always welcome to join us here in prayer. Why was it placed on the body?'

'Because the killer was sending a message.' Carys's voice rang out clearly in the echoing space of the church as she read from the open book. 'Ecclesiastes chapter nine, verse five. "The living know at least that they will die, the dead know nothing; no more reward for them; their memory has passed out of mind."'

The words hung in the air, bleak and ominous.

Carys handed the Bible back to Anthony, still sealed in its plastic bag. 'Do we have any identification for the victim yet?'

'I can help you with that,' said Brother Cadoc. He gestured for an elderly woman sitting at the back of the church to join them. 'This is Sister Monica. She looks after the guests staying at St Philomena's.'

The elderly nun rose to her feet and walked towards them with a surprising sprightliness. She was rosy-cheeked and bright-eyed. If she hadn't been wearing a nun's habit, Rhodri would have characterised her as an idealised grandmother figure – warm and caring but with a wickedly fun side. He was willing to bet she played a ruthless game of Monopoly.

Sister Monica cast a glance in the direction of the body on the altar before addressing Carys, speaking with a pronounced European accent. 'The poor girl. She's one of the retreatants staying at St Philomena's. Her name is Sarah Black.'

Rhodri reached for his notebook and wrote the victim's name.

'What can you tell us about her?' asked Carys.

'Not much,' answered Sister Monica. 'She kept to herself most of the time. That's not unusual. Our guests come here for peace and quiet. We gather together at mealtimes, but there are no fixed activities during the day. People often spend time alone in their room or walking the island.'

'Did Sarah come to the island alone?'

'She arrived with the current group of retreatants. Five people came over on the boat from Tenby two days ago, but they were all travelling solo. I don't believe that any of them knew each other before arriving.'

'We'll need to obtain her full details from you,' said Carys. 'Her next of kin will need to be informed.'

'Of course,' said Sister Monica. 'I've already gathered together all the information I have.' She held out a few sheets of folded paper.

'Thank you,' said Carys.

Rhodri felt it was about time he made a contribution to the investigation. 'How often is the church used for services?' he asked.

It was Brother Cadoc who answered. 'Eight times every day. The services follow a strict timetable, based on the canonical hours. The monastic day begins at half past three in the morning with Matins, and the last service, Compline, finishes at eight in the evening.'

Rhodri raised his eyebrows as he made a note of the times. *Half past three.* He hadn't been up that early since Lila was a baby. 'And was that when the body was found? At Matins?'

'That's right.'

'Who discovered it?'

'It was all of us, together,' said Cadoc. 'The monks, that is. We entered the church as a group, although Father Anselm was the first to see the body.'

'Presumably you didn't notice anything out of the ordinary when the last service of the previous day took place?'

'Correct.'

Eight services a day seemed excessive to Rhodri, but at least they now had a window of just over seven hours during which time the murder must have occurred.

'We'll need to speak to everyone on the island,' said Carys. 'The retreatants, the monks and the islanders. I'd like to start with the abbot.' She looked at Brother Cadoc, clearly expecting him to arrange a meeting immediately. 'Can you show me to his study?'

The monk cleared his throat. 'That would be rather

difficult.'

'In what way?' Carys's voice was sharp, with an edge as keen as the blade used to murder Sarah Black.

Rhodri wondered if he should speak up. With his local knowledge, he was aware that the abbey was an all-male environment and that women were strictly forbidden from entering the building. But a quick sideways glance from Carys caused him to hold his tongue. She clearly already knew, and her eyes held a defiant glint. She waited, challenging the monk to spell out the obvious.

'According to the Rule of Saint Benedict,' said Brother Cadoc stiffly, 'women are barred from the cloister. However, if you will permit your sergeant to conduct the interview, I can arrange to–'

'No.' Carys silenced him with a word. 'I am the Senior Investigating Officer and I will conduct the interview myself.'

Rhodri looked anxiously from Carys to Brother Cadoc. For a moment the air crackled with the tension between them. Carys might have the power of the law on her side, but the monk clearly believed he had the power of God on his.

It seemed that neither was willing to back down, but the situation was saved by the intervention of Sister Monica. 'If you don't mind me saying, Brother Cadoc, there seems to be a very simple solution to this problem. If the detective inspector cannot go to the abbot, then surely the abbot can come to her?'

Cadoc nodded in relief. 'Would that be acceptable to you?' he asked Carys.

She rewarded him with a smile that lit up her face. 'Of course.'

The monk humbly bowed his head. 'I'm sure a reception room outside the cloister can be made available. I will make the necessary arrangements immediately.'

'Thank you,' said Carys.

As Cadoc hurried off to arrange a meeting room, she gave Sister Monica a wink. The old nun turned away, hiding a grin.

Rhodri couldn't help but be impressed. Brother Cadoc was a formidable man, but Carys had decisively won that battle of wills. Yet he still didn't know what to make of her. She wasn't like any DI he had come across before, dressed in what looked like charity-shop castoffs and quoting from the Bible as if she knew the text by heart. He couldn't see her getting on very well with DCI Gareth Pritchard. Pritchard was an old stick-in-the-mud who liked things done the proper way. Rhodri still wasn't sure if he liked her very much himself. Time would tell.

One thing was certain, though. Having seen what she was capable of during the argument with Brother Cadoc, he would be sure to watch his own step carefully. He didn't want her bossing him around like that.

CHAPTER 6

The arrival on the island of two strangers in the company of Brother Cadoc had not escaped the notice of Nia Armitage. Neither had the presence of uniformed police officers and scene of crime investigators. As postmistress in charge of the island's small post office, there was little Nia didn't know about the comings and goings of the monks and islanders.

It was rare to see one of the monks out and about. They usually spent their days cloistered in the abbey, doing whatever monks did all day long. Yet while opening up the post office that morning, Nia had spotted Brother Cadoc walking past with a man and a woman in the direction of the abbey church. Although they were dressed in plain clothes, Nia suspected they were police detectives. That had been nearly an hour ago and they had not yet returned. What were they doing now? Curiosity was eating away at her. She would have loved to be a fly on the wall inside the abbey, but sadly that part of the island was closed off to her.

And there was another thing. Where were the tourists today? Admittedly, it was a blustery day in October but there were always a handful of hardy souls who braved the bumpy crossing to enjoy the delights of Caldey Island. If the weather was particularly bad, they would usually take shelter from the wind and rain by coming into the post office which doubled as a small museum. There was no doubt in Nia's mind – the police must have closed the island to visitors.

She pretended to sort the postcards in the display stand while looking out across the village green, waiting to see what would happen next. She didn't have long to wait. A familiar figure with a grey canvas bag slung over his shoulder appeared by the fishpond across the green and made his way towards the post office. Oh good, Eifion had mail for her. He usually brought the post over from the mainland two or three times a week and she enjoyed his visits even though he wasn't much of a talker. Today, especially, he might be a useful source of information if she could prise it out of him. She hurried back behind the counter so it wouldn't look as if she'd been waiting for him.

The door opened with a ring of the bell, and a gust of wind preceded the boatman's entrance.

Nia looked up. 'Oh, hello, Eifion. I didn't know if you'd make it across today. The sea's quite choppy, isn't it?'

He stamped his boots on the mat and closed the door behind him. 'Well, I had to come, didn't I? To drop those two detectives off.'

Detectives. She'd known it! 'Has something happened, then? In the abbey, perhaps?'

Eifion shrugged, as if the matter were of little interest to him. 'A death.'

Well, yes, any idiot could have worked that out. You didn't send a whole bunch of police officers and a SOCO team over to the island unless something very serious had happened. 'Who's dead, then, Eifion?'

'I don't know. I didn't ask.'

Nia suppressed a sigh. How could Eifion be so infuriatingly incurious? If she'd been stuck on a boat with two police detectives she would have asked so many questions that by the time the boat landed, there would be nothing she didn't know about their reasons for being there.

'Have you got some post for me, then?' she asked.

Eifion reached inside his canvas bag. 'Just a few bits and bobs.' He handed over a small pile of envelopes.

Nia worked quickly through them. A gardening supplies bill for Dafydd Rees, a bank statement for Sister Monica, a letter from Withybush hospital addressed to Father Anselm. Oh, and a postcard for Bethan Rees, Dafydd's wife. Nia turned it over and read the message. *Having a lovely time in Sicily. Visited Etna on a coach trip. Love, Auntie Joan.* Not many people sent postcards these days – they posted pictures of themselves on social media for the whole world to see, and Nia devoured those Facebook and Instagram posts avidly – but Bethan's Auntie Joan always sent a postcard from wherever she went. Nia read them all.

She set the post aside and handed Eifion more letters to take back to the mainland.

'You got your boat working again, then?'

'For now, touch wood,' said Eifion, tapping the side of the counter. He stowed the outgoing post into his bag. 'She needs a proper service and I want to pick up some new parts when I can get over to Pembroke Dock, but I've got to take the police back and forth all day, see?'

Nia leaned across the counter, dropping her voice to encourage Eifion to come closer. 'So, what are they like, these two detectives? Is one of them that boy who worked for you a few years back? Rhodri, is it?'

'Rhodri, that's him. And there's a woman in charge.' Eifion chuckled. 'I think Rhodri's a bit scared of her.'

'What's her name?'

'Carys. New, she is.'

Carys. Nia stored that nugget of information in her mental repository of facts. 'And she's new, you say?'

'From Cardiff.'

Some hotshot from the city. No doubt this new

detective would want to question everyone on the island. Nia could hardly wait.

The door opened and the bell rang again as another gust of wind rattled the postcard display. It was Novice Thomas, the newest monk at the abbey. So well-mannered and nice, it seemed a waste for him to be shutting himself away with a bunch of old men for company. At his age, he ought to be out in the world, making the most of his life. But it took all sorts, Nia supposed, and she had never understood what made a man decide to become a monk. He gave her a cautious smile, hanging back when he saw the gruff old boatman standing by the counter.

'Come on in,' said Nia kindly. 'Don't be frightened of Eifion, now.' She had a soft spot for Thomas and looked forward to the times when he popped in to collect the post for the abbey. 'You've got perfect timing today. Eifion's just brought the post, and there's a letter here for Father Anselm.'

Thomas approached shyly and she held out the letter addressed to the abbot. The novice reached for it, but she wasn't willing to let him take it without first answering a few questions. She held onto the letter, keeping it out of his reach. 'I hear the police are on the island. What are they doing at the abbey?'

Thomas cast a nervous look in Eifion's direction before returning his gaze to Nia. 'Looking around. Asking questions. They're speaking to the abbot next.'

'Are they, indeed?' said Nia. 'And what do you know about this suspicious death?'

Eifion heaved out a grunt of irritation. 'I never said it was suspicious.'

Nia shot him a dismissive glance. 'Away with you, Eifion James! Of course it's suspicious – why else would the police be here?' She turned her attention back to Thomas. 'Well?'

Thomas shrugged. 'I don't know anything. Not really. A woman was found dead in the church at Matins, that's all.'

'A woman? What can you tell me about her?'

Thomas shook his head. 'Nothing. Can I have the letter now?'

Nia sighed. Extracting information from this pair was like drawing blood from a stone. She would have to employ more direct methods if she was going to find out more about the police investigation. 'Go on then,' she said, letting him take the letter for Father Anselm. She watched as he scurried away, the bell tinkling once again as he left.

CHAPTER 7

'The abbot will see you now,' said Brother Cadoc, beckoning for Carys and Rhodri to follow him out of the church.

She accompanied him through a gate marked *Private*, across a raised terrace bordered by a high stone wall, beyond which the roofs of the villagers' cottages could be glimpsed, and into a square tower on the far perimeter of the abbey buildings. A steep and narrow spiral staircase led upwards, but it was into the ground-floor parlour that Cadoc showed the two detectives.

'Father Anselm will be with you shortly,' said the monk, before bowing his head and leaving. The heavy oak and iron door banged shut behind him.

Rhodri swept a disparaging look around the starkly furnished room. 'Is this the best they could come up with? The cells at the station are more comfortable than this. At least they're heated.'

It was true that the room was cold and austere. The floorboards were bare, the rough, whitewashed walls were decorated only by a large wooden crucifix, and the narrow slits of the windows permitted little more than a glimmer of light to enter. There was a sense that someone might be sent to this place to do penance. The only furniture was a stack of wooden chairs in one corner, and Rhodri began to arrange them into a circle in the middle of the small space. He was attempting, Carys realised, to regain control of the situation.

There was clearly a power struggle at play between herself and Brother Cadoc that was not simply a tension between the religious and the secular. As a woman – a daughter of Eve – Carys was not welcome in the all-male world of the abbey. This inconvenient and uncomfortable tower room, physically separated from the main abbey building, only served to emphasise her exclusion.

Yet Carys didn't feel as disgruntled as Rhodri obviously did. The stark austerity of the tower room struck a chord with her, reminding her of the Welsh folklore her grandmother had shared with her and her sister – tales of imprisonments and banishments, fairy abductions and magic circles. Rather than waste her energy resenting the monks and their archaic prejudice against the female sex, she decided instead to claim this space and make it her own. She helped Rhodri arrange the chairs and prepare the room for the coming interview.

When they were done, the big iron ring of the door handle creaked as it was turned slowly from the outside. Rhodri went to the door and heaved it open to reveal an elderly monk standing outside. He leaned on a walking stick, slightly out of puff.

'Thank you,' said the monk, entering the room and making his way slowly to the nearest chair. He eased himself gratefully into it, gripping his stick with knobbly, arthritic hands and panting from the exertion. Once he had recovered his breath, he introduced himself. 'I am Father Anselm, and it is with great sadness that I welcome you to Caldey Island. Brother Cadoc says you wish to speak with me. How may I be of assistance?'

The abbot was dressed in the same garb as Brother Cadoc – a white tunic unembellished by any form of decoration, and a plain cowl. Not for nothing were the Cistercians known as the white monks. The simplicity of their habits symbolised poverty and austerity. Carys judged Anselm to be in his seventies or eighties. She noted his kind eyes and forlorn expression and found herself wrongfooted, having expected the abbot to be more adversarial. She should keep an open mind at this early stage of the investigation, but it struck her immediately that Father Anselm was no murderer. He was far too frail to have attacked a young woman and hauled her body onto the altar, and his concern seemed sincere.

All the same, he was the figure of authority on this island, a potential obstacle to the police investigation, and a hazard to be navigated with care.

'DI Morgan and DS Evans. Pleased to meet you,' she said, mirroring the abbot's own formal style. 'Thank you for agreeing to speak to us at such short notice. And thank you for making this room available for our use.'

She felt Rhodri stir in the seat beside her, and sensed his lingering feeling of indignation at being consigned to this outbuilding. But it was important to put that matter behind them and move on. There would be other battles to fight, and as far as Carys was concerned, this room would serve as well as any other. 'Perhaps you could take notes, Rhodri?' she suggested.

She waited until he had taken out a notebook and pen before continuing. 'Before we get on to the events that brought us here, Father, perhaps you could tell us a little about the island and the monastery.' She kept her request deliberately open-ended to encourage the abbot to speak freely. She wanted to get the measure of the man before moving on.

Father Anselm gave a brief nod. 'The most important thing for me to say is that Caldey is a holy island, much like Iona in Scotland, or Lindisfarne in Northumberland. And by that, I mean it is a spiritual place, a place of faith and belief. A place where one comes to find God.'

'I see.' Carys didn't contradict him, despite the

evidence in the church indicating that not everyone on the island was obeying the Ten Commandments. She ran through them in her head. *Thou shalt not murder* came in at number six. Personally, she would have placed it higher up the list.

'The roots of Christianity run deep on Caldey,' continued the abbot, gazing wistfully out through the narrow window rather than directly at Carys. 'Celtic monks first settled here in the sixth century, at which time the island was known by its Welsh name, *Ynys Bŷr*. The Vikings came later, giving it its present name, which is said by some scholars to mean *Cold Island*. Monasticism returned in the twelfth century, when St Illtud's church and the old priory were built.'

Rhodri's pen remained idle in his hand, and he was clearly bored by this historical detail, but Carys knew that in order to fully understand someone you had to find out what they cared about. What she had learned already was that Father Anselm cared deeply about the long tradition of monasticism on the island.

'Perhaps you are aware of what happened to British monasteries during the sixteenth century?' queried the abbot.

'The Dissolution under Henry VIII,' supplied Carys.

Anselm nodded sadly. 'Those were dark days for monastic communities all across the country. Caldey Priory was closed and the monks expelled. For over three hundred years, the island remained in secular hands. But God did not forsake Caldey. An order of Benedictine monks purchased the island in 1906 and built the current monastery buildings. The island was then sold to our order of Reformed Cistercians in the 1920s and the first new monks arrived from the mother house of Notre-Dame de Scourmont in Belgium.'

'And monks have been here ever since,' concluded Carys. 'How many currently reside in the monastery?'

The abbot's face fell. 'Our numbers have dwindled in recent years. Old age is catching up with us and now just six remain, including myself. Brother Cadoc you've already met. He handles all aspects of our relations with the outside world. Brother Gregory cooks for us and looks after us when we're sick. Our youngest recruit is Novice Thomas, our hope for the future.' His face glowed for a moment with the hint of a smile. 'Brothers Mark and John, I'm afraid, are too frail these days to leave their rooms except at mealtimes and the canonical hours.'

Rhodri looked up from his notebook. 'Brother Cadoc mentioned those. What are they, exactly?'

'That is the name we give to the services around which the Cistercian day is structured: Matins, Lauds, Terce, Sext, None, Vespers, and Compline.'

'Do all the monks attend every service?' asked Rhodri.

'Yes,' said Father Anselm. 'As well as holy mass each morning.' He frowned. 'Although now I think about it, Brother Cadoc retired early yesterday evening, complaining of an upset stomach. He stayed in his room and did not attend Compline. But he was present at Matins this morning.'

Rhodri noted it down. 'And in between these services, what do you do all day, if you don't mind me asking?'

'We work,' said the abbot simply. 'The Rule of St Benedict urges us to live by the work of our hands, and those of us who are physically able to, tend the vegetable garden and prepare meals. The rest of the time we read and write. The Rule encourages us to speak only when necessary, although contrary to popular belief we do not take a vow of silence.'

'And what do you do after Compline?'

'Compline brings the day to a close, and we retire to our cells. Most of us are in bed by nine. After all, the bell for Matins rings at half past three in the morning.'

'It sounds like a hard life,' said Rhodri.

The abbot's lined face broke into a gentle smile. 'It is intended to be. The Order of Reformed Cistercians is founded on the principle of penitence. When a man commits his life here, he quite literally becomes a new person in Christ. That's why we adopt a new name on taking our vows – in my own case, I chose the name Anselm.'

Carys had heard enough from the abbot to understand that his prime concern was the continuity of the monastic tradition here on Caldey. The monks were growing old, their numbers dwindling, and the monastery faced a genuine threat to its long-term existence. The gruesome murder of a young woman in the abbey church would do nothing to still his fears. From that perspective, it was in both their interests to solve this crime as quickly as possible.

'Let's move on to the other islanders. How many ordinary people – if I can put it like that – live on the island?'

'Not many,' Father Anselm admitted. 'There's Dafydd Rees and his wife, Bethan. She runs the café and he maintains the woodland and planted areas around the abbey. And there's Nia, our postmistress. The gift shop staff and other workers live in Tenby and come over by boat each day.'

'And finally, there are the guests at St Philomena's.'

'We call them *retreatants*,' said the abbot, 'because they come here on retreat, seeking spiritual renewal or just a period of solitude away from the stresses of the modern world. I like to think that Caldey offers them what they are looking for.'

'Do they mingle with the monks?'

'Oh no. The monastery and St Philomena's are kept entirely separate. Have you met Sister Monica? She runs the guest house for us.'

'I have.' Carys paused a moment before continuing, aware of how her next words might be received. 'The church where the murder took place is one of the locations that is open to all three groups – monks, islanders, and retreatants.'

The abbot frowned, lifting his eyes to Carys's for the first time during the interview. 'I don't quite follow your meaning, Inspector.'

Carys held his gaze unwaveringly. 'My meaning is that we cannot exclude anyone from our inquiries.'

'But surely a monk–' Anselm began to protest.

'– is as capable of sin as any other person,' she concluded.

Beside her, Rhodri shifted uneasily in his seat. He disliked conflict, Carys realised. And talk of sin and other religious matters unnerved him. He would have to grow a thicker skin if he was going to pull his weight in this investigation.

'I'd like to consider the circumstances of the murder,' Carys continued. 'Why commit a murder in a church? Why place the body on the altar? Why arrange the victim's hands in a position of prayer?'

Father Anselm appeared dismayed by the questions. 'I cannot picture the mind of someone who would do such a thing.'

'Are you aware that a Bible was placed on the victim's chest?'

The abbot shook his head. 'I do not recall the details of how the victim was arranged.'

Carys leaned forwards. 'It was left open at Ecclesiastes chapter nine, verse five.'

A look of horror flitted over the monk's features. '"The living know at least that they will die, the dead know nothing,"' he murmured. 'This was surely the work of a madman.'

'I don't think so,' said Carys. 'I think the killer intended to convey a message, and I intend to find out what and why. To do that, I will need to interview everyone on this island. Monks, retreatants and islanders.'

'Then this room is at your disposal,' said Anselm, 'but I cannot allow you any further into the abbey.'

Helpful as the abbot had been, Carys would not allow this remark to pass unchallenged. She leaned forwards and spoke with steely determination. 'Father Anselm, may I remind you that this is a murder investigation. If the police need access to any part of the monastery, then we will obtain a warrant and go wherever we please.'

She held the abbot's gaze until he dropped his to the tiled floor. 'Very well.'

Carys stood up. 'First of all, we'll go to St Philomena's.'

'I'll arrange for Brother Cadoc to take you there,' said the abbot, struggling to his feet.

'Thank you, but there's no need.' Carys didn't need a minder, nor did she want Brother Cadoc following her about, knowing where she went and who she spoke to. 'We know where it is. We'll make our own way there.'

CHAPTER 8

Rosalind Greaves was still unnerved after her encounter with Paul Roberts. She wasn't easily spooked, but inside St Illtud's church with the overbearing schoolteacher, she had felt... *trapped*. Yes, that was the word. *Trapped*. He had made her feel vulnerable, standing too close, breathing down her neck. Lecturing to her on the history of the island, as if she couldn't possibly know it already! She didn't need him telling her what to think. Besides, she didn't trust people who hid behind a smokescreen of knowledge but refused to reveal anything about themselves.

She hurried back in the direction of St Philomena's, glad to be out in the open air where she could breathe more freely. She had always loved nature. It was a trait she shared with her fictional protagonist, Brother Aidan, who knew the name of every plant and animal he encountered on his travels. The flowering season on the island was largely over, but she spotted a few stubborn wild roses still in bloom, and a tapestry of autumn colour – ferns turning rusty-brown, hawthorn adorned with bright red haws, the dry seed pods of sea campion, and green holly berries ripening towards winter red.

On an impulse she turned and headed into the woods. The trees were dense and the path wound gently uphill through oak, hazel and rowan until she found herself at the foot of the Calvary Cross.

Occupying a clearing on a patch of high ground with a view across to the mainland, the cross bore a life-size carving of Christ, arms outstretched, feet crossed at the ankles. It unsettled her, this depiction of a dying man, every rib clearly visible through his torso, the muscles in his arms taut with the strain. Her own religious upbringing had been more sanitised. She remembered a sermon from her childhood where the vicar in her local Anglican church had explained that the empty cross above the altar represented Christ's resurrection – that was why it was empty. She had been reassured by this simple explanation. He was no longer dead but alive. This Catholic obsession with death and suffering was a little unhealthy.

She heard approaching voices and two men emerged from the trees on the opposite side of the clearing. She recognised them as the two other male guests at St Philomena's – a young man called Samir Khan, in the company of an older man, Rick Styles. It seemed that solitude was going to elude her this morning, but at least Paul Roberts wasn't with them.

Samir, clean shaven and dressed in skinny black jeans and a waxed waterproof jacket, was sucking on a vape. Rick, a somewhat grizzled character with a few days' worth of stubble on his face and wearing faded jeans and a black woollen work jacket, was smoking an old-fashioned cigarette. They came to a stop when they saw her.

'Hope we're not intruding,' called Rick in his Brummie accent. He took one last drag on his cigarette then dropped it on the grass and ground it out beneath the sole of his trainer.

'Not at all,' said Rosalind. She crossed the clearing, refusing to allow the skirmish – or whatever it had been – with Paul to upset her. 'I just came up here to stretch my legs.'

When she'd first met Rick, she hadn't been sure what to make of him. He wasn't at all the type of person she'd expected to encounter on a religious retreat. His demeanour was gruff and his manners were rough and ready. Yet despite his appearance, she had found herself warming to him over dinner the previous night. He came across as genuine, as if what you saw was what you got, and he saw no reason to apologise for it. She suspected he had an interesting story to tell and was hoping to draw it out of him. Collecting people's life stories was her hobby – perhaps even part of her job as a novelist.

Of Samir, she had yet to form a strong impression. He hadn't said much and seemed to spend most of his time scrolling on his phone. He was probably just shy. Or maybe he, too, had secrets to hide. In Rosalind's experience, most people did.

Rick approached the crucifix in the middle of the clearing and crossed himself. That was something Rosalind hadn't anticipated. Her surprise must have shown because Rick gave a shrug and said, 'I was brought up a Catholic but I let it lapse. Went a bit off the rails, to tell the truth. But you know what they say – once a Catholic, always a Catholic.'

'Well, we all go a bit wild in our youth,' she said with a laugh, remembering her own days as a student at Cambridge, discovering drink, drugs and sex. Those years hadn't lasted long, but she'd thrown herself into the hedonistic life with gusto and enjoyed them to the full, although her examination results had suffered somewhat as a result. Still, everything in life was experience that she could draw on when writing her books. She had no regrets.

'Most people don't go quite as wild as me,' said Rick darkly. 'What I did landed me in prison.'

'Prison?' Samir sounded shocked. 'What did you go to prison for?'

Rick shook his head. 'Doesn't matter. That's all in the past.'

Rosalind was eager to learn more but decided she would have a better chance of drawing the full story from Rick if she could speak to him alone.

'And what do you do for a living, Samir?' she asked, seeking to cover the uneasy silence that had descended.

'Me? Oh, I work in tech.' The young man took another pull of his vape.

'Tech?' Rosalind waited while he puffed out an aromatic cloud of vapour like a dragon. She was never going to be satisfied with such a brief reply. 'Then I expect you work for one of those big corporations that keep us all so busy tapping away on our phones these days.'

Samir shook his head. 'Not really. My company's more niche. You won't have heard of it.'

'I see,' she said, although that still didn't give her any clue about what he did. 'And where do you live?'

'London.'

'So what brings you to Caldey?'

He seemed taken aback by the question and his hand darted to the pocket of his waxed jacket as if checking for something. The action didn't escape Rosalind, who was a consummate people watcher. She often included little details like this in her books when creating characters. Unless she was very much mistaken, Samir was hiding something there.

'You're not thinking of becoming a monk, are you?' she joked.

'No,' said Samir. 'I don't believe in all that stuff. I just... I needed to get away for a bit, that's all.'

'Hmm.' Rosalind's imagination was again working in overdrive, but she feared that further questioning might make the shy tech worker clam up completely. He was another dark horse, and she would have to take her time with him.

It started to spot with rain and Rick suggested they go back to the guest house and put the kettle on.

'Excellent idea,' said Rosalind. She had grown cold with her wanderings around the island.

She fell into step behind him and walked the short distance back to St Philomena's. When they reached the guest house, Rick held the door open for her. Not many men still did that, and Rosalind was once again wrong-footed by the Brummie. She thanked him and headed straight to her room to jot down notes while her memory was still fresh. The morning had been very productive. Not only had she met a creepy schoolteacher who for some reason wasn't at school, but she had also spoken to a lapsed Catholic with a criminal past, and an evasive tech worker desperately concealing some object in his clothing. She could already feel her creative juices starting to flow.

*

'Any chance we could grab a coffee and a bite to eat?' asked Rhodri as he and Carys left the tower room and made their way down to the village green. DCI Pritchard's unexpected early-morning call had robbed him of that third slice of toast, and his stomach was starting to rumble. Breakfast was a distant memory, and if he'd been at the station he would have made his way through at least three coffees, a plate of biscuits and a packet of crisps by now. Amy was always telling him to take a banana to work but who was she trying to kid? Bananas weren't a patch on chocolate Hobnobs.

To his relief, Carys agreed to a quick pit stop at the island's café.

They walked past the post office and Rhodri noticed a face in the window, observing them. He caught the woman's eye and she immediately turned away, pretending to re-arrange the postcard display. But when he looked back a moment later, she was watching them just as intently as before.

'The locals are nosey,' he said to Carys. 'This is probably the biggest thing that's happened on the island in years.'

'Some people never miss a trick,' said Carys. 'But nosey

neighbours can be useful.'

The café was a single-storey, wooden-clad building tucked away under the trees. A large grassy area in front of it was full of garden furniture and picnic tables. Today, however, the only visitors were a pair of ducks from the nearby pond.

The woman behind the counter seemed glad to see them. 'Oh, good morning. I was wondering if we were going to get any customers at all today.'

Rhodri inclined his head in the direction of the abbey church. 'I'm sure the SOCO team will drop in before the morning's over. They had an early start.' He scanned the menu on the wall. 'Any chance of a coffee and a bacon roll? Maybe a chocolate muffin too, and I'd better have a bag of cheese and onion crisps.'

Carys eyed him with amusement. 'Will that be enough? I'd hate to see you starve on my watch.'

'Best to be safe, boss. In this job, you never know when you might get your next chance for food.'

'I'll just have a green tea,' said Carys.

'Coming right up,' said the woman. 'Take a seat. I'll bring everything over when it's ready.'

They found a table with a good view across the green towards the abbey. Rhodri took a seat, admiring the view. The monastery was a large building that looked big enough to house a hundred monks. Most of the rooms must be empty if there were only six monks currently in residence. It must be creepy living there, especially on a dark winter's night with the wind howling and the rain lashing against the windows. It was hard for him to imagine what made someone become a monk.

'So, what do you make of it so far?' Carys asked.

He could tell from her tone that this was some kind of test, and he sat upright, focussing on what he had seen and heard. 'Well, boss, my best guess would be that the murderer is one of the other people staying at St Philomena's.'

Carys's expression gave nothing away. 'Why do you say

that?'

'Just seems obvious. The murder happened after the last boat returned to Tenby, so it must be someone staying on the island. And I can't see why one of the monks or villagers would suddenly go from zero to carnage on an innocent bystander.'

Carys stared across the lawn, her gaze fixed on the tower where they had interviewed the abbot. 'You're making too many assumptions, Rhodri. We don't know anything about the backgrounds of the monks or the islanders, and all we know about the victim is her name.'

'Well, what's your best guess?'

Carys turned to him. 'I don't make guesses, Rhodri. I look at the facts. What do you make of the location of the crime scene, the staging of the body and the placing of the Bible?'

Rhodri mulled it over. 'Some kind of religious connection. But what did that Bible passage mean? All that stuff about "the dead know nothing?" You told Father Anselm that the killer was sending a message.'

'I think so, and I think we can also assume that the killer is familiar with scripture. In this context, the quotation suggests to me that the victim knew something and the killer wanted to silence her because of it.'

'Or it could just be random,' suggested Rhodri. 'The work of a lunatic.' He shuddered as he recalled the violence of the attack. The blood on the floor. The placing of the body on the altar, hands folded across the victim's chest. What kind of person would do such a thing?

The woman who had taken their orders appeared carrying a tray. She came over to the table and laid out their food and drinks.

'Thanks,' said Rhodri.

'If you're not too busy,' said Carys, 'would you care to join us?'

The woman smiled. 'I'd like to. Thanks.'

Rhodri hesitated, surveying the soft floury roll with its mouthwatering bacon aroma, the milky coffee, crisps and generously proportioned muffin. He was keen to get stuck in but didn't want to appear greedy. Reluctantly he left the food untouched.

The woman settled in next to him. 'I'm Bethan Rees. I manage the café. My husband is Dafydd. He takes care of the woodland and the gardens around the monastery.'

'We saw him when we first arrived,' said Carys. 'Chopping wood with an axe.'

'That will have been him. He has a lot of clearing to do at this time of year, see, cutting back all the dead wood and burning leaves.'

'I understand there aren't many people living on the island,' said Carys.

Bethan shook her head sadly. 'Apart from the monks and Sister Monica, it's just me, Dafydd and the postmistress, Nia. There was more of a community when we first moved here. But a lot of the older folk have passed away and there are no children anymore. The school closed a few years back. Dafydd enjoys the solitude, but to be honest with you, it can feel quite lonely at times.'

'You don't have any children yourself?' asked Carys.

'Dafydd and I weren't blessed that way.'

Rhodri eyed his bread roll, knowing that the crispy bacon inside was growing cooler with every passing second. He longed to sink his teeth into it, but Carys hadn't touched her tea and it would look rude if he broke ranks now.

'Since the community is so close-knit, I take it that everyone gets on well together?' he asked.

Bethan pursed her lips. 'Not really. Nia's a real busybody, always poking her nose into other people's business. I keep my distance from her, I do!'

Rhodri glanced across the green to the post office and fancied he could see a shape in the window where the postmistress was still watching.

'What about the monks?' asked Carys. 'Do you have much contact with them?'

Bethan shook her head. 'Not really. They keep

themselves to themselves. It's a separate world, up there in the monastery.'

'And what about St Philomena's?'

Bethan smiled. 'Yes, you get to know a few of the retreatants – some of them come back year after year. And Sister Monica is friendly. She pops in now and again for a tea and a chat.'

Rhodri's gaze returned to his plates of food. Carys still hadn't made any motion to pick up her tea, but this was becoming ridiculous. He reached for the bacon roll and took a large bite, feeling a sensation close to bliss as he chewed the soft roll and crisp bacon inside.

'Do you know any of the current visitors?' Carys asked Bethan.

She shook her head. 'I've seen them about, but I don't recognise any of them. I think they're all here for the first time.'

'Have you spoken to one of them – a woman named Sarah Black?'

'She came to the café on Saturday, but I haven't seen her since. She seemed nice enough.' She stood up. 'Anyway, I'll let you eat your food in peace.'

Rhodri waited until she had gone before speaking again. There was something he needed to say. 'Boss, do you have a grudge against the monks? You were a bit hard on Father Anselm. And Brother Cadoc too. They both seemed like decent blokes. For monks, I mean.'

Carys didn't look at him, but took a tiny sip of her tea, blowing to cool it down. 'They tried to stop me from entering the monastery.'

'Well, there is that,' he conceded. 'But only because you're...'

'A woman?'

Rhodri knew immediately that he'd put his foot in it. It would have been better if he'd kept his mouth shut. He hated arguments. 'I know it's not exactly a diversity-friendly policy, but to be fair, the abbot was probably just doing his job.'

Carys turned the full force of her gaze on him, and he felt those green eyes boring into his. 'You know your problem, Rhodri? You're too trusting. Just because someone's in a position of authority, it doesn't mean they act with the purest of motives. In fact, you should make a point of not trusting them. Believe me, their interests don't always align with yours.'

A hard edge had entered her voice, as if her words were born from personal experience.

Rhodri sighed and turned away. He really didn't think she was going to hit it off with DCI Pritchard.

CHAPTER 9

After returning from the abbey church, Sister Monica set about restoring some order to her day. She put away the breakfast things, tidied the guest house kitchen, and began to make tea. Everyone needed a strong cup of tea after they'd had a shock, didn't they? The retreatants – those who still remained, now that Sarah Black was dead – had returned from their morning walks, and Sister Monica braced herself to tell them what had happened.

How was she going to break such shocking news to her guests? She felt herself to be personally responsible for the wellbeing of all who stayed at St Philomena's. Many returned year after year and she regarded them as friends. The current batch of five – well, there were only four of them now – were all visiting for the first time. They had arrived on Saturday, and she had done her best, as always, to make them welcome. None of them had known each other prior to their arrival. And now one of them was dead.

While she waited for the kettle to boil, she dropped two tea bags into a large, brown pot. Then she arranged an assortment of mismatched cups on a tray with a jug of fresh milk and a bowl of sugar cubes.

'Can I help?'

Sister Monica turned around. 'Ah, Rosalind, dear. That's very kind of you.' She had warmed to the novelist from the very first evening. There was something about her that made you want to confide your innermost thoughts, although of course Sister Monica had been careful not to. You had to watch what you said to a writer or you'd find your story turned into a book.

'Let me take the tea things through,' said Rosalind. She picked up the tray and carried it through to the sitting room.

When the kettle boiled, Sister Monica poured the water into the pot and went to face her guests.

The sitting room at St Philomena's was a comfortable, if somewhat dilapidated room, with faded floral sofas and scenic paintings of Caldey Island on the walls. Everyone had gathered in the communal space as if in anticipation of some announcement. Was some sixth sense at work? Probably they had noticed the police on the island and were curious about what was happening. She paused in the doorway and studied her guests.

The schoolteacher, Paul Roberts, was pacing beside the window, pausing every few seconds to peer outside. Sister Monica didn't like to judge, but in her estimation Paul was an odd fellow. Unlike Rosalind, who put everyone at ease, Paul was one of those who put you on edge. She had caught him staring at people when he thought he was unobserved. Watching silently, like a spider regarding a fly.

Sister Monica always did her best to see the good in people, but the Bible taught that out of the heart of man came evil thoughts, sexual immorality, theft, murder, adultery, greed, malice, deceit, lewdness, envy, slander, arrogance and folly. You didn't need to go looking for the devil in order to find evil. It was present everywhere that people went.

'That teapot looks heavy,' said Rick Styles, standing up from his armchair and coming to help. 'Let me take that,

Sister.'

She gave him a warm smile. 'Oh, thank you, Rick.'

She was still unsure what to make of this bearded and rather scruffy man. He carried an air of menace and wasn't someone you'd want to meet in a dark alley. His build was lean and wiry, he was quick-eyed and carried himself with the wary confidence of a man who knew trouble and wouldn't shy away from it. Yet despite his rough appearance, there was a disarming directness in the way he spoke, as though he had no talent – or desire – for pretence. The very first evening, he'd confided in her that he'd spent time in prison but was now a reformed character. Paradoxically, the revelation made her think of him as a very honest person. She had told him there was more rejoicing in heaven over one sinner who repented than over ninety-nine righteous people who did not need to repent, and he had answered, 'Very true, Sister!'

Despite his large hands, he poured the tea with the delicacy of a waiter at the Ritz. Not that Sister Monica had ever been to the Ritz, but she imagined such things to be so. Watching him pass around the cups with an easy smile, she was filled with positive feelings. For indeed, she mused, the fruit of the Spirit is love, joy, peace, longsuffering, gentleness, goodness, faith, meekness and temperance. With Rick, you needed to look beyond the rugged exterior to see the light within. Once you had, it drew you like a candle shining in the darkness. Nevertheless, her intuition told her to keep her wits about her whenever she was with him. An edge of danger lurked beneath the surface and she sensed instinctively that it would be unwise to rouse it.

She accepted a cup of tea from him and felt a shiver run down her spine as their fingers brushed. It hadn't escaped her notice that Sarah Black had also been drawn to Rick. She had noticed the younger woman watching him that first evening over dinner. Sister Monica had never been in a relationship with a man, but she could understand how Sarah would have been attracted to Rick. He exerted a raw charisma that was most compelling. *A rough diamond.*

Once everyone had been served, she cleared her throat. 'I have something to tell you all. I'm afraid that it's very sad news.' She glanced around to make certain she had everyone's attention before continuing. 'There isn't an easy way to break this to you, but the body of Sarah Black was found in the abbey church this morning. The police are treating her death as suspicious.' Her thoughts darted to an image of the young woman arranged atop the altar, her throat and torso red with blood, her hands folded across her chest as if in prayer. "Suspicious" was something of an understatement, but it was what the police had asked her to tell the retreatants. 'Detectives from the mainland will be arriving shortly to speak with each of you.'

She looked up to see how her announcement had been received. As expected, there was a mix of stunned silence and horrified gasps.

Rosalind's eyes were wide – with shock? or interest? It was impossible to say.

Paul wore the same slightly superior expression he always wore, as if he were above such matters and normal rules didn't apply to him.

Samir was more of an open book, his face aghast. But Sister Monica detected more than mere horror at learning of another's misfortune. His expression betrayed a sense of fear. His hand crept to his pocket as if checking something was there. She had noticed that gesture before. From his arrival, Samir had been on edge, constantly checking his phone, looking over his shoulder, starting nervously whenever anyone entered the room. He had told Sister Monica he worked in "tech", but when she had suggested it would be good for him to escape from phones and gadgets for a few days, he had stared at her as if she were speaking a language he didn't understand.

Yet it was Rick who gave the most surprising reaction to the news.

'Murder,' he pronounced solemnly. 'Or suicide. That's

what the police mean when they say a death is suspicious. Which was it, Sister?'

Sister Monica gave a quick shake of her head, startled by the bluntness of his question. 'They asked me not to discuss the circumstances.'

'Murder, then,' said Rick grimly, and a silence descended over the room.

Sister Monica's gaze drifted around the assembled retreatants. She knew what each of them was thinking – was a killer among them right now? She sensed them moving apart, putting a safer distance between each other, and in particular from Rick.

'Will they be here soon?' blurted Samir, looking at his smart watch. 'The detectives, I mean.'

Rick turned to him. 'Why do you ask, mate? Do you have an appointment? Somewhere you need to be? And what have you got hidden in your pocket that you're so worried about?'

Samir stared at him, open-mouthed. 'It's nothing. I'm not hiding anything.'

'Yeah?' said Rick. 'Well you seem very jumpy.'

When Samir didn't respond, Rosalind spoke to the room at large. 'I've always wanted to be interviewed by the police. Just to see what it's really like. I'm sure it will be fascinating.'

She was trying to smooth over the awkwardness, and Sister Monica was grateful for her intervention. Yet Rick scoffed at the idea. 'It's not like in books or on the telly, I can tell you that, love. Brace yourself for some tough questioning and be careful what you say. The police show no mercy.'

Paul set his cup down with a clatter. 'I don't require mercy from the police. They deal in laws made by men. Dust and ashes. I've no interest in that.'

An uneasy silence descended on the room as everyone turned to look at him.

'Judgment belongs to the Lord,' Paul went on, his voice steady with assurance. 'Scripture's very clear on that.

Vengeance is mine, saith the Lord. Not theirs.'

Rick gave a short laugh. 'Mate, try telling that to the judge. If you've done something–'

'I've done nothing wrong!' bellowed Paul.

Sister Monica cleared her throat. 'Paul, the Church teaches that repentance–'

'Repentance is for sinners,' he cut in. 'For those who've knowingly turned away from the teachings of the Bible.' His gaze moved round the room, daring anyone to speak, before finally settling on Sister Monica herself. 'But what about those who are accused of a crime they never committed?'

Sister Monica felt a prickle of unease. Paul was undoubtedly speaking about some crime he had committed. Yet this was no confession, it was a sermon – one carefully designed to absolve its speaker. But before she could find a response, or decide whether one was wise, Rosalind's voice cut across the uneasy atmosphere of the sitting room, the relief plain to hear.

'The police have arrived,' she said, nodding towards the window.

Thank goodness. Sister Monica went to answer the door, glad to have avoided answering Paul's question. She just hoped the police wouldn't ask her too many questions of their own.

CHAPTER 10

St Philomena's was quite different in style to the main monastery buildings and village. Unlike the abbey with its white walls and tiled roof, the guest house was built from a dark grey stone.

'It looks like a miniature castle,' remarked Rhodri, gazing up at the crenellated tower that stood at the front as if to fend off unwanted visitors.

The building was austere, but not unattractive. With its arched windows, it reminded Carys of a chapel, and the gardens that surrounded it were enclosed and welcoming – more evidence of Dafydd Rees's work.

The front door opened as they walked up the path, and Sister Monica welcomed them inside. Carys followed her into a communal lounge and found a group of people gathered in expectation, some sitting, some standing. All eyes turned to her and Rhodri, and she quickly assessed the occupants of the room.

A middle-aged woman was studying her with undisguised fascination. A young British Asian man averted his gaze as soon as her eyes came to rest on him. A thin man with the pinched appearance of a life lived hard returned her stare unflinchingly. And an older man regarded her with a distinct look of superiority. Carys wondered how the victim had got along with this motley crowd.

'Is everyone here?' she asked.

Sister Monica nodded.

Carys introduced herself and Rhodri and thanked them for their patience. 'I must ask, however, that none of you leave the island until we have completed our inquiries.'

The middle-aged woman nodded her willing assent, the young man scowled, the older man looked as if he resented the request, and the thin man seemed resigned, as if that was exactly what he'd expected. He'd had dealings with the police before – Carys could tell.

'Right,' she said, 'my colleague DS Rhodri Evans will take a statement from each of you. Sister Monica, could you show me to the victim's room, please?'

'Come with me.' The nun gestured in the direction of the hallway and stairs. 'It's this way.'

The upstairs room that Sarah Black had occupied for just one night was simply furnished with a single bed, a small armchair, a wardrobe and a desk with a wooden chair tucked underneath. Old-fashioned floral curtains hung at the window which looked out onto the woodland. A thin trail of smoke was still rising from the remains of Dafydd's bonfire, the smell of woodsmoke seeping in through the ill-fitting window panes. The sparseness of the room reminded Carys of student accommodation in the older halls of residence in Cardiff. Although to be fair, the students probably had nicer rooms. There was a shared bathroom, she noted, down the corridor.

'Thank you,' she told Sister Monica. 'I'll take it from here.'

The nun took the hint, bowed her head, and withdrew.

Carys pulled on gloves and began to search the room.

The wardrobe standing beside the window looked as though it was on its last legs. Carys opened it carefully, but there was nothing inside except a few clothes hangers.

Sarah hadn't even had time to unpack properly, or else had chosen to keep everything in her bag. She hadn't brought much with her. A holdall on the bed contained a few changes of underwear and some spare tops. She'd packed miniature toiletries – just the bare essentials – and a battered copy of a psychological thriller. Carys couldn't find a mobile phone, but there was a tablet on the desk. A quick check revealed that it was locked with a password, so it would have to go to digital forensics to be examined.

She checked beneath the bed and ran her hands under the mattress, but there was nothing concealed there. She returned to the holdall and removed all the items, placing them on the bed.

In an interior pocket of the holdall she found a small leather wallet. It contained a credit card, a library card, and a driving licence. Carys removed them and laid them out on the desk next to each other. The black-and-white photo on the driving licence showed a woman with dark, shoulder-length hair. It was definitely the face of the victim she'd viewed earlier that day, although the hair colour had changed since the photo was taken.

But here was the thing. The name on the driving licence, credit card and library card was not Sarah Black.

CHAPTER 11

'Boss!' Rhodri ran up the stairs, taking two at a time. He didn't know which room Carys was in. But she wasn't going to like what he had to say. She would probably put the blame on him for what had just happened.

A door opened at the end of the landing. 'I'm here,' said Carys. 'What is it?'

Rhodri braced himself. 'One of the witnesses has done a runner.'

'What? Who?' Carys stepped into the corridor and he braced himself for a dressing down, but she seemed remarkably calm.

'The rough-looking bloke. Rick Styles. He said the others could be interviewed first, making it sound as if he was being polite. But by the time his turn came, he'd buggered off.'

Rhodri was furious with himself for allowing a suspect to get away with such an obvious ploy. He wished again that DC Elen Vaughan was here. Elen played rugby for her local women's team and never let anyone get away with anything. She was like a human cannonball.

Sister Monica appeared anxiously at the top of the stairs. 'Is there a problem?'

'Which room was Rick Styles staying in?' asked Carys.

'That one,' said the nun, pointing at the door next to the bathroom.

Rhodri pushed it open to reveal an empty room that looked as if it had been cleared in a hurry. A lone sock lay on the floor. Everything else, including its occupant, was gone.

'Well, he can't have got far,' said Carys, heading for the stairs. 'Let's find him.'

Rhodri followed her out through the front door, glad to be taking action, and relieved to be outside again. He hadn't been impressed by the spartan comforts of the guest house and hoped the residents hadn't paid too much for their rooms. Amy would have been out of that place so fast, her suitcase would have left skid marks on the welcome mat. His wife certainly liked a bit of luxury when they travelled, although all Rhodri really wanted from a holiday was some decent surf and a chance to put his board to use.

'If Rick wants to escape,' he called, 'he'll need to take a boat to the mainland.' A worrying thought ran through his head – Eifion. The old sailor would be no match for a desperate man trying to make a getaway.

They sprinted through the woodland down to Priory Bay, Rhodri taking the lead, but Carys keeping pace close behind. When they emerged from the trees, Rhodri's worst fears were confirmed.

'There he is,' he panted, pointing to a figure on the jetty who was shouting at Eifion and gesturing at the boat.

Rhodri put on an extra burst of speed, his lungs burning. He'd failed to keep Rick at St Philomena's. He damn well wouldn't let him get away from the island. And he certainly wasn't going to allow Eifion to come to any harm.

To his relief, Eifion stepped back and allowed Rick free access to the boat without attempting to stop him. Rick untied the mooring rope from around the bollard and threw it into the boat. Then he stepped on board.

Rhodri arrived just in time to intercept him. 'Oh no, you don't,' he said, grabbing hold of Rick's arm.

An incoming wave nudged the boat away from the jetty and the distance between Rhodri's feet grew wider. For one precarious moment he stood poised between land and sea, not fully anchored in either realm. Then his surfing instincts kicked in and he pushed himself forward. Rick resisted, but Rhodri was the stronger of the two and a moment later, Rick was in handcuffs, lying face down in the back of the boat, his clothing soaked in salty bilgewater. Rhodri was about to read him his rights when it occurred to him that the man hadn't actually committed an arrestable offence.

He looked up and saw Carys standing on the dockside, a smile playing at the corners of her mouth. 'If you two have finished playing boats, I suggest you come back inside and get dry.'

Rhodri looked down, realising that his own shoes and trousers were also soaked with seawater. He sighed, then tossed the mooring rope to Eifion, who secured the boat to the jetty. Then he hauled Rick to his feet and marched him back to dry land. Rick was meek as a lamb now, his head bowed, his earlier escape attempt forgotten.

'Why did you run off?' asked Rhodri.

'I'm sorry,' said Rick. 'It was a stupid thing to do. I just panicked.'

'Let's go and sit down,' said Carys. 'Uncuff him, Rhodri. He's not going to do a runner again.'

Rhodri released his prisoner and led him to a low wall that looked out across the beach. He was surprised at Carys's reaction. She'd shown no anger at Rick's escape attempt, and yet when challenged by Brother Cadoc and then by Father Anselm she had displayed a steely resolve. He couldn't make her out. Personally, he hoped that by catching Rick he'd done enough to redeem himself in her eyes.

They sat together on the jetty wall. A seal flopped

across the sand with her pup. The clouds parted briefly, allowing weak sunlight to dry Rhodri's trousers a little.

'What made you panic, Rick?' asked Carys.

'I thought you were going to arrest me for murder.'

'Why would you think that?'

'Because I have a previous conviction for manslaughter.'

Figures. Rhodri had known there was something fishy about Rick. You could just tell.

Rick stared at his feet, his cheeks glowing pink with shame. 'I ran over a man while driving a stolen car. I served five years and spent every minute inside regretting what I'd done. Believe me, I'm a reformed character now. I've paid my debt to society, although I know I can never make amends to the man I killed. Every day I pray for forgiveness and I'm determined never to go back to the life I lived.'

Rhodri had heard it before. A convicted criminal who'd found God in prison. He supposed it happened, but mostly he reckoned it was a ploy to secure early release. If Rick really was a reformed character, he should have cooperated with the police instead of making a dash for it.

The man was right about one thing though – with a convicted killer on the island and a dead woman in the church, it didn't need a maths genius to make two plus two add up to four. If they could get him to confess, they'd have everything wrapped up by teatime.

'What did you do between seven o'clock yesterday evening and three o'clock this morning?' he asked.

'I had dinner in the guest house with the others,' said Rick. 'Sister Monica cooked a Bolognese.'

This fact at least was consistent with what Rhodri had heard from the other interviewees. All five guests had sat down to dinner at six. They had shared a meal, then according to Samir, he and Rick had stepped outside for a smoke. Sister Monica had served tea in the lounge at seven, and the group had mostly sat in the lounge chatting and getting to know each other a bit. They had drifted up to their bedrooms at various times between nine and eleven, although Sarah Black had disappeared earlier – probably around eight.

'What time did you go to bed?' Rhodri asked.

Rick shrugged. 'I don't keep a close track of time, but I was the last to go upstairs. I had one last smoke outside and then I headed to my room.'

'What about Sarah Black?'

'I didn't see her much. I got the impression she was avoiding me for some reason. But after I got into bed, I heard the front door of the guest house open and close.'

Rhodri frowned. 'You're saying someone went out?'

'In or out. I couldn't say which.'

'And what time was this?'

'Probably after midnight.'

Rhodri raised a sceptical eyebrow. None of the other retreatants had reported hearing the door open and close that late, although it was conceivable that they were all asleep by then. He looked at Carys. Did she believe Rick's story?

Her expression gave nothing away. 'Rick, I'd like you to return to St Philomena's and remain on the island until I say you can leave. If you want to convince us that you're innocent, it's in your best interests to cooperate with us from now on.'

Rick shrugged, then gave a lopsided grin. 'That's fine with me. It's not like I have anywhere else I'd rather be.'

CHAPTER 12

The seal pup nestled against its mother's side, sucking contentedly. The role of male grey seals ended after mating and they played no part in the rearing of their offspring. The mothers, too, would leave not long after the birth of their pup. It was a situation that Carys could all too easily identify with.

She tore her attention away from the seals and back to Rhodri. 'I know you think I let Rick off easily, but I'm confident he won't try to escape again. If we need to question him, we'll know where he is.'

'I guess.' Rhodri's boots were still wet, and he walked along the path leaving a trail of muddy footprints behind him.

'You did well catching him, though,' said Carys.

'Thanks.'

'And I have some information for you. The victim's name wasn't Sarah Black.'

Rhodri ground to a halt. 'What?'

'Her real name was Veronica Emmett. I found her driving licence and credit card in her room.'

Confusion flickered across Rhodri's face. 'Why would

she lie?'

'Good question,' said Carys. 'I'll need you to take everything from her room – including her tablet – back to Haverfordwest. Her phone is missing, by the way. But before you go, I think we'll have a chat with Sister Monica.'

At St Philomena's they found the nun in her study, a small, cramped room that smelled of old paper and furniture polish. Shelves sagged under the weight of books and more were stacked in tottering piles across the floor: mostly religious texts, commentaries on scripture, and thick biographies of saints and mystics. A narrow desk occupied the only free wall, its surface lost beneath notebooks, rosaries, and a chipped mug of tea. She was peering at the screen of an old-fashioned desktop computer.

'I'm afraid there's nowhere for you to sit,' she said. 'Shall we go somewhere more comfortable?'

'Don't worry,' said Carys. 'This won't take long. The thing is, it appears that Sarah Black was here under a false name.'

She scrutinised the nun's face for a reaction and saw she had known the truth all along.

'Ah, yes,' said Sister Monica. 'I did have an inkling that something was amiss. There was a discrepancy with the booking, you see. She called herself Sarah but paid under the name of Miss V Emmett.'

'And you didn't think to mention this to the police?' Carys glared at her, but the elderly nun returned her gaze without a hint of shame.

'You must understand that people – especially women – sometimes come here to escape from abusive partners. I always respect our guests' privacy.'

'I understand that perfectly well,' said Carys. 'But this is a murder investigation. Whose privacy did you think you were protecting by concealing the victim's identity?'

Sister Monica appeared unrepentant. 'Perhaps I should have mentioned it. But in all honesty, it slipped my mind.'

Carys continued to fix her with a hard stare. Why

would the nun conceal the victim's true identity? She was getting on in years, so maybe it really had slipped her mind. But Carys was growing tired of this lack of cooperation, first from the monks and now from the nun. 'Very well,' she said. 'I'm going to ask my sergeant to clear Veronica's room. We're taking everything back to the mainland. And if there's anything else you think might be relevant to our investigation, please be sure to mention it.'

*

A solemn silence hung over the refectory. The only sound was the squeaking of a wheel as Novice Thomas pushed a trolley into the room. The refectory was a large, wood-panelled space with a high vaulted ceiling and a log burner at one end that did little to dispel the chill in the air. Now, in October, the temperature was tolerable, but Thomas knew that in the depths of winter it would become glacial.

The monks stood mutely at their places around the edge of the room while he unloaded the dishes onto the central table. According to the Rule of Saint Benedict, monks were entitled to two meals a day. They were allowed a choice of dishes, but meat was not traditionally on the menu. Saint Benedict had prohibited the eating of red meat from four-legged animals because it was believed to cause sexual temptation – never a good thing in a monastery. Chicken, on the other hand, was considered safe in this respect.

Yet the monks' diet was no longer as austere as that of their forefathers. Red meat was now enjoyed – without apparent detrimental effect – once or twice a week. In fact, shepherd's pie on a Tuesday had become a firm favourite. Today's meal consisted of buttered potatoes, green beans, sliced ham, boiled eggs and tinned peaches.

It was practically a feast, although not at all the sort of fare Thomas had been used to before joining the monastery. In his former life he had survived on a diet of fast food, takeaways and sugary drinks. At first, he had missed the burgers and chips, late-night curries and fry-ups. But under Brother Gregory's tuition in the kitchen, he was quickly becoming an advocate of simple meals prepared with fresh ingredients. And there was never a shortage of food. Not with Brother Gregory in charge of portion sizes. Gregory had the appetite of two men and made sure there was always plenty to go round. When Thomas had finished laying out the food, he moved the trolley out of the way and took his place at the end of the long table.

Father Anselm cleared his throat and mumbled the Grace in Latin. Then the monks shuffled forwards to serve themselves. As was customary, no one spoke.

Being the youngest and fittest in the room, Thomas could easily have been the first to the food. But he knew his place and allowed those who were less able to go ahead. As the monks crowded around the table, he waited patiently behind Brother Gregory. The older monk had taken Thomas under his wing when he first arrived, and he considered him a father figure, although all the monks were brothers, and only Father Anselm was the head of the household. Still, Thomas couldn't help the way he felt.

Brother Gregory was just about to help himself to the potatoes when Brother Cadoc reached for them too. Gregory withdrew his hand and gestured for Cadoc to go first. But instead of graciously taking his turn, a spark of antagonism flashed in Cadoc's eyes. 'Are you trying to poison me again?' he hissed.

The accusation detonated in the silence. Mealtimes were not occasions for social interaction, and certainly not for the airing of grievances. The older monks shook their heads as if they couldn't believe what had happened. Yet none of them said anything. It was forbidden.

Thomas watched to see what would happen next.

Brother Gregory raised his eyes to Cadoc's and said in a whisper nonetheless audible to everyone present, 'You liar! I didn't poison you. You're the one with something to hide.'

Father Anselm gave each of them a stern look and they withdrew with their plates to opposite corners of the room.

Thomas took his own share of food before returning to his place and sitting down to ponder what he had just witnessed. He didn't know much about Brother Cadoc except that his parents were Nigerian and that his name before becoming a monk was Ignatius. It was true that the previous evening, Brother Cadoc had become ill and missed Compline. Had he been poisoned? Brother Gregory would never do such a thing. But what did Gregory mean when he said that Cadoc had something to hide? It was well known that the two monks were rivals for the position of abbot when Father Anselm passed from this world to the next. But there were undercurrents in the monastery that Thomas was only dimly aware of.

Still, he knew that this was the vocation he wanted for himself. He chewed his food, and the rest of the meal proceeded, as it should, in silence.

CHAPTER 13

An inky twilight had descended by the time they returned to the mainland in Eifion's boat. Rhodri had brought Veronica's possessions bagged and labelled, and Carys arranged with him to reconvene the following morning at Haverfordwest. It would be her first day at police HQ since transferring from Cardiff.

There were no lights to guide her through the thickness of the gloom on the narrow country road back to Manorbier. The passenger door of her Isuzu Trooper brushed against overgrown hedges, and the wheels jolted into potholes. Welcome to Pembrokeshire, a county where no two towns were more than thirty miles apart, yet every journey seemed to take at least an hour.

She pulled up outside her cottage, turned off the ignition, and sat for a moment listening to the slow ticking of the engine as it cooled. The Trooper was twenty-five years old – a real old lady – but Izzy, as Carys had nicknamed her, was still going strong. Carys had taken a course in car mechanics with the aim of keeping Izzy on the road. With the tools she kept in the back – socket set, spanners, torque wrench, jump leads – she could sort out most problems on her own and thus the two of them continued to enjoy a long and happy relationship. Longer than most of the human relationships in Carys's life, but that was another story.

She hopped out of the car, locked it, and threaded her way up the overgrown path to the front door. Her nan, Olwyn, had always kept the small garden tidy, but there had been no time since moving back for Carys to trim the brambles that snaked across the path or clear the fallen leaves that were giving off a mellow, earthy smell of compost. The house where she had grown up was starting to resemble a witch's cottage straight out of a fairy tale. Carys had a list of jobs that needed tackling before winter set in – clear the guttering, fix a broken downpipe, check for cracked or missing tiles on the roof. She would do what she could herself and only call in professional help if absolutely necessary. She hated being dependent on anyone and didn't like strangers invading her personal space.

She unlocked the front door and lingered just long enough to take a pinch of salt from the earthenware pot she kept by the entrance and sprinkle it over the threshold. Then she went inside and shrugged off her outer garments, hanging them in the hallway. The wool coat still smelled of her nan – a soothing blend of rose and lavender. A coat like this could last for years and Carys could never bear to throw anything away. Even if a garment was worn, it could usually be fixed, and she was adept with a needle and thread. People sometimes gave her funny looks at her mismatched wardrobe, but she cared little for fashion

The cottage wasn't large, and there were just two doors leading off the hallway – one to the sitting-room, and one to the kitchen. She pressed the latch of the kitchen door and stepped inside, ducking her head to avoid the low oak lintel.

The room held a lingering warmth from the oil-fired cooker, but it wasn't what most people would call comfortable. Growing up, Carys had learned that a chunky-knit jumper was the way to keep warm in the old stone cottage, and a long-sleeved vest and even a scarf or gloves might be needed too in the depths of winter. Her nan had worn thick stockings and a shawl most of the year round. Only during the height of summer was the quarry-tiled floor warm enough to walk on in bare feet, and sometimes not even then.

'I'm home, Nan,' Carys called softly, wishing with all her heart that her grandmother was still here to greet her. Nan would have had a cawl – a hearty meat and vegetable stew – simmering in the cast-iron pot on the stove. She would have summoned Carys and her sister, Esme, over to the range, where they would have filled their bowls and eaten it with crusty homemade bread spread thick with butter from the local farm. And Nan would have told them the old, familiar stories, of Welsh saints who sailed across the sea to perform miracles, and the *Tylwyth Teg*, or faerie folk, who came from the Otherworld to take lovers or steal children. Myths, legends and history all jumbled together, becoming one and the same.

The memory filled her with a sudden, sharp longing for all that was lost. But her nan was no more and neither was the cawl.

'It'll have to be scrambled eggs on toast, Nan.'

The eggs came from the same farm as the butter and were fresh that morning. Carys whisked them in a chipped bowl, added a generous knob of butter, and set the mixture to cook on the range. She cut a slice of bread and opened a tin of sardines. Her nan had grown up during the war and had been evangelical about the benefits of a cupboard stocked with tinned food. It was a habit she had instilled in Carys, who had duly topped up her supplies of sardines, mackerel, baked beans, and custard powder on moving back to Manorbier. Cheap, wholesome food that never went off – what was not to like?

She ate her makeshift meal at the kitchen table and mulled over the day. Working with new people always presented a challenge for her. Or perhaps it was Carys who presented a challenge for them. At school, her favourite teacher had praised her for being *an independent thinker*. Others had been less flattering. *Not a team player* was a comment that peppered her old school reports. She hadn't made friends easily at school and still didn't. But for Carys, making friends mattered less than her mission – to help the hurt and the lost, the scared and the damaged. Not to mention the dead.

This present murder was particularly cruel and twisted – not what she'd expected to encounter in rural Pembrokeshire. But she would approach it as she always did, calm and practical, never losing sight of the victim. In this case, the young woman at the centre of it all wasn't who she had claimed to be. Yet whether her name was Sarah Black or Veronica Emmett, Carys felt for her and would stop at nothing to identify and apprehend her killer.

As for her new colleague, Rhodri had impressed her with the energy he had put into intercepting Rick Styles at the jetty. Of course, he had been trying to make up for the fact that one of the witnesses had done a runner on his watch. And she wasn't blind to his need to show off his physical prowess. He was clearly a man of action. But after the shaky start to their working relationship down at the harbour, she thought they would rub along well enough. Besides, action could be very important, when the time came.

She finished her meal and brewed a mug of chamomile tea to help her relax before bedtime. Nan had taught her all the herbal remedies – peppermint and fennel to aid digestion, rosehip and ginger in the winter months to ward off colds. As a child, Esme had refused to drink it, but then Esme had always been a rebel.

A difficult child – Carys had overheard the words whispered in the local shop by a pair of gossiping women. Aged four, she had known they were talking about her sister, then just two and a half, by the way they had given Esme disapproving stares as she made a grab for the sweets on display. Carys had approached the women, tugged at the coat of the nearest and asked, 'Is that why our mother left us?' Too shocked to speak, the women had turned away, and Carys had learned that sometimes the truth was too difficult to mention. Nan had rescued the situation by blithely asking after the women's husbands and children as if nothing untoward had occurred. Nan had known how to walk with her head high. Yet Carys had never forgotten the look of disdain on those women's faces.

Esme, of course, had been oblivious. She had learned later, though, that her family was a topic of village gossip. Perhaps that's why she had become such an outlaw. Or perhaps she had been born that way.

Curled up on the sitting-room sofa with her tea, Carys picked up a framed photograph that stood on a side table. In the image, Carys and Esme were standing on top of a tower at Manorbier Castle, playing at princesses, their long hair blowing in the wind. Carys must have been about eight, Esme six and a half. They were wearing matching dresses that Nan had made on her Singer sewing machine.

It had always been just the three of them – Carys, Esme and Nan. The girls were half-sisters, and their mother, Dawn, had left when Esme was a baby. She had walked out one day and never returned. Carys's recollection of her was vague, and she couldn't tell whether she remembered anything at all or had simply reconstructed her mother's image from old photographs and Nan's tales. There was nothing left of her now except a few photos, a jumble of strange items and the iron key that Carys carried in her pocket at all times to ward off evil.

Esme's father had belonged to a community of Travellers who came and went with the seasons. He moved on before Esme was born. As for her own father, Carys had never known him.

She had grown up believing her father had wings. Not angel wings, but faerie wings, cobweb-thin and glinting in moonlight. It was a story she had told herself, at first to feel special, and later to feel safe. Immersed in Nan's peculiar blend of myth and legend, she had constructed a world in which her father was the faerie king, Esme a changeling, and her mother a prisoner in the Otherworld beyond the sea. But when the truth came – brittle, mundane and heavy with human failure – she stopped believing in faeries. And in fathers.

She gave the photo a quick polish with her sleeve and placed it back on the table.

'They're all gone, Nan,' she murmured. 'Now it's just me.'

*

The monks processed in single file along the darkened path, passing graves marked by simple wooden crosses, the final resting place of so many of their brethren. As he led the way, Father Anselm felt the ache in his bones and knew that he too would lie here one day. Perhaps that day was not far off.

With the monastery church out of bounds, sealed with crime-scene tape that fluttered and snapped in the wind, he had decided that the service of Compline would take place here in the nearby St David's church instead. The important thing was that the monks should continue to follow the canonical hours as laid down in their tradition and according to their faith.

The grey stone church stood alone in the churchyard, the only light the flicker of candles through its stained-glass windows, a symbol of hope amid the darkness.

The congregation rose as the abbot entered the church and led the monks down the aisle to the sanctuary. Father Anselm was pleased to see that for once it was not just the monks who had come to pray for a peaceful end to the day. The tragic events of the morning had drawn the religious and secular worlds together.

He recognised all of the locals – Bethan and Dafydd Rees, Nia Armitage the postmistress, Eifion the boatman from Tenby. The retreatants, who sat as a group on the left-hand side with Sister Monica, he did not know.

Brother Gregory acted as cantor, leading the chanting with his strong baritone voice. 'O God, come to my assistance.'

The other monks responded with, 'Lord, make haste to help me.'

As the chanting of the familiar words proceeded, Father Anselm found his mind beginning to wander. It had been a long and trying day. First had been the shocking discovery in the church. His mind reeled with the horror of finding that poor woman's body laid on the altar, and he couldn't begin to fathom what kind of person might commit such an atrocity. Next had come his encounter with DI Morgan, a woman clearly determined to get her own way, even if that meant overturning centuries of monastic tradition. And finally there had been the unprecedented outburst in the refectory between Brothers Cadoc and Gregory.

He had observed for some time the growing rivalry between the two men and felt his own failure keenly in this respect. He could have done more to prevent it, and bowed his head in shame at his lack of action. He had been weak when he should have been strong.

Forgive me, Father, for I have sinned.

The two monks were worthy contenders for the position of abbot, but neither was without fault. Gregory was a glutton, and Cadoc vain and ambitious.

Could Gregory really have tried to poison Cadoc? If such a thing could happen in his own monastery, Anselm was unfit to be abbot. Yet he knew that if he stood aside now, he would unleash a battle between his two rivals, fiercer by far than what had already occurred.

His thoughts turned darker, as he perceived that some great evil had taken root within the monastery. Feuding monks was just the beginning. He lifted his head and let his gaze fall silently on each person present. Monks, islanders, retreatants. They had gathered together in prayer, yet one of them was a murderer.

CHAPTER 14

DCI Gareth Pritchard often wished he could have lived in an earlier, more elegant age. It would always be a matter of regret to him that Pembrokeshire Police, to give the force its historic name, no longer operated out of Castle House, the former gaoler's house in the grounds of Haverfordwest Castle. The crenellated stone building with gothic windows – now the local museum – would, he felt, have been a much more inspiring building to work in than the flat-roofed, redbrick 1960s block that now housed Dyfed-Powys Police – to use the new and correct name of the institution that he worked for. But he had suffered the misfortune of being born into the latter half of the twentieth century and had watched with growing despondency the decline of all the values he held dear – duty, tradition and respect. Not to mention the construction of monstrous edifices such as his present place of employment.

It was raining – again! – and as he dashed from his Mercedes C300 saloon to the shelter of the entrance, he covered his thinning hair with a black, leather folder. He loved Wales, but God, how he hated the weather! It was always bloody raining. Today was worse than usual, as there was fog as well as drizzle. What did you call that kind of weather? Fizzle? Drog? Whatever it was called, he damn well hated it.

It was all the work of the *Pembrokeshire Dangler* – that peculiar meteorological phenomenon that so often brought misery to Pritchard's life. The wind had swung to the north during the night, bringing with it a raw, salt-bitten chill that met the mild, maritime air rising off the Irish Sea. By dawn the coast sat under a strange, shifting gloom, heavy with impending precipitation, as if someone had drawn a ruler-straight line from Anglesey to St Govan's. And by the time Pritchard set off on his morning commute, the grey mist clinging low to the hedgerows had given way to lashings of rain so thick that as he drove across the Cleddau Bridge, the little town of Neyland on the shore of the estuary remained hidden from view. He had almost driven into the back of a white van so smeared with grime that it was indistinguishable from the weather. In short, he was not in the best of moods for the meeting with his new detective inspector from the bright lights of Cardiff. A young and ambitious "hotshot" no less – his least favourite kind of police officer.

He fetched a coffee from the vending machine, hoping to grab five minutes in his office before the day's work began, but a woman in a long wool coat, knitted scarf and beret was already sitting outside waiting for him. A Celtic cross dangled around her neck. Her feet were encased in shiny Doc Martens. Who on earth was this, now?

As he approached, she stood up, matching his height.

'You'll need to book an appointment with my secretary,' he informed her briskly. 'I have a meeting right now.'

She held out her hand. 'I know. DCI Pritchard? You asked to see me first thing. I'm DI Carys Morgan.'

He stared at her, reevaluating his first impressions, and arriving at exactly the same conclusion. An eccentric, that's what she was. Pritchard loathed eccentrics. Freethinkers, nonconformists, mavericks. Couldn't bloody stand them.

'Yes, all right. Do come in.'

He was flustered and knew he was showing it. He hated being agitated before a meeting. He liked to get himself settled, check his notes, and then proceed calmly, with control.

'Would you rather I come back later, sir?' Her eyes radiated concern.

'No, now is fine,' he snapped. 'Please come in and take a seat.'

They entered his office – a dull room with a desk, gunmetal filing cabinets, and a view of the car park. It didn't normally bother Pritchard that the room was so functional and boring –he preferred it that way – but in the presence of this outlandishly-dressed woman, he became conscious of its shortcomings. Should he personalise it with photos of his wife and his dog? He brushed the idea aside. There was no room for sentiment in his job.

She took the chair facing his desk, unwinding her extravagantly long scarf in a distracted manner. But she kept the beret on her head. The action seemed calculated to annoy him.

'So,' he said, settling himself down and removing Carys's personnel file from his leather folder. He'd taken it home the previous night to familiarise himself with its contents, so at least he was up to speed. 'You've come all the way from Cardiff.'

He regretted the words as soon as they were out of his mouth. Cardiff was only a hundred miles away, but he made it sound as if she'd travelled halfway round the globe.

'I lived in Manorbier until I was eighteen.'

'A local girl,' he replied, feeling a sense that he was getting on top of things again.

She made no reply, just studied him with those eyes that were as green and dark as bottomless pools.

'Hmm.' He retreated to the safety of the personnel file. 'So you joined the police straight after finishing university and were fast-tracked into Major Crime.'

'That's correct. I was selected for the accelerated training programme.'

She said it without any hint of boasting or false modesty but stated it matter-of-factly, as if confirming her date of birth. Pritchard liked that quiet confidence and found himself warming to her. In any case, facts didn't lie. She had clocked up an exceptional track record during her time in Cardiff and her file made impressive reading. Promoted to detective sergeant at twenty-six, then to detective inspector aged thirty-two. She was now just thirty-six and had already led a series of successful high-profile investigations.

He closed the file. 'Your last case in Cardiff was a missing girl.'

She looked away and a flicker of emotion passed across her face. 'Yes.'

There was no need to go into details. They both knew that the girl had been found alive but holed up in her abductor's basement having been subjected to horrifying sexual and physical abuse. According to her previous boss, Carys had demonstrated "a relentless and almost obsessive determination to find the victim and arrest her captor."

There was nothing wrong with that in Pritchard's opinion – far from it – but it was a red flag, given Carys's personal history. He tried to find a tactful way to phrase his next question. 'I know you've returned to Pembrokeshire under difficult circumstances.'

Her eyes flicked back to his and held them steadily. 'Sir, I can assure you I'm quite capable of doing this job. My personal circumstances will not affect my ability to carry out my work.'

'I hope not.'

After going through the file, he'd called his opposite number in Cardiff who had told him that Carys got results but could be unconventional. Looking at the way she dressed, Pritchard could well believe it. She was also suffering a deep personal loss. Her sister had tragically died in Manorbier while Carys was caught up in the recent investigation. Her boss had concerns about Carys's mental health and had insisted she take compassionate leave.

'I've attended counselling sessions,' said Carys, 'and I'm fit to return to work.'

Pritchard nodded. He'd gathered from the phone call that Carys felt personally responsible for her sister's death, having been so involved with work. Her transfer to Dyfed-Powys was presumably a direct response to her bereavement. But despite that, Pritchard couldn't begrudge her arrival at a time when experienced detective inspectors were thin on the ground. Just as long as she could handle the pressure.

He pushed her personnel file aside and leaned back in his chair. 'Caldey Island, then. Sounds like a strange one to me. Anything to report so far?' Pritchard would have been the first to admit that he preferred more regular cases – trouble in Milford Haven on a Saturday night, the recent spate of burglaries across the county, the sort of thing he was used to dealing with.

Some kind of ritualised killing on a holy island – that wasn't what his training at police college had prepared him for.

Yet at mention of the investigation, Carys's face came to life. 'We have a positive ID for the victim. She was one of the pilgrims staying on the island, but she was there using a false name. I don't know why yet, but I believe that the location and manner of the murder are significant. The body was placed on the altar of the monastery church with an open Bible on her chest.'

Pritchard wrinkled his nose. 'I imagine that your degree subject may prove useful here.' He had never in his life heard of a graduate of theology joining the force before.

She gave him an enigmatic smile.

'Hmm,' said Pritchard, standing up. 'Well, we'd best be cracking on. Come with me. I'll introduce you to the rest of the team.'

*

Rosalind was the first down to breakfast as usual. She had developed the habit of rising early when her children were young. The quiet hours before eight o'clock had been the only time she could get any writing done. Now, her children were grown up and long gone, but she still found that mornings were the best time for creative work – before the demands of daily life intruded on her thoughts.

She found Sister Monica already setting out the breakfast things in the dining room.

'You're another early riser, Sister,' said Rosalind. 'Let me help you with that.' She took a heavy-looking tray laden with butter, jam, marmalade, and island honey out of the nun's hands.

'Thank you, dear. I'll make the tea.'

Rosalind put the spreads on the table, then joined Sister Monica in the kitchen. She was glad it was just the two of them. She had lately conceived the idea that her protagonist, Brother Aidan, should encounter on his travels a female mystic and visionary along the lines of Hildegard of Bingen or Julian of Norwich, and Rosalind was keen to speak with a woman who had experienced life within the walls of a convent.

'Did you always want to be a nun?'

'Oh, yes,' said Sister Monica. 'I grew up in a small village in Latvia and there was literally nothing else for a girl to do, apart from get married and have babies.'

Rosalind had detected a foreign accent in Sister Monica's speech but had been unable to place it. 'And you didn't want to have babies?'

Sister Monica gave a rueful smile. 'I would have liked a baby. It was the husband I didn't want.'

Rosalind laughed. 'Surely there were other options?'

The nun's expression turned serious. 'Not in my country at that time in history. I saw how my mother lived, and my aunts too, and I knew I didn't want that life for myself. But I was a good student and came from a very devout family, so it wasn't too unusual to consider going into a convent. My parents were very proud when I took my vows.'

Rosalind nodded, trying to put herself in the nun's shoes and understand how she experienced the world. This was what made being a novelist so fascinating – the creative act of imagining yourself living another person's life. While writing, you could become anyone you wanted to, at any time or place. 'When did you leave your home country?'

'During the 1990s. So much was changing during that decade, it was a thrilling time to be alive. I wanted to travel and see other places, so I asked my Mother Superior if I could transfer to another convent abroad. I didn't expect to be granted permission, yet God has a plan for each of us, so here I am.'

Rosalind grinned, marvelling at the alignment of coincidences that had brought a poor Catholic girl all the way from her village in Latvia to an island off the coast of Wales. It struck her, as it so often did, how life was stranger than fiction.

Their conversation was interrupted by the deep grunt of a man clearing his throat. Paul Roberts stood in the doorway, a scowl darkening his features. 'Is breakfast ready?'

'Not quite,' said Rosalind coolly. 'But you could help. Rather than leaving it all to the women.'

She turned away from him, giving Sister Monica a wink. She felt the two of them had bonded over their shared conversation. And Paul had given her an idea for another character – a misogynistic zealot who would be a thorn in the side of her female mystic. *He would surely get what was coming to him.* The story was already taking shape in her mind and she began to imagine interesting ways to kill him off.

CHAPTER 15

The incident room at Haverfordwest wasn't quite up to the modern spec that Carys had come to expect during her time in Cardiff, but it would have to do. Anyway, it wasn't facilities that made the difference, it was the team, and she was keen to meet the detectives she would be working alongside.

Her introductory meeting with DCI Gareth Pritchard had gone as well as expected. He obviously didn't know quite what to make of her, but she was used to that. Pritchard's smart suit and functional office devoid of personal touches signalled his conservative nature, and she had noted his silent disapproval of her dress code. Yet he had said nothing about it. He was a pragmatist, and she could work with that.

She knew what her previous boss in Cardiff would have told him – that she blamed herself for Esme's death and was still dealing with bereavement. Still, Pritchard had accepted her assurance that she was fit for the job, and that also boded well. She might not yet have earned the unquestioning loyalty of her new boss, but she sensed he would back her as long as she delivered results.

The room fell silent as they entered. Rhodri slid off the desk where he'd been sitting, chatting to the others. He'd been gossiping about her, no doubt. Probably telling them how he had mistaken her for a tourist. It was only natural that they'd be curious.

'DS Rhodri Evans you already know,' said Pritchard. 'This is DC Hugh Hughes and DC Elen Vaughan. Well then, I'll let you get on. Any problems, you know where to find me.' He left the room, retreating to the safety of his office.

Carys regarded her new team with interest. Rhodri, tall and athletic, but squeamish when confronted with the body in the church, was the most senior, though she could tell from the way he had been chatting to the others that he regarded himself as one of the gang. He'd been at ease in the company of the boatman, Eifion, too, so he had a talent for fitting in, although he'd displayed discomfort in the abbot's presence. Carys, by contrast, would never allow herself to be intimidated by authority. Rhodri showed potential, but he would need to toughen up.

The other two were an unknown quantity.

Hugh Hughes, in his late twenties, appeared bookish with sloping shoulders and silver-framed glasses. His skin was as pale as milk, as if he had never ventured outdoors. He stared at her through his thick lenses, like a rabbit caught in the headlights.

Elen Vaughan looked to be in her early to mid-twenties. She wore her long ginger hair tied back in a practical plait and had a bright, open face with a splash of freckles over her cheeks and button nose. She was dressed in black trousers, a navy blouse and sensible shoes. Short and stocky, she looked like the sort of person who would hold it together in an emergency.

Carys gave them a brief smile. 'I'm DI Carys Morgan, just transferred from Cardiff. I'm originally a Pembrokeshire girl, so don't worry about having to explain any local customs to me. My background is in Major Crime, especially kidnapping, abduction and murder. Any questions, or shall we get started?'

She was greeted by complete silence. Either nobody had any questions, or they were too intimidated to ask. Carys looked around the room to see what facilities were available to her. An old whiteboard on wheels stood in one corner. She pulled it to the front of the room and picked up a marker pen from the tray. She tried to write with it, but the ink had dried up.

'Try this one,' said Hugh, passing her a new pen.

'Thanks.' She tossed the old pen into a wastepaper basket and wrote two names on the board.

Sarah Black and *Veronica Emmett.*

The right place to begin any investigation was always with the victim, a point that Carys sometimes found she had to remind her colleagues and even her superiors of.

'The body of a young woman was found by monks on Caldey Island yesterday morning when they entered the abbey church for Matins. She had been stabbed multiple times' – Carys retrieved a photograph of the murdered woman and pinned it to the board – 'and placed on the altar. She told other people on the island that her name was Sarah Black, but documentation recovered from her room indicates that her real name was Veronica Emmett. Her parents have been notified and her body was formally identified last night. It has been taken to the mortuary in Haverfordwest and the post-mortem is scheduled for later today.'

Carys had put the wheels in motion during the boat trip back from Caldey the previous day. She wished she could have been present to meet the parents, but it wasn't possible to be everywhere, and the logistics of the current investigation didn't make things easier. It was, she had to admit, the first time she had investigated a crime that hadn't taken place on the mainland.

Hugh reached for his notebook and pushed his glasses up his nose. 'I started looking into the victim's background as soon as I received confirmation of her ID yesterday. Veronica Emmett was thirty years old, originally from

Cardiff but she'd been living in Swansea for the past twelve years. She was single and worked in a building society as a cashier. No criminal record. But this is where it gets interesting.'

Hugh's voice was high-pitched and reedy, but there was an intensity to him that Carys immediately liked. She could tell that he took his job seriously and did it well. He might lack Rhodri's physique and easy charm, but there was a lot to be said for his attention to detail. 'What is it, Hugh?'

'Her brother, Jack Emmett, was killed seven years ago after a fatal collision with a stolen car. The vehicle in question had been involved in a break-in at a High Street jewellers. The driver was arrested and convicted of manslaughter. He was given a sentence of ten years but served five. The parole board recommended him for early release, partly on the basis of a favourable report from the prison chaplain. The driver's name was Rick Styles.'

'Rick is one of the other retreatants staying on Caldey,' explained Carys for Elen's benefit. 'Good work, Hugh.'

'There's more,' said Hugh. 'I came in early this morning to start looking at the victim's tablet and found this.' He brought the screen to life and swivelled it around so they could all see. Then he clicked *play* on a video.

Veronica Emmett was dressed in the same clothes she'd been wearing when Carys had seen her in the abbey church, and she was sitting at the desk in her room at St Philomena's. Speaking directly to camera, her gaze was unflinching.

'Right, so as you know, I've been keeping tabs on Rick Styles ever since he was released from jail. I stalk him online, I know where he works, where he hangs out, who his mates are. I've even followed him in real life once or twice. He never shuts up about how he's a changed man. But we all know that people don't really change – not deep down. Reformed character, my arse! He's a killer and he should have been given a much longer jail sentence. Five years for killing Jack!' She tossed her hair angrily over her shoulder. 'This is what I'm going to do. I've followed him to Caldey Island – he's been posting online for weeks about this trip – and he hasn't recognised me. I dyed my hair blonde and gave the people here a false name. I even sat next to him on the boat, and we had dinner together in St Philomena's, and I'm sure he has no idea who I am. So here's my plan. I'm going to have it out with him. Then I'll tell everyone on the island who he really is and ruin his life, just like he deserves. There's a schoolteacher here, and a novelist, and a guy who works in London, not to mention the nun who runs the guest house. I'll tell them all what he did, and they can decide for themselves if he's truly repented. And this is just the beginning. Yeah, Rick Styles is going to pay for what he did.'

The video ended.

'This video was recorded on Sunday evening at 8:15pm,' said Hugh. 'There are earlier videos but nothing later than that.'

'Very good,' said Carys, impressed with Hugh's diligence. 'Rick Styles tried to make a run for it yesterday. When Rhodri apprehended him, he admitted to serving a manslaughter sentence. He didn't mention the robbery, though.'

'I wonder what else he kept to himself,' said Rhodri. 'I had a bad feeling about that guy from the start. Are we going to bring him in?'

'Yes,' said Carys. 'Elen, you come with us to Caldey. Hugh, keep looking through the data on the laptop and run a background check on all the other retreatants at St Philomena's. I don't want any more surprises.'

'Will do.' Hugh returned to his computer keyboard.

As they were about to leave, Rhodri's phone rang. 'DC Rhodri Evans speaking.'

Carys couldn't hear the caller's voice, but as Rhodri listened to what they were saying, the colour drained from his face. He hung up then turned to face her, his mouth hanging open.

'What is it?' asked Carys.

'Boss, another body's been found on the island.'

CHAPTER 16

The season was as good as over, and Bethan Rees wasn't expecting to do much business today, unless those police detectives decided to pop into the café later. Even if the island hadn't been temporarily closed to day-trippers, the weather was turning, becoming increasingly autumnal, churning up the sea and making boat crossings challenging for all but seasoned seafarers.

Since she had no customers, she armed herself with rubber gloves, a bucket of hot soapy water and a sponge, ready to set to work scrubbing the plastic chairs in the café garden. Afterwards, she'd get Dafydd to put them away for the winter. If they were left out, the first storm of the season would blow them all across the island.

But as soon as she stepped outside, her attention was caught by a commotion by the gift shop. A group of people had gathered next to the fishpond, their backs to her. They were looking at something in the water. Bethan set down her bucket, removed her rubber gloves, and walked over to the pond.

The staff from the gift shop were all there – they didn't have any customers either. And the retreatants from St

Philomena's too. She hadn't met all of them, but she recognised Rosalind who had popped into the café a couple of times for coffee, cake and a good old chinwag. Bethan liked Rosalind and had found herself revealing all sorts of personal stories she didn't usually share with other people. She hoped she wasn't going to find herself in Rosalind's next book. The novelist was standing between Sister Monica and two men who Bethan hadn't yet met. Brother Cadoc and Novice Thomas were kneeling at the water's edge. And there, thigh-deep in the pond, wearing his waders, was her own husband, Dafydd.

'What's going on?' The voice in her ear made her jump and she spun around to see Nia from the post office, trying to peer over the heads in front of her.

Bethan shivered. She disliked Nia and always kept well out of her way.

The manager of the gift shop turned and whispered loudly, 'Dafydd's found a body in the water.'

Bethan could see it now, a man's body floating among the dying waterlilies, face-down in the pond.

'Who is it?' asked Nia. 'Who's dead?'

'Must be another one of the retreatants,' said the gift shop assistant. 'Everyone else is here.' She dropped her voice. 'Did you hear? The woman who was found in the church? She wasn't who she claimed she was. Called herself Sarah Black, but her real name was Veronica Emmett?' Her voice rose in pitch with the questioning tone favoured by the young.

'Veronica Emmett, you say?' repeated Nia, eyes open wide with interest. 'Is that with two Ts or one?'

'No idea.' The girl turned back to the pond where there was a great deal of splashing as Dafydd dragged the body towards dry land. His feet slipped in the mud and a collective gasp rose from the watching crowd, but he quickly steadied himself.

Then Brother Cadoc's voice called out, loud and clear. 'All right, Dafydd, push him this way. That's it – a bit further. Okay, got him. Ready, Thomas?'

Together, Cadoc and Thomas hauled the body out of the water, getting their habits soaking wet in the process. They lifted it onto the grass and rolled it over. The dead man stared blindly at the sky, his face as pale and grey as the clouds that scudded overhead.

Bethan screamed. Novice Thomas bent double and retched into the reeds at the water's edge. Dafydd climbed out of the pond and peeled off his waders, his face expressionless as if what he'd just done was all in a day's work.

'Oh my God,' said the gift shop assistant, turning away. 'Gross.'

Brother Cadoc held up his hands. 'Please everyone, stay calm. The police have been called and are on their way.' His booming voice and steady composure reassured the crowd and set Bethan's own nerves at ease. There was no one else on the island quite like Cadoc to bring order to a difficult situation.

Sister Monica began to pray aloud in a quavering voice. 'Eternal rest grant unto them, O Lord, and let perpetual light–'

But she was interrupted by one of the male retreatants who shouted across her. 'Never mind all that! Can't you see what is happening here?' All eyes turned to him. He was late middle-aged, scruffily dressed in corduroy trousers and a checked shirt, and his grey hair was long and unkempt. He held their attention like a preacher as he bellowed, 'Evil walks among us! Sin has returned to the fold!'

Bethan had seen and heard enough. She turned to leave and was surprised to see that Nia was already hurrying away across the village green. What could be so urgent that she would miss a single moment of this drama?

⋆

On this second trip to the island, Rhodri sat up front in the bow with Elen while Carys sheltered in the cabin with

Eifion. The arrangement suited Rhodri well enough. He was glad of the chance to catch up with his friend and compare notes.

'So what do you think of the new DI?'

Elen clutched the side of the boat as it rose on the swell of a wave. 'Carys? She seems sharp enough.'

Rhodri gazed across the shifting grey water to the island that lay ahead of them. From the sea, the abbey was hidden from view, but the lighthouse on the far side peeked out above the tops of the trees. 'Bit weird though, don't you think?'

The front of the boat crashed downwards, sending a spray of salt water over them. Elen scrunched her eyes tight shut. 'I don't mind weird.'

'Figures.'

'What's that supposed to mean?'

'Well, you know… you're a weirdo yourself. You and Hugh. I'm the only normal person in the team.'

Elen punched his arm. 'Oi! Just because I play rugby. Girls do, these days. Get used to it! And Hugh's not weird, just a bit nerdy.'

'Ouch!' Rhodri rubbed his arm where she'd hit him. That hadn't exactly been a playful punch. Elen packed some serious muscle and wasn't afraid to throw it about. 'Do you lift weights or something?'

'Of course. You don't get to play prop unless you've done the hard work in training.'

Rhodri shrugged. He was more a football fan himself. Rugby was too rough and muddy for his liking, although he was happy enough to watch a match down at the Three Mariners if pints were involved. And who was he kidding? At the Three Mariners, pints were always involved.

'She wears weird clothes too,' he continued.

'You mean she doesn't dress in order to please men.' Elen glanced down at her own waterproof jacket and black trousers that completely hid her figure. 'I hate to break this to you, Rod, but not every girl looks like she's about to audition for Love Island.'

'I didn't mean that. I just meant…' Oh, what was the point? Elen just liked to argue for the sake of it. She was always picking fights.

She dropped her head to her knees. 'Oh God, I feel sick. I hate boats.'

'Raise your head and look towards the horizon,' said Rhodri. 'It'll help to steady you.'

She did as he suggested, turning to face the approaching island.

'Now that's a first,' he said.

'What?'

'You doing something I told you to.'

His reward was another punch on the arm.

'Bloody hell, Elen. That hurt.' Rhodri would never hit a woman and wondered why it was okay for her to hit him. Now that he thought about it, it probably wasn't. 'I could report you to HR for assault.'

'Go on then. Dare you.'

'Nah, I'll let it go this time.' He could imagine the consequences if he did. He'd never be able to show his face at the Three Mariners again. Jon Jenkins would laugh him out of the pub. 'Though I've got to warn you, Elen, I'm seriously considering crossing you off my Christmas card list.'

'Go ahead. I can handle it. I'm a big girl.'

Brutal. He considered a sarcastic response but thought better of it, not wanting to risk a third blow. He gave his arm another rub. There would be bruising there in the morning. How would he explain that to Amy?

'Anyway,' he went on, 'be careful not to get on the wrong side of Carys. She gave a couple of those monks a hard time yesterday. When one of them suggested I should do all the interviews because I was a man, she practically bit his head off. She even laid into the abbot when he offered to help, and the poor old bloke's practically got one foot in the grave.'

Elen nodded her approval. 'Sounds like she gets the job done.'

'Or gets other people to do the job for her,' Rhodri moaned. 'She made me drive the evidence bags over to forensics after we got back from Caldey yesterday, and then I was too late to pick up Billy from football club. Amy had to ask her mum to collect him instead and gave me a right earful when I got home. I forgot to buy the milk and bread too. The only upside was that I earned some overtime so I wasn't completely in the doghouse.'

'You need to grow a pair, Rod. Toughen up a bit. Why don't you take up rugby?'

Rhodri made no reply. He was growing tired of Elen's banter and the day had hardly started. If he'd been hoping for sympathy from a mate, he'd have been better off in the wheelhouse chatting to Eifion. He was thinking of downgrading his rating of Elen as a friend.

Frenemy was perhaps closer to the truth.

A loud retching sound brought him out of his self-reflection as she heaved over the side of the boat.

Rhodri suppressed a grin. He had never been sick at sea. 'I didn't think you were such a lily-livered landlubber.'

He shouldn't have been too surprised when she rewarded him with a punch on his other arm.

CHAPTER 17

The sea was a lot rougher than the day before, and even Rhodri was glad when they landed on Caldey. He'd taken enough of a battering from Elen, never mind the waves slapping against the prow of the boat. He sprang onto the jetty, leaving his colleague looking green in the bow. *Serves her right for hitting him.* Elen might be in her element on the rugby pitch, but she was all at sea in a boat.

He tied the rope to the bollard and offered her his hand. 'See? No hard feelings.'

'Thanks.' She accepted his help and stepped off the boat, stopping with her hands on her knees and taking in great gulps of air like a pair of bellows. *Or a dragon.* Then she straightened up, smiled, and announced she was okay. 'We're good, Rhodri?'

He bumped fists with her. 'We're good.'

Carys and Eifion followed. 'You wait here with the boat, Eifion,' said Carys. 'I don't know how long we'll be.'

'That's fine with me,' said the boatman. 'I've nowhere else to be.'

Brother Cadoc was waiting at the end of the jetty to

meet them. The hem of his habit was wet and covered with green vegetation.

'I see you've been in the water this morning, Brother,' said Rhodri. 'Bit cold for a bath, isn't it?'

The monk didn't smile at Rhodri's weak attempt at humour. 'Novice Thomas and I helped Dafydd Rees pull the body out of the fishpond.'

Carys's face soured at the news. 'You moved the body? You should have left the crime scene undisturbed for the SOCO team to examine.'

Cadoc's expression remained impassive. 'It seemed disrespectful to leave the man in the water.'

'With respect,' said Carys icily, 'I will be the judge of how this investigation is conducted.'

Rhodri nudged Elen and gave her a *told you so* look. She didn't respond.

They set off through the woods in silence, Brother Cadoc leading the way. On arriving at the village green, Rhodri saw that the SOCO team had erected a white tent over the body and were busy searching the surrounding area.

Anthony Davies emerged from the tent and strode across the lawn towards them. Even in his white protective suit, he carried himself with an effortless grace and Rhodri couldn't help noticing Elen's look of admiration, even though she was the one who had told him Anthony was gay.

Carys, however, seemed unaffected by the SOCO boss's good looks. 'What have we got this time?'

Anthony pulled off his gloves and ran a hand through his wavy hair. 'Looks like a blow to the back of the head from a blunt object. And then the victim either fell or was pushed into the water.'

'Did he drown? Or was it the blow that killed him?'

'I can't say,' said Anthony. 'You'll need the pathologist to confirm one way or the other.'

'It's a different MO to the first victim, though,' said Rhodri. 'Different murder weapon. No religious symbolism this time.'

'I don't know about that,' said Anthony. He held up a plastic evidence bag. 'We recovered this Bible from the breast pocket of the victim's coat. It's a bit soggy, but it was bookmarked at Acts, chapter twenty-two, verse sixteen, if that means anything to you.'

Carys gave a sharp nod. '"And now why delay? It is time you were baptised and had your sins washed away while invoking his name."'

Rhodri looked at her in bewilderment. How did she know all these Bible quotes? He could barely remember anything from his Sunday School days, and certainly not by chapter and verse.

'Can we see the body?' asked Carys.

'Of course.' Anthony set off in the direction of the tent.

Brother Cadoc was loitering nearby, and Carys turned to him. 'Thank you for your help, Brother. We'll take it from here.'

He moved away reluctantly and Carys waited for him to leave before following in Anthony's wake.

Rhodri gave Elen another nudge. 'See?' he whispered. But she said nothing about Carys's dismissive treatment of the monk and set off towards the tent. Rhodri groaned inwardly but hurried to catch up.

Anthony was holding open the tent flap so that the three detectives could look inside. The dead man lay on the grass where he had been dragged from the pond. The corpse's arms and legs were tangled with reeds and slim tendrils of vegetation. The man's face was puffy and grey, the lips a mottled blue. But his features were unmistakable. Rough grey stubble, mid-length hair, a strong jawline and a determined look, even in death.

Rhodri had seen enough. 'It's him, boss. Rick Styles. The man we were going to arrest.'

'How was the body discovered?' asked Carys.

Anthony allowed the flap of the tent to fall closed. 'Dafydd Rees was in the pond, cutting back the dead reeds ready for winter. When he found the body, he called for assistance, and two of the monks helped to drag it out of the water. Unfortunately that means there's no chance of recovering any footprints from the scene.'

'What have you managed to find?'

Anthony gave a shrug. 'We found the victim's phone and the Bible tucked into his pocket. But nothing resembling a murder weapon. We'll need to dredge the pond, and I'm waiting for a specialist team to come from the mainland. If they find anything, I'll let you know.'

'Thank you,' said Carys. She turned back to Rhodri and Elen. 'I'd like the two of you to take statements from all the islanders and the retreatants at St Philomena's. Find out when and where they last saw Rick Styles. Let's see if we can establish a window for the time of death.'

'Will do, boss,' said Rhodri. 'And what about you?'

Carys turned her head in the direction of the abbey. 'I need to speak to the abbot.'

*

'I must say, I am dismayed,' said Father Anselm, shaking his head as he lowered himself slowly into the chair.

It was colder in the tower room today. The morning rain had penetrated deep inside the stone walls, producing a damp musty smell. Carys kept her coat and beret on and was glad of her long scarf. The abbot, too, was dressed for the weather, with a heavy black cloak over his white tunic. She wondered if the main abbey building had any form of heating, or if a cold, comfortless existence was all part of the monastic life.

'Dismayed?' It wasn't the first reaction she had expected after informing him that a second murder had occurred on the island. Sorrow, empathy, compassion; these were emotions she would have understood. But dismay?

Father Anselm fixed her with his watery eyes. 'I dread to think what this will do to the reputation of the monastery and the island. The person responsible for these terrible crimes must be caught as quickly as possible. Do you have any leads?'

'I can't comment on the progress of the investigation, other than to say that we're not excluding anyone from our inquiries. We'll need to re-interview all the monks, in addition to the island's residents and the people staying at St Philomena's.'

The abbot shook his head slowly. 'None of the monks or islanders could have committed such dreadful crimes. It must be an outsider – one of the retreatants.'

'Outsiders?' said Carys sharply. 'Is that what you call them? I thought they were your guests. The Bible says, "Do not forget to entertain strangers, for by so doing some people have entertained angels without knowing it."'

The abbot's expression betrayed a grudging respect. 'I see you are well versed in scripture.'

'As is the killer. The first victim was found with an open Bible on her chest, the second with a bookmarked copy in his pocket.'

Father Anselm nodded miserably. '"The living know at least that they will die, the dead know nothing; no more reward for them; their memory has passed out of mind."'

'"And now why delay?"' added Carys. '"It is time you were baptised and had your sins washed away while invoking his name."' She waited while the abbot digested the implications of the words. 'Father,' she continued, 'these are not random verses. They are messages from the killer. That killer has demonstrated a clear biblical knowledge. They may even be familiar with the monastic or liturgical life.'

'Scripture is vast,' countered the abbot, refusing to acknowledge the possibility that a monk may have been involved. 'People pluck lines from the Bible all the time. They misunderstand them, twist them, use them to justify actions no faith would ever condone.'

'Exactly,' said Carys, leaning forward. 'That's what worries me. Someone with knowledge of this place is using your symbols. The altar. The pond. The texts. There is method here, not madness.'

The abbot's voice dropped almost to a whisper. 'Inspector, I understand you have a job to do. But I must ask you to tread with the utmost care. This has been a place of prayer for over a thousand years, and yet its future is not certain. You cannot know how it is to shepherd a community that's already fragile. A scandal like this... it could destroy us. Pilgrims would cease their visits. Vocations would dry up. My own brothers would become objects of suspicion.' His eyes glistened. 'We are simple men trying to live quietly, in service of God. That is all.'

Carys studied him, hearing the tremor beneath the dignity. There it was, as plain as day – his fear for the abbey's reputation. She sympathised but couldn't allow his concerns to restrict her investigation. She had personal experience of how the desire to protect institutions could ride roughshod over the rights of individuals. She would not permit that to happen here. She leaned forward, appealing one last time for his cooperation. 'Father, I'm not trying to destroy anything. I'm here to help you. So help me find this killer.'

A silence settled between them. But when the abbot eventually spoke, he had shed all trace of vulnerability. 'Inspector, I will say this again: if you think the murderer is within these walls, you are badly mistaken. You must turn your gaze elsewhere.'

He leaned on his walking stick, knuckles white, and rose slowly to his feet. Then he walked from the room without another word.

CHAPTER 18

The specialist search team arrived at the pond just as Carys returned from her meeting with the abbot. Rhodri and Elen were sitting in the café, an assortment of bacon rolls, packets of crisps and cups of coffee spread before them. Elen was obviously feeling better after her bout of seasickness on the boat trip over. Carys ordered a green tea and an egg roll and joined them.

'Boss,' said Rhodri through a mouthful of bacon bap. 'How did you get on with the abbot?'

Carys took a sip of the tea. 'He wasn't very helpful but that doesn't matter. We'll carry on with our job with or without his cooperation. How did you two get on with the interviews?'

Rhodri swallowed his food and took a loud slurp of milky coffee. 'We spoke to everyone at St Philomena's and they all told us pretty much the same thing. Everyone on the island attended Compline in St David's church yesterday evening – monks, islanders and retreatants. That finished just after eight o'clock. Rick Styles walked back to St Philomena's in the company of Paul Roberts.'

'What did they talk about? Did Paul say?'

'He was a bit vague on that.'

'Evasive, more like,' remarked Elen.

Carys nodded. 'And then?'

Rhodri checked his notes. 'Samir and Rick stayed outside for a smoke. According to Samir, Rick was in a subdued mood. But then everyone was, after what happened to Sarah – that's what they're still calling Veronica, even though they know it wasn't her real name.'

'So was Samir the last person to see Rick alive?'

'No,' said Elen. 'Rosalind Grieves encountered him when she went out for a short walk before bed.'

'What time was this?'

'About ten, she says. As far as we know, she was the last person to see him alive.'

'I'd like to hear for myself what she has to say.' Carys finished her breakfast while she collected her thoughts. Rosalind Grieves had struck her as both perceptive and inquisitive. Perhaps that came from being a novelist. Her impression of Paul Roberts and Samir Khan had been less favourable. There was something off about both men, and she would need to speak to them later.

She stood up. 'Rhodri, you come with me. Elen, can you supervise the dredging of the pond?'

'Sure thing, boss.' Elen trudged off in the direction of the fishpond. Her squared shoulders announced her intention to get the job done and Carys concealed a small smile. Elen was like a tractor chugging in low gear – not fast, but unstoppable.

At St Philomena's they were met by an anxious Sister Monica. 'Any news?' she enquired.

'The investigation is proceeding,' said Carys. 'We'd like to speak to Rosalind next.'

The nun ushered them inside. 'I'll show you to her room.'

The novelist's room was at the top of the stairs, directly opposite the room that Veronica Emmett had occupied. Sister Monica knocked and waited for the door to open. 'Rosalind, dear, the police would like to speak to you.'

'Again? That's fine, Sister. Send them in.'

They entered the room and Carys closed the door behind them, waiting until she heard the nun's soft footsteps retreating down the staircase. Sister Monica was like a shadow flitting through the old stone building – barely seen or heard, yet somehow everywhere and missing nothing. She had known Sarah Black's true identity from the start, yet had said nothing to the police. What other secrets might she be keeping to herself?

Rosalind's room resembled Veronica's both in size and style and contained a similarly mismatched assortment of furniture. The novelist was seated before the latticed window, a glimmer of sunshine peeping through the clouds and casting a crisscrossed shadow across the open notebook on her desk. Unlike Veronica's room, which faced the trees, the view here was southerly, looking out across a small but neatly tended garden lawn.

Rosalind closed her notebook and turned her chair to face them. She was wearing a tartan skirt with walking boots and a knitted jumper. She gestured to an armchair. 'I can offer you a seat, but I only have one spare.'

'That's quite all right,' said Carys. 'We're happy to stand. I know that you've already spoken to my sergeant here' – she nodded in Rhodri's direction – 'but I'd just like to go over everything once more.'

'Of course,' said Rosalind. Unlike the abbot, the novelist seemed only too willing to help. She crossed one leg over the other and began to talk. 'So as I explained, I saw Rick at Compline with everyone else but we didn't speak then. I was hoping to have a word with him afterwards, but as soon as we left the church, Paul collared him, and so I left them to it.'

'What are your impressions of Paul?' asked Carys.

'I can't say I feel very comfortable in his presence, but perhaps that's just his personality. There's an intensity to him, and an unhealthy fixation on religion. He's always banging on about sin and judgement. Frankly I try to avoid him. Anyway, I left the church alone and came back to my room to catch up on my reading. But I always like to take a short walk before bedtime, so I stepped out for some air at about ten o'clock. I was pleased to find Rick outside, just finishing a cigarette. I asked if he would like to join me for a walk and he said he'd love to, so we went for a stroll through the woodland. It's quite magical on the island at night. We heard an owl hoot.'

'You said you'd been hoping to speak to him,' said Carys. 'What about?'

'He told me he'd spent some time in prison. I was curious to find out why.'

'You asked him directly?'

Rosalind chuckled. 'Not immediately, no. You can't just dive into a conversation with something like that. Well, not unless you're the police, I suppose. At first we just chatted generally. He was very interested in my books. Did you know I write a medieval mystery series? That's why I'm here on this retreat. I'm not particularly religious, but I like to immerse myself in a place before I write about it. Anyway, Rick wanted to know all about my writing and how I get published.' She paused. 'But that was really just a pretext.'

'A pretext? For what?'

'Just as I'd hoped, Rick quickly got on to talking about himself. He practically told me his entire life story there and then, or at least the juiciest parts. You see, I think he was hoping I would ghost-write his memoirs.'

'What did he reveal to you?'

'Lots. All about his difficult childhood growing up in the West Midlands. He got embroiled in minor criminality, mainly burglaries to finance his growing drugs habit. It all came to a head when his getaway car killed a pedestrian during a diamond robbery. At first I thought he was making it up, or at least embellishing it, but he showed me an article about the robbery on his phone – a smash-and-grab at a jewellers in Birmingham. The diamonds have never been recovered, and Rick claims he doesn't know what happened to them. But he pleaded guilty, was sent to prison and rediscovered God. Now he does voluntary work and raises money for charity. I could see how his story could make a compelling read – from troubled childhood to convicted criminal to reformed character. A classic redemption arc. Unfortunately, I don't have any experience at ghost-writing other people's stories, but I encouraged him to have a go at writing it himself and said I would read it and offer suggestions for improvement.'

'Did Rick say anything to you about Veronica Emmett – that's the woman who called herself Sarah Black?'

Rosalind raised a long finger to her chin. 'Well, Inspector, Rick didn't actually say anything, but I do have a novelist's practised eye for observation. I saw that Sarah, or Veronica rather, seemed – how shall I put it? – keenly interested in Rick. I assumed she found him attractive. Despite being a few years her senior, he was a very good-looking man, if a little rough around the edges.'

'And did he pay her any attention in return?'

'None whatsoever,' said Rosalind. 'It was as if he didn't even notice her. Perhaps he didn't – it wasn't as if Veronica paid him any attention directly. I just caught her watching him whenever he was around.'

'As if she was spying on him?'

Rosalind brightened. 'I didn't want to frame it that way, in case you thought I was saying it to add drama. But yes, it was exactly as if Sarah – or Veronica – had come to Caldey to spy on Rick. Do you think that might be why she was murdered?'

CHAPTER 19

Elen always got lumped with the crap jobs, but she didn't really mind. That was to be expected when you were the most junior member of the team, and every job was a learning opportunity if you approached it with a positive mindset. She stood at the water's edge, watching as a team of officers dressed in long waterproof waders divided the pond into a grid with string tied to pegs in the ground. They then began the painstaking task of sifting through the mud, section by section. When a square had been thoroughly searched, Elen ticked it off on her clipboard.

The search team started at the edge of the pond and worked their way towards the middle. The muddy bottom was slippery and one of the officers almost lost his balance and fell in. It was a brief moment of amusement in what was otherwise a slow, tedious job.

Elen consoled herself with the thought that at least she wasn't standing up to her waist in cold water, sticking her hands into the mud. In her case, she was so short that the water would be halfway up to her neck.

She wasn't looking forward to the boat ride back to the

mainland. She had grown up and still lived in the tiny Welsh-speaking village of Crymych, at the eastern end of the Preseli Hills. Despite living only ten miles from Pembrokeshire's north coast, she had never been a water lover and couldn't understand Rhodri's obsession with surfing. Being at the mercy of the waves was her idea of hell. She preferred to have both feet planted on solid ground. That was probably what made her so good in a scrum.

A shout went up from the centre of the pond. 'Found something!'

Everyone stopped what they were doing and looked up as an officer delved into the murky depths and held aloft a metal object a foot long with a broken-off wooden handle. The metal gleamed dully, trailing strips of dripping pond weed.

'Bring it over here,' Elen called, holding out a large evidence bag.

The officer waded to the edge of the pond and held up his find for her to see.

'Bloody hell,' she said. 'It looks like a scythe.'

'Reckon the Grim Reaper dropped it on his way by,' said the officer. He placed it carefully into the bag and Elen sealed it and recorded the find on her clipboard, noting the grid square where it had been discovered.

Now that something had been found, a new urgency gripped the search team and it didn't take much longer to recover a garden spade. The tool was a heavy-duty piece of equipment with a tarnished blade and a solid wooden handle. It reminded Elen of the tools her grandfather kept in the shed on his allotment – decades old and weighing much more than the lightweight models you could buy from the garden centre. She'd offered to get him a new spade and trowel for his birthday but he swore by his old tools.

Elen catalogued the find and waited to see what other treasures might be recovered from the murky pond, but it seemed there was nothing else to be found. The first murder victim's phone was still missing. But they did now have a scythe and a spade. Were these the murder weapons? Or just random tools tossed into the pond? Hopefully the forensics lab would be able to tell.

*

The cottage was one of half a dozen whitewashed, red-roofed buildings lined up in a neat row on the village green, lying in the shadow of the abbey that loomed above it on higher ground. It was a bit like having God watching over you all the time. Carys knocked loudly at the door and waited for a response.

It was Dafydd Rees who answered. His eyes narrowed as he leaned against the door jamb, filling the space, arms folded across his broad chest. He was tall, with the toughened skin of a man who spent his time outdoors in all weathers. He regarded the detectives with a cool, almost hostile gaze, his eyes the colour of a stormy sea.

'Mr Rees?' said Carys. 'Can we come in for a chat?'

In view of the discovery of the scythe and garden spade in the pond, she had logically decided to switch her focus from the retreatants to the woodsman. The tools almost certainly belonged to the abbey and Dafydd of all people ought to be able to confirm that. But he was going to have a hard time explaining what they were doing at the bottom of the fishpond.

'If you're wanting to talk to Bethan, you'll find her at the café.'

'No, it's you we'd like to speak to, Mr Rees.' Carys had spotted Dafydd's wife cleaning the tables and chairs outside the café on her way over from St Philomena's so she knew Bethan wasn't at home. That was good – she wanted to speak to Dafydd on his own. 'So can we come inside?'

He held her gaze for a few seconds longer, before grunting and turning aside to allow her and Rhodri to enter.

The cottage's interior was small but comfortable and Carys recognised a woman's touch in the décor. In the sitting room, bright, flowery curtains framed a box sash window that looked onto a small cottage garden, the borders neatly trimmed back for winter. A vase on the window sill contained a bouquet of dried plants, their seedheads architectural, each stem carefully chosen and arranged.

Dafydd followed Carys's gaze. 'Bethan picks them,' he explained. 'In summer I bring her fresh blooms every day. She's always loved flowers.'

'Perhaps that's why she married you,' suggested Rhodri. 'You being a gardener and all.'

Dafydd turned to face him, his expression betraying nothing. 'Perhaps.'

Carys gestured to a small sofa and matching chair arranged in front of the fireplace. 'Do you mind if we sit?'

Dafydd nodded a grudging assent, and Carys took one side of the sofa, Rhodri sitting next to her. Dafydd lowered himself uneasily into the armchair as if his large frame was unused to being so constrained. He leaned forward, meaty forearms resting on his knees, saying nothing, just waiting to be questioned.

The woodsman was in his forties, Carys guessed, although his weatherbeaten features made him appear older. Bearded, with dark hair and angular features, he possessed a brooding presence. His still mouth suggested calm, and yet she sensed a fierce passion in his watchful eyes. He seemed a man at once aloof and emotionally volatile. She wondered how he would behave if roused to anger.

'We have a few questions to ask you, Mr Rees. My sergeant will take notes.'

'You can call me Dafydd,' he answered. 'Nobody calls me Mr Rees.'

'Dafydd, then,' she said as Rhodri produced a notebook and pen. She gestured to a framed photograph on the mantelpiece that showed a much younger Dafydd and Bethan. 'How long have you and your wife lived on Caldey?'

'Seven years. We lived on the mainland when we were first married. I worked on the Stackpole Estate.'

Carys gave him an encouraging smile. 'You've always been a gardener?'

'I like to work with my hands.' He held them up as if to demonstrate their capability. They were large, calloused and strong. Capable of care or harm. His blunt fingers and palms were stained with earth, but she could easily imagine them red with blood.

'I understand that you discovered the body in the pond this morning.'

'I was cutting back the reeds. They die off at this time of year and if you don't remove them, they rot.'

'What time was this?'

He shrugged. 'I don't wear a watch. I rise with the sun.'

His manner was gruff, curt, as if he resented this intrusion into his home and his life. Carys wondered how someone as chatty as Bethan got on with him.

'I'd like to show you a couple of photographs, Dafydd. Do you recognise these tools?' She held up her phone and flicked through two images – the spade and the blade that had been recovered from the pond.

He frowned, his heavy brows knitting together. 'That's my best spade, that is. And that's an old scythe blade. Haven't used it since the handle broke off, but it's one of mine, yes.'

'They were found in the pond. Do you know how they could have got there?'

'No.'

'Where are they usually kept?'

'In the storage shed.'

'Could you show us?'

'Now? All right.' Dafydd levered himself out of his chair, glad to reclaim his freedom. Outside the cottage, he led them along a path to a windowless shed at the back of the monastery. A rickety wooden door creaked on its hinges when he heaved it open. He stood aside and gestured. 'In here.'

A thick smell of mulch, engine oil and petrol emerged from the shed. Rhodri poked his head around the door, shining the light from his phone into the darkness. Thick strands of cobwebs hung from the rafters, and the floor was strewn with dead leaves. The space was crammed with gardening equipment, including at least three enormous petrol-powered lawnmowers, various sized wheelbarrows, chainsaws, hedge trimmers, and an assortment of spades, rakes, forks, shears, secateurs, and plant pots of every size. Some of the gear looked as old as the abbey itself.

'When were you last in here, Dafydd?' Carys asked.

'This morning. I came to fetch my gear for the pond, then brought it back afterwards.'

'And did you notice any sign of disturbance?'

'No.'

'How could you even tell if something was disturbed?' said Rhodri. 'This place is a mess. And it's not even locked. Don't you have a padlock or anything?'

Dafydd folded his brawny arms across his chest. 'Nobody's going to steal anything on the island.'

Rhodri shook his head in disbelief. 'Then how did the tools find their way into the pond?'

He was met with a stern gaze and a shrug.

Carys opted for a softer approach. 'Dafydd, who has access to this shed besides you?'

'Brother Gregory is in charge of the monastery garden, and Novice Thomas helps him. I'm not allowed to go in there.'

You and me both, thought Carys. Aloud she said, 'So, just the three of you?'

'That's right.'

Rhodri shook the flimsy wooden door. 'Boss, anyone could have got in here. There's no padlock. Nothing.'

Carys nodded. Rhodri was right. The spade and scythe could have been taken by anyone on the island. But Dafydd was still the most likely suspect.

'Dafydd,' she said, 'where were you last night and on Sunday evening?'

'At home. Where else?'

'Can your wife vouch for that?'

'Bethan and I don't spend much time together. She was in the other room. She likes to watch TV.'

'So she can't provide you with an alibi for the time of the two murders?'

He shrugged his broad shoulders. 'I suppose not.'

'Dafydd,' she asked, 'have you noticed anything unusual on the island these past few days? Something about the behaviour of the retreatants staying at St Philomena's perhaps? Have any of them said or done anything suspicious?'

He fixed her with his grey, fathomless eyes. 'Can't say I've paid them much attention. There are always strangers on Caldey and this lot are no different. I blame Brother Cadoc for bringing them here. The island can't handle so many tourists. Its ecosystem is too fragile.' He turned his gaze to the sky. 'This place is special, see? Look at the birds, the seals, the rare plants. Rock sea-lavender, golden samphire, dotted sedge... well, they should matter more than tourists.'

It was the longest speech he had made and it revealed to Carys what he was passionate about. 'You love this island, don't you, Dafydd?'

'I do.'

'But you don't like visitors and you don't like Brother Cadoc.'

He shrugged. 'I prefer Brother Gregory. He's a true monk. He knows his plants, too.'

'All right,' said Carys. 'Thanks for your help. But Dafydd?'

'What?'

'Get a padlock for that shed.'

CHAPTER 20

Brother Gregory was at his happiest tending plants in the monastery garden or preparing meals in the abbey's kitchen. St Benedict himself had written extensively on the subject of food and its preparation, stating that all utensils should be regarded as if they were sacred vessels of the altar. And hadn't St Augustine counselled his followers to care for their physical bodies as if they were going to live forever? In Brother Gregory's opinion, if cleanliness was next to godliness, then good food was close behind.

The kitchen was a big, airy space with grey-tiled walls and a terracotta floor. Stainless steel pots and pans were lined up on open shelving, and a row of ladles and spoons hung from hooks on the wall in order of size. The facilities were basic by modern standards but Gregory knew that fancy gadgets weren't needed to produce good meals. What mattered was a feel for food – what those in the secular world might call a passion.

Gregory's skills in the kitchen and garden were a gift from God and improved with practice, like all gifts. He took pride – though aware that pride was a mortal sin – in serving dishes that were made from simple ingredients, but which were nevertheless nourishing and wholesome. And plentiful too. Monks should not be expected to endure long days of prayer and work on nothing but a slice of bread and a bowl of watery soup. This was a monastery, not a prisoner-of-war camp.

'Where do you want these, Brother?' Novice Thomas entered with a basketful of apples freshly picked from the tree in the garden.

Gregory was particularly fond of apples. The idea that the apple was the forbidden fruit eaten by Eve, leading to loss of innocence, expulsion from the Garden of Eden, and separation from God, appeared to have originated from a mistranslation of the Latin word *malum* which could mean both "apple" and "evil". In Brother Gregory's book there was nothing evil about apples – they were a source of pure goodness. He considered it much more likely that Eve had eaten a pomegranate, which were devilishly fiddly fruits to prepare and eat.

'Leave them by the sink,' he told Thomas. 'We'll make a crumble later.'

He chopped four large homegrown onions, his knife flashing in quick, economical strokes, then slid them into a pan of sizzling butter and oil. He inhaled the heavenly scent as the onions spat and hissed. Then he gave them a stir, clamped a lid on the pot and turned the heat down.

'What would you like me to do now?' asked Thomas, fastening a navy and white striped apron over his habit.

Father Anselm had recently appointed Thomas to be Gregory's assistant chef. 'He should learn how all aspects of the monastery work,' the abbot had said. Thomas had proven to be an enthusiastic, though not always helpful apprentice. Yet Gregory knew he must show patience, for how else would Thomas learn and improve?

'You can grate the cheese,' said Gregory, indicating a large block of cheddar on a wooden board. 'It's for the sauce.' Cauliflower cheese was a firm favourite with the monks. Their diet was still largely vegetarian even though meat was consumed more regularly than it had been when Gregory had taken his vows.

For a few minutes they worked in peaceful silence, Thomas grating the cheese and Gregory breaking a cauliflower into florets, dropping the pieces into a large pan of boiling water.

'Can I ask a question, Brother Gregory?' said Thomas, once he had finished the cheese. A frown creased his youthful forehead.

'Of course.' In addition to supervising Thomas in the kitchen, Gregory had taken on the unofficial role of mentor. He enjoyed having the novice around and being able to impart the benefit of his wisdom. 'That is how we learn.'

'That man this morning... the one I helped Dafydd Rees and Brother Cadoc pull out of the pond?'

'What about him?'

'There was a Bible on his body, just the same as the first victim.'

'Was there?' said Gregory. He checked on the onions. They were softening nicely. He stirred in some flour to make a roux for the cheese sauce.

'It's just... it was marked at a page that talked about washing away sins. Was his death some sort of divine punishment?'

Gregory stopped what he was doing and looked across at Thomas. 'Whatever gives you that idea?'

'I don't know, I just thought...' He trailed off.

'Let me tell you something,' said Gregory gently. 'God doesn't punish people by drowning them in fishponds. Only wicked men do that.'

Thomas nodded. 'Yes, you're right. I'm sorry.'

'No need to apologise,' said Gregory. 'Ask as many questions as you like. You know you can always speak to me if there's something bothering you.'

'Thank you.'

Gregory checked the roux. 'This looks ready. Do you want to make the sauce? You remember what I taught you?'

'Yes, Brother. I can do that.'

Gregory turned down the heat on the cauliflower while Thomas went to the fridge. He returned with a large bottle of milk and was about to pour it into the roux when Gregory reached out and grasped his arm.

'Stop! What are you doing?'

Thomas looked at him in confusion. 'Making the sauce?'

'With cow's milk? Remember that Brother Cadoc is lactose intolerant.'

Thomas looked stricken. 'I forgot!'

Gregory took a deep breath and silently prayed for patience. 'Have you done this before, Thomas? Used cow's milk in a shared dish?'

The novice's neck flushed pink. He nodded.

'Then this explains why Brother Cadoc was ill the other night,' said Gregory. 'And why he believed he had been poisoned.'

Thomas hung his head with shame. 'I am so sorry, Brother. I must beg his forgiveness.'

'Never mind,' said Gregory, patting the young novice's shoulder. 'Cadoc survived, and I do think he went a bit overboard accusing me of poisoning him.' He chuckled. 'Put this back in the fridge and fetch the soya milk instead. We'll say no more about it.'

When Thomas had his back turned, Gregory slipped a couple of apples into the voluminous pockets of his habit. They would come in handy later.

*

Carys, Rhodri and Elen stood on the jetty, buffeted by the wind as the lifeboat docked at Priory Bay. The body of Rick Styles lay at their feet, bagged and secured to a stretcher. The scythe and spade were in separate evidence bags along with Rick's phone. They still hadn't found the phone belonging to Veronica Emmett.

The Coastguard in Tenby had dispatched a Tamar-class all-weather boat, a sturdy vessel with a navy hull and bright orange cabin to pick up the body and return it to the mainland. Carys could hardly ask Eifion to ferry a dead body in his passenger boat, like Charon ferrying the souls of the dead across the River Styx. They were already imposing on the boatman to transport the police to and fro and hang around all day.

The coxswain and two of the crew hopped ashore in their yellow waterproof suits and red lifejackets.

'Thank you for coming out,' said Carys. The lifeboat crew were all volunteers but you wouldn't meet a more professional bunch.

'We'll get this done quickly,' said the coxswain, indicating the body. He was a tall, bearded man with a commanding voice. 'There's a squall brewing out there. It won't be a smooth crossing.' He nodded to his crew who swiftly and methodically tied the stretcher to a hoist and lifted it onto the deck where they secured it with straps.

Carys turned to Rhodri and Elen. 'The coroner's officers will meet you in Tenby. Can you take the evidence bags to forensics?'

'No problem,' said Rhodri.

Elen eyed the lifeboat with trepidation as a wave crashed into the side of the jetty, sending up a spray.

'You'll be all right,' said Rhodri to Elen. 'You'll be in safe hands on the lifeboat.'

The crew helped the pair climb aboard and fitted them with lifejackets – a safety measure that wasn't available on Eifion's boat. Then the boat cast off, swinging around as it pulled away from the jetty. The engine note deepened as it powered away across the grey water leaving a broad ribbon of surging foam in its wake.

Carys headed back up the path through the woodland, enjoying this rare moment of solitude after a day spent in the company of others. The light was starting to fade and she took a moment to appreciate the twilight, that liminal period between day and night – the time when faeries came out to dance and do their mischief. All around her, the trees stood sentinel, their trunks and branches black against the dimming sky. As a girl, she had believed this was when her mother would return. She had always given up hope when darkness fell completely.

She continued on to St Philomena's, not wishing to keep Eifion waiting any longer than could be helped. At the entrance to the guest house, two uniformed police officers – a man and a woman – were waiting for her and she greeted them and led them inside.

She found the three remaining retreatants gathered in the lounge. Sister Monica had made tea and served sandwiches. They sat in silence around the dinner table, nibbling the food and sipping their tea. Two of their number were now dead. It wasn't surprising that the mood among the survivors was subdued.

Sister Monica offered her a seat. 'Shall I pour you a cup of tea, dear?'

'No, thank you. I won't be staying long.' Carys sat down at the table, feeling suddenly weary. Rosalind and Samir looked at her with anxious faces. Paul Roberts regarded her from beneath heavy brows, his expression severe. Sister Monica alone seemed calm, as if a lifetime of service had taught her the value of patience. Or perhaps it was her faith that bolstered her during this time of crisis.

Samir broke the silence. 'What's going on? Have you made an arrest yet? Do you have any suspects?'

'I'm afraid I can't tell you that,' said Carys.

'You must appreciate how stressful this is for us,' said Rosalind. 'I'd like to know how much longer we have to stay here.'

'I want to leave now,' chimed in Samir. 'This place isn't safe.'

Carys could sense their unease, pressing in like a tangible presence in the room. 'I understand that you may wish to leave the island –'

'Of course we do,' declared Paul. 'When the angel passes over a house marked for blood, the wise man does not linger at the threshold.'

Carys frowned. She would definitely need to dig deeper into Paul Roberts's past in the morning. She held up a hand. 'I'm afraid that I must refuse your request. The police investigation is ongoing, and I would like everyone to remain here for the moment.'

'You can't keep us prisoner!' blurted Samir, though his voice lacked conviction.

Carys beckoned to the two uniformed police constables to come into the room. 'I have asked these officers to stay at St Philomena's tonight to ensure your safety. Nothing will happen to you while they are here, and they can offer you support if you need it. Think of them as family liaison officers.'

Paul gave a humourless chuckle. 'Families are where the worst sins are always hidden. Scripture's clear on that.'

'Shut up!' snapped Samir, turning on him. 'I'd rather be alone than locked up with you!'

'Me?' said Paul, turning his gaze first on Samir, then on Rosalind and Sister Monica. 'The murderer could be anyone. We'll not know until the sword is drawn. Until then, trust no one.'

'I don't intend to,' said Samir.

'Please,' begged Sister Monica. 'Stay calm, all of you! This bickering is getting us nowhere.'

Carys didn't intend to discuss the matter any further. 'I advise you all to lock your bedroom doors during the night, and not to go out.' She rose to her feet. 'I'll be back in the morning. And remember, if you have any concerns, you can share them with the police.'

She left the room, lingering just long enough to whisper to the uniformed officers as she walked past. 'Keep an eye on all of them, especially Paul Roberts, and don't be shy about eavesdropping. Let me know if you notice anything suspicious.'

Outside, the wind tugged at her scarf and she placed a hand over her beret to stop it blowing away. The weather was turning again, growing windier as the night closed in.

In the distance, a single light from the village twinkled through the swaying trees.

CHAPTER 21

'I'm going to be sick again,' moaned Elen, leaning over the side of the lifeboat and wailing into the howling wind.

Rhodri shifted away from her along the bench, creating a safer gap between himself and his sea-green colleague. What did you call those singing mermaids who lured fishermen to their death? *Sirens.* Elen was one great honking siren, although the way she looked, he didn't think there would be much luring occurring in her present state.

'Not much further to go,' he said, doing his best to reassure her. Mates looked out for each other, didn't they? He had, however, made certain he was sitting upwind of this particular mate. He didn't fancy getting reacquainted with that bacon butty Elen had eaten at the café.

In truth the lifeboat was taking a lot longer to reach Tenby than it would have done in calm waters. The sea was a roiling mass and they were still some way from the harbour. The coxswain had slowed the boat, prioritising safety and stability over urgency. After all, Rick Styles was dead and in no hurry to get to the mortuary.

Yet despite the slow progress, the boat crested and

dipped with every wave, sending white foam spraying over the railings. Rhodri didn't mind that – it reminded him how much he missed surfing – but the way the body bag slid and shifted about the deck was setting his nerves on edge. It was as if the man inside was alive and struggling to get out.

A huge wave surged into view and broke over the bow, showering them in cold water. The drenching seemed like the last straw for Elen and she retched violently over the side.

'Get it out, El. You'll feel a lot better afterwards,' Rhodri told her, although he wasn't completely convinced by his own words. One thing was certain – he was going to be the one who would have to drive the evidence over to forensics again.

He checked his watch and sighed. It was going to be another late finish and Amy wouldn't be pleased. She'd want him to help with the children's bathtime and bedtime routines. And he was happy to help – of course he was. He enjoyed reading Billy and Lila a bedtime story. And dinner with his wife was always a pleasure, even if it came with a breathless debrief from the hair salon – which romances were blossoming, which marriages were hanging by a thread, and whose kids had gone feral.

But he didn't feel as bad about being late as maybe he should have done. The fact was, this murder case was far more interesting than his usual investigations. And he was warming to Carys. His new boss was tough when she needed to be, but he'd seen a softer side to her, too.

They sailed past St Catherine's Island before finally easing into the safety of the harbour. 'You'll be all right now, Elen,' he said, giving her a hearty slap on the back as they berthed. She shot a murderous glance his way, but said nothing, just clambered ashore, leaving him to deal with the handover of the body. Fortunately, the coroner and a police escort were waiting on the jetty to meet them. Rhodri was glad to see the back of the body bag as it was taken away to the mortuary. He thanked the coxswain for the crew's help and watched as the boat sailed back to the lifeboat station.

To his surprise, Elen was waiting for him at the top of Pier Hill. 'I can drop the stuff off at forensics if you want,' she said.

'Are you sure?'

'Of course.' She seemed to have recovered her poise now they were back on dry land. 'It makes sense. I have to drive past Haverfordwest anyway. Silly for you to go all that way now that you're back in Tenby.'

'You're a pal,' said Rhodri, handing her the bags containing the scythe, spade and phone. He checked his watch again as she headed off and found that he wasn't late after all. At this rate, he'd be back with time to spare. He started up the hill, taking St Julian's Street into the town centre. Most of the shops were closed, and there was no one sitting outside the bars and pubs. Everyone was inside, sheltering from the weather.

He turned left at St Mary's church, walking briskly. He'd be home in a couple of minutes and Amy would be pleased. He'd tell her about his day, although he obviously wouldn't share the details of the murders and the suspects, otherwise they would be broadcast all over Tenby in less than twenty-four hours, such was the efficiency of the hair salon grapevine.

'Rhodri, mate!'

He turned at the sound of his name. In the doorway of the Five Arches Tavern, Jon Jenkins was smoking a cigarette. He was wearing a new leather jacket and black jeans, and when he lifted the hand holding the cigarette, a chunky silver watch strap gleamed under the cuff. Jon was Rhodri's oldest mate, but he was such a show-off.

'Jon, how you doing?'

'How you doing, Rod,' said Jon in reply, dropping his cigarette on the ground and grinding it out with the heel of his black boot. 'What you been up to then?'

'Oh, you know,' said Rhodri. 'Work. Wife. Kids.'

Jon gave a throaty laugh. 'Mate, you got hitched up too

young. Didn't I always tell you?'

Rhodri shrugged. Amy didn't care much for Jon, who had been best man at their wedding and had organised one hell of a stag do. Jon had told him he was daft to be getting married instead of continuing to play the field. But Rhodri had been so head over heels that nobody could have talked him out of it.

And yet some days lately, Rhodri had begun to fear that Jon was right. He loved Amy more than anything, and he loved his kids too. But it was terrifying the way life was flashing past so quickly. Twenty-eight years old and he was shackled with a job, a mortgage and a family.

'The boys are inside having a beer,' said Jon, 'Come and join us.'

'No, I can't. I've got to get home.'

'What for? Amy can handle the kids. Come on, just a quick pint.'

It was a Tuesday evening and Rhodri really ought to be heading home. Amy would be glad to have him back at a decent time. He had work the next day, and Billy had school. But it had been a long and stressful couple of days and he deserved a bit of unwinding. One quick pint wouldn't hurt.

'Go on then,' he said. 'But not a word to Amy, all right?'

'Scout's honour,' said Jon, pushing open the door.

It was pleasantly warm in the pub and Rhodri shrugged off his coat. The seawater had left white stains down the front and back.

'Been surfing with your coat on?' teased Jon.

'Just got off the lifeboat from Caldey.'

'Yeah, I heard about that. What are you having?'

'I'll have a pint of Worthington's.'

He waited as the beer was poured and Jon ordered a double whisky for himself. They took the drinks over to the table where the lads were sitting. They'd already had a few rounds judging by the number of empties.

'Hi, guys,' he said, taking a sip of his pint as he pulled

up a chair. 'How's everyone?'

'All right, Rod,' said Sam. 'How's this case, then? Two bodies now, we heard.'

'Two, yeah.'

He was saved from having to elaborate by Matt leaning across the table, glass in hand, his beer tilting at an alarming angle. 'Jon here's been showing off about his new boat. You seen it yet, Rod?'

'What's this then?' asked Rhodri. Jon had been bragging for ever about buying a fast boat, but he was always talking about some scheme or other. They rarely amounted to anything.

Jon took out his phone. 'Here she is.'

Rhodri stared in amazement at a photo of a sleek new speedboat moored at the harbour. 'No way! Is this yours?'

'Would I lie to you, Rod?'

'God, she's a beauty,' said Ben. 'Just look at that.'

'She goes from idle to full plane in under four seconds,' said Jon. 'Top speed just shy of sixty knots. Twin outboard engines with a total output of 600 horsepower.'

Rhodri shook his head in disbelief. 'You win the lottery or what?'

Jon smiled and slapped him on the back. 'It's a business venture, Rod. I'll take you out for a spin, one day. Just let me know when you're free.'

'I'll do that. Cheers, mate.' He sipped his pint while the talk moved on to football and then rugby. At some point a second pint appeared in front of him and before he knew it, his watch told him it was eight o'clock. How had that happened? He downed the last of his beer and rose to his feet. 'Sorry, lads. I've got to be off now.'

'Stay for another!' said Matt, but Rhodri shook his head with determination. It was all right for the others. None of them had wives waiting at home. They were still living the life he had once enjoyed, spending their cash on clothes and going to festivals. Now Rhodri bought stair gates and mowed the lawn on Saturday mornings.

'Next Tuesday,' called Jon. 'Curry night?'

'Yeah, count me in,' he said as he made his way to the door. He left the pub and headed off along the familiar route home. How was he going to explain this to Amy? He would have to blame it on Jon.

CHAPTER 22

The roads were wet on the drive back to Manorbier. Izzy's headlights reflected in black rainwater pooled in roadside ditches, like corpse candles foretelling death. Carys tried to suppress an image of the dead man, Rick Styles, his sightless eyes staring, his blue lips sealed. What had those eyes witnessed during his last moments? What truth would those lips never speak?

Two deaths now in as many days, and she was still no nearer to discovering who was responsible, or why. She ought to have arrested a killer by now, yet all she had was a list of suspects and a handful of tantalising clues. Someone on the island was engaged in a twisted enterprise, but as yet she could discern no motive or pattern.

She wondered what DCI Gareth Pritchard made of her. She wanted – needed – to prove she was an effective detective. So far, she'd failed.

And what about Rhodri and Elen?

She wasn't sure they liked her much. But so what? She hadn't returned to Pembrokeshire to make friends.

She was here for Esme.

She recalled the night the two police officers had come

knocking on the front door of her flat in Cardiff. She knew immediately why they had come. The police didn't call at eleven o'clock at night unless they had to. A woman's body recovered from the sea at Manorbier. Drowned. Could Carys come and identify the body? She had known at that instant that she would have to return to Manorbier, abandoning the life she'd made for herself in Cardiff.

Esme was only her half-sister, yet blood was the strongest tie, and when your parents were gone you had to cling to whatever family was left. Now that Nan was dead, Esme was all Carys had.

Wild, chaotic Esme – who was no more.

Her only regret was that she hadn't returned sooner.

She pulled up at the roadside and parked a short distance away from her cottage.

A man called to her from across the street as she stepped out of the car. 'Carys, is that you? I thought I recognised that old car of yours.'

Dan Chandler.

She'd known she was going to have to face Dan eventually. You couldn't move back to a village as small as Manorbier and not run into your ex-boyfriend sooner or later. She fixed a smile to her face as he crossed the road.

'How're you doing?' he asked, searching her face. 'I heard you were back.'

'Yeah, good thanks. You?'

'Yeah, things are great.' He pushed a lock of hair away from his forehead and gave her one of those broad smiles that lit up his entire face.

Same Dan. He hadn't changed one bit.

'How's work?'

'Quiet at this time of year. We're running the holiday park now, me and Pete. It's seasonal work, but it's doing fine. During the summer months it's hectic.'

'Glad to hear it.' Carys forced herself to ask the next question. 'How's Lauren?'

His smile dimmed for a fraction of a second but he recovered quickly. 'Yeah, she's fine.'

Carys had learned a year ago that Dan and Lauren had married. Lauren was a village girl from Lydstep, the nearest settlement along the coast in the direction of Tenby. Carys and Esme had known her when they had summer jobs at the castle during school holidays. Lauren had been loud and pushy and they hadn't much liked her.

But Carys could hardly blame Dan for finding someone else. After all, she was the one who had pushed him away.

'So, are you with anyone?' he asked.

'Not at the moment.' Now wasn't the time to go into details. He didn't need to hear about the boyfriend she'd so easily abandoned in Cardiff when she'd decided to return to Manorbier. Nor about the string of short-lived relationships before that. There was no need to tell him that she'd never been with someone for as long as she'd been with him.

He nodded thoughtfully. 'Well, it's good to see you back in the village. Catch up soon?'

'Perhaps.' She turned to go, but his hand reached out and touched her arm. It was like an electric shock that ran through her body.

'I just wanted to say, I was so sorry to hear about Esme. The drowning, I mean. Terrible accident.'

'Yes. It was.'

'The currents are so strong in the bay.'

'Yes.'

He dropped his hand. 'Well then, I'd better be off. See you around.'

She nodded. 'See you.'

He walked away up the hill, his strong, broad back and long legs making the climb look easy. Lauren was lucky to have a man like Dan. She imagined their future – a whole brood of mini-Dans and mini-Laurens building sandcastles on the beach and running into the waves. She shut that thought down quickly.

Instead of going straight home she took the long, steep path up to the parish church of St James the Great. The old church with its tall, square tower stood on top of the hill and afforded stunning views down to the castle and the bay. This evening, it was too dark to see far, but Carys picked her way across the sloping churchyard to the stone that marked the grave of her grandmother and sister. The two women lay together overlooking the valley below.

Olwyn Morgan and Esme Morgan.

Carys knelt down on the wet grass in front of the stone. 'Hi Nan, it's me.' She wrapped her fingers around the iron key in her coat pocket, feeling the reassuring coolness of the metal. In Celtic folklore, cold iron was believed to repel spirits and faeries and to bring good luck to those who wielded it.

Superstitious nonsense, some claimed, but Carys believed in the old ways – of pagan rituals, of Celtic rites. The earliest Christians in Wales had mingled their new beliefs with the old – adopting feast days as religious festivals, recasting local spirits as saints, and building churches on ground long sacred to nature worshippers. Carys had done the same at a deeply personal level. Her studies in theology had offered up a smorgasbord of spiritual delicacies, and she had chosen from it hungrily, tossing in a few of Nan's crazy inventions too. Christianity, Buddhism, neo-paganism… if you were wired to believe in a world beyond the material, why stop at one religion? Why not take them all and fashion a belief system of your very own?

'You understood well enough, didn't you, Nan? The world's too complex for a single explanation. Nothing's ever quite as it seems.'

She fished out her phone and thumbed to the text Esme had sent the night she'd gone missing – the night before her body had been washed up on the beach at Manorbier.

I need you, Carys. I'm so scared.

Carys should have been with her sister that night. If she had, everything would have been different. But she'd been too busy in Cardiff to offer help to the one person who needed it most. The missing girl case that DCI Gareth

Pritchard had alluded to that morning had kept her at her desk, morning, noon and night. By the time Carys had arrived in Pembrokeshire, there was no one to greet her but a cold corpse washed up by the sea.

The coroner concluded that Esme had drowned while swimming. A terrible accident, Dan had called it. That was what everyone thought.

Carys was happy to let them go on believing that.

*

The detective had given clear instructions not to go out, but Samir couldn't sleep. It was too quiet on this island. No people. No cars. Nothing. Just the relentless rattling of the window panes as the wind shook them. His hand reached instinctively for the small package beneath his pillow.

Safe.

No one suspected him of hiding a secret. Only Rick and the girl – Veronica, or Sarah, or whatever her name was – and they were both dead.

He checked the time on his phone. Gone midnight. He slipped out of bed, dressed quickly and slid the package into his pocket. Then he crept into the corridor and tiptoed down the stairs. The police officers who were supposed to be keeping everyone safe were dozing in the sitting room, the man with his head tilted back on a cushion, the woman snuggled up on the sofa. Neither heard him as he lifted the latch and stepped outside.

He needed a vape but he didn't want to hang around St Philomena's. Instead, he took the path that led to Priory Bay and to the jetty where they'd all arrived just four days ago. Four days? It felt more like four months. How could so much have happened in so short a time? Five of them had got off that boat and now only three remained.

He wished he'd never come to Caldey.

His feet sank into the sand as he followed the gentle curve of the bay. Waves crashed against the shore and the wind tore at his hair.

His hand went to his pocket again as it had so often since leaving London. It had become a compulsion. He looked over his shoulder. There was no one on this deserted beach. No one to see.

He withdrew the package and held it tightly. It fitted so snugly into the palm of his hand. A small brown paper parcel containing a memory stick. Such a tiny device, and yet it held a wealth of damning information. It was like walking around carrying an unexploded bomb. If he threw it in the right direction it would bring down the company he worked for and send its owner to jail for a long time.

But like a bomb, it might also explode in his hand and take him down instead.

Could he take that risk?

Did he dare?

He had come to Caldey Island to lie low while he gathered his thoughts and gained some perspective on his problems. But now he found himself trapped.

In the distance, pinpricks of light marked the line of the mainland. How far was it across the sea from here? A mile at most.

He could swim that distance. He'd done it at his local swimming pool. Sixty-four lengths. It wasn't that far. But that was in a heated indoor pool, not in the Bristol Channel in October. How cold would the water be? And how long would he survive without succumbing to hypothermia? He was young and fit, but even so, it would be a huge risk. A safer option would be to bribe the boatman into taking him back to Tenby. Yes, that was a wiser choice.

Feeling calmer for having arrived at a decision, he turned to head back to the guest house.

A shape moved in the shadows, maybe fifty yards ahead of him where the trees met the path at the edge of the beach.

Samir froze. He stood and listened but heard only the wind, the waves, and the pumping of his own blood in his ears. He could see nothing.

But he had definitely seen movement.

'Who is it?' he called, but the sound was lost on the wind.

He peered into the darkness and this time made out the shape of a crouching figure.

'I see you!' he called, sounding bolder than he felt. 'Who's there?'

There was no reply, but then the figure rose and began to run. Samir braced himself to flee, but it was the watcher who was fleeing.

Summoning up all his courage, Samir began to run towards the trees. He was a quick sprinter and had always won the hundred metres at school. But by the time he reached the path, the figure had vanished.

CHAPTER 23

Carys sat in the warmth of her car, the windows misted with condensation, listening to the dreamy voice of Hope Sandoval floating ethereally above the acoustic guitar and cello backing of Mazzy Star's *Into Dust*. Good music for a post-mortem. Carys would have preferred to listen to the song on vinyl, but as Izzy's dashboard lacked a turntable, she had to compromise with a CD when driving. At least that was better than streaming. Various boyfriends had branded her "old school" for still buying vinyl, but the simple truth was that she preferred tangible objects to ephemeral digital nothings.

There were already far too many ghosts in Carys's life. She needed things she could hold onto. Her record collection was going nowhere. 'And neither are you, Izzy,' she murmured, patting the steering wheel of the old car.

She wiped a small circle in the fogged windscreen with her sleeve and peered out at the squat rectangular building that was Withybush General Hospital in Haverfordwest. Its grey concrete render and uniform rows of windows didn't make it an inspiring or welcoming sight, and Carys had personal reasons for disliking the hospital too.

It was where she had come to identify her sister's body.

But there was no getting away from the fact that she would have to go back there, and if she chose to remain in Pembrokeshire, it was likely to become a regular haunt.

When the song drew to a close, she got out of the car and entered the hospital. The pathology department was conveniently situated off the main corridor on the ground floor next to the hospital shop. Everything you needed in life – drinks, snacks, magazines and phone chargers – side-by-side with everything required in death – a refrigerated drawer and a cold mortuary slab.

She was glad of her scarf and beret as soon as she walked into the chilly air of the mortuary and resolved to keep them on. She fished in her pockets for a pair of handknitted fingerless gloves and pulled those on too.

The lead pathologist was also donning a pair of gloves – blue nitrile in his case. 'DI Carys Morgan?' He looked up and frowned, recognition slowly dawning. 'Ah, yes, I thought I knew that name. You're here this time in a professional capacity, I believe.'

Carys didn't welcome this reminder of her previous visit. Then, she had been just plain Carys Morgan, half-sibling of a woman lying dead on a trolley beneath a blue sheet. Next of kin and bereaved family member. A junior police officer had accompanied her, more anxious than Carys, and she had looked steadily into the dead woman's face and said, 'Yes, that's Esme. That's my sister.'

'You're quite sure?' the police officer had asked her.

'Of course,' said Carys. 'Tell me exactly how she died.'

Now, she forced a smile and faced the man who had performed the previous post-mortem and was about to examine the murder victims from Caldey Island. 'Dr Fowler, how nice to meet you again.'

She had got the full measure of Dr Graham Fowler during their previous encounter. One wall of his office was adorned with framed certificates, assembled and displayed in the way other enthusiasts might collect stamps or coins

– ordered, curated and intended to be admired. He needed everyone to know how qualified he was: first-class degrees in science, medicine and surgery from Imperial College, London; a post-graduate diploma in pathology from Cardiff; an antiquated parchment-style certificate in gothic script admitting him as a fellow of the Royal College of Pathologists; his Home Office registration certificate; and a letter appointing him to the post of consultant forensic pathologist with Hywel Dda University Health Board.

His achievements were impressive.

But they weren't enough for Carys.

The qualities she valued most in her colleagues were intuition and empathy. A good detective – and a good pathologist – followed their instincts and, above all, they *cared*. Carys had found the missing girl in Cardiff because she cared enough to keep pushing and digging when other people had urged her to give up.

Her only regret was that she hadn't had enough time and energy left over to save her own sister.

She turned her attention now to the bodies lying side-by-side on two trolleys. 'Ready when you are, Dr Fowler.'

The pathologist's assistant folded back the blue sheets, revealing the corpses of Veronica Emmett and Rick Styles.

Carys moved closer for a better view, being careful not to step into the "splash zone". It was her job to find out who had killed these two people. But it was who they had been in life that gave the job meaning.

In life, Veronica Emmett had been a woman with a mission. She had known precisely who Rick Styles was – the man who had hit and killed her brother driving at speed from the scene of a jewellery robbery. She had disguised herself as Sarah Black, her stated objective to "make him pay" for what he had done. Rick had been to prison for his crime, but Veronica evidently felt the sentence he had served was inadequate. She had been a vigilante of sorts, although how far she would have taken things would never be known.

What was unclear was whether Rick had recognised

Veronica. Had he even known that the man he killed had a sister? People changed, and Veronica had dyed her hair and used a false name. And although Rick may have had a motive to silence Veronica, why would anyone have wanted him dead too?

Carys's heart went out to them both although she managed to retain her professional demeanour. It was a trick she had learned over the years – to feel deeply while appearing detached. It demanded a lot of emotional energy from her, this being true to herself while playing the role that people expected from a police detective.

'I expect you'll want to know the time of death,' said Fowler, peering at her over the mask that covered the lower half of his face.

'That's always a good place to start,' said Carys.

'I can narrow it down to a range, but not an exact time. In my professional opinion, I would say that victim number one –'

'You mean Veronica. Let's not depersonalise her. She's not a slab of meat.'

Fowler's eyes narrowed. 'Very well, then. *Veronica* died on Sunday night, between eight and midnight. If pushed I'd go for the earlier hour.'

'And Rick?'

'On Monday evening, with a similar time range. Now, as for the cause of death. The first victim' – he stopped himself when he caught Carys's look – '*Veronica*, shows signs of defensive wounds. These slashes on the underside of her forearms suggest that she raised her arms to protect her face from the blade.' He lifted Veronica's pale white arms, revealing several deep cuts that Carys took in silently, though her chest tightened in grim resolve. The woman had faced her attacker – and must have known who did this to her.

'What can you say about the nature of the weapon used?'

Fowler gave a curt nod. 'I'm glad you asked. This wasn't a typical knife-style attack. The blade was single-edged and curved, used in a way that produced sweeping, lateral cuts. It was heavy and wielded with some force – the wounds show deep penetration with bone damage in places. You could say they were more slashes than thrusts.' He pointed out the three wounds that Carys had already seen – near the heart, throat and belly.

'A small scythe was found close to the crime scene,' said Carys. 'Could that have been the murder weapon?'

'An agricultural tool? Yes, I would say the wounds are consistent with a weapon of that type. As for the cause of death, I can say with some degree of certainty that it was the final chop-type wound – to the anterior of the neck – that proved fatal. This wound transected underlying muscle and severed both the left and right carotid arteries. Death would have been rapid due to catastrophic blood loss. Do you have any further questions?'

Carys eyed him impassively. Fowler undoubtedly knew his job, but as for empathy, he had displayed no evidence of any. 'Yes, two questions. Was the attacker left- or right-handed? And how can you be certain that the neck wound was the fatal blow?'

His eyes brightened, as if he relished the opportunity to further display his knowledge. 'The wound trajectories suggest a lateral sweeping action from left to right, so the killer is most likely right-handed. As for which blow was the fatal one, that's really quite elementary. The other wounds may look nasty to the untrained eye' – Fowler turned his gaze meaningfully in Carys's direction – 'but they're quite superficial. The victim – *Veronica* – would have continued to struggle after receiving them.'

Perhaps he had hoped for more challenging questions from a worthier opponent, for that was clearly how he regarded Carys – a sparring partner in some kind of perverse competition. He cocked his head to one side. 'You know, the first documented post-mortem examination in history was conducted on Julius Caesar immediately after his assassination. Caesar's physician, Antistius, carefully examined the body, documenting each wound. Out of a total of twenty-three stab wounds, only one had proven fatal.' He tapped his shoulder. 'It was near the left shoulder blade and severed a major artery. Antistius's conclusions were presented in the Roman forum, and this is the origin of our modern term "forensic".'

'Fascinating,' remarked Carys dryly. The pathologist's compulsion to show off his expertise was becoming an irritation. Yet she had learned one important fact – that what had appeared to be a frenzied attack was in fact a controlled series of slashes that Veronica had attempted to block or dodge. Only the final cut to her neck had been sufficient to cause real harm. And once it had been delivered, the killer had ceased their attack. This was no deranged slasher but someone intent on committing cold-blooded murder.

She turned to the second body in the room. 'And what about Rick?'

'Ah yes,' remarked Fowler. 'A completely different type of attack. The deceased sustained blunt-force trauma to the posterior aspect of the head from a weapon with a relatively broad, flat surface.'

'A garden spade?' suggested Carys.

He arched an eyebrow. 'That would do it.'

'And was that the cause of death?'

'No. The blow may have been sufficient to cause momentary loss of consciousness, but the victim's lungs contained a significant volume of water.'

'He drowned?'

'Yes. But not without a struggle.' Fowler gently lifted Rick's neck, displaying for the first time a genuine respect for the deceased. He pointed out a thumb-sized bruise on the left side of the neck and multiple smaller bruises on the right. 'These bruises suggest that he was held underwater for an extended period.'

'He was drowned deliberately.' Carys kept her expression neutral, but in her heart a quiet anger was burning. Someone had deliberately and ruthlessly claimed the lives of two people. What had Veronica and Rick done to deserve such brutal deaths in the peaceful setting of Caldey Island?

She thanked Dr Fowler for his help and returned to the car park, where Izzy was waiting for her. Three questions were uppermost in her thoughts. What was the meaning of the Biblical verses? Why had the killer singled out Veronica and Rick? And had they completed their murderous spree?

CHAPTER 24

At times of difficulty, Rosalind always asked herself the same question. *What would Brother Aidan do?* Her protagonist was in many ways her alter ego, or at least the person she wished she could be. The resourceful monk combined bravery with compassion and wisdom. If he had a flaw – and every character in a novel required one flaw to make them relatable – it was that he had a tendency to overestimate his abilities, often ending up in deep water as a result.

There was that time Aidan had challenged the tyranny of a feudal landowner on behalf of the local peasantry and had found himself fleeing for his life from the landowner's private army. Only his knowledge of secret tunnels beneath the city of Norwich had enabled him to escape by the seat of his habit. That book had done particularly well, with one reviewer calling it "a gripping page-turner". Rosalind had been hoping to repeat the success of that early novel ever since.

Now, as she helped Sister Monica clear away the breakfast things, she found herself asking this exact same question: *What would Brother Aidan do?*

She was trapped on an island where two people had died in horrible circumstances and her fellow retreatants were behaving very suspiciously. Would Brother Aidan cower in the safety of St Philomena's under the watchful eye of uniformed police officers?

Or would he head out to see what he could find?

If Brother Aidan put consideration of his own safety first, her books would be very short and boring. So after finishing in the kitchen, she fetched her coat from the hallway and pulled her walking boots on. 'I won't go far,' she promised the policeman who came to check what she was up to. And that was true – on such a small island, it was impossible to venture more than half a mile in any direction.

'I could come with you if you like,' the policeman suggested, but Rosalind refused his offer with a smile.

'No thanks, I'll be quite all right.'

'Just keep to the main paths, then.'

She agreed to this and set off.

It had been raining earlier but now the clouds were clearing and a tentative sunlight was making the wet grass and foliage sparkle. Caldey Island was a beautiful place. So peaceful, so… She came to the pond and stopped abruptly. The area was still sealed off with crime scene tape, even though the temporary tent that the CSI team had erected had now been taken down. Such a tragedy that Rick was dead – she'd really warmed to him. In a way, he reminded her of Brother Aidan – dashing and reckless but basically a good man. And she was pleased that she'd discovered his secret before he died.

Rest in peace, she murmured, then hurried on past the gift shop, following the sign for the lighthouse and old priory.

She glanced over her shoulder as she walked, but there was no sign of Paul Roberts today. She lingered a while outside St Illtud's church, tilting her head to marvel at its crooked spire, but didn't go in. Memories of her earlier encounter there with Paul were still vivid in her mind.

There was a darkness within the schoolteacher, as if he carried the burden of a great wrong. Had something been done to him or had he done wrong to others? Rosalind strongly suspected the latter.

She pressed on quickly past the medieval fishpond – an unpleasant reminder of the village pond in which Rick's body had been found – and set off in the direction of the lighthouse. The path sloped gently upwards and she soon left the tree-covered part of the island behind. The ground to either side became open farmland with horses grazing in a field, oblivious to the chilly wind that tugged at their manes.

The lighthouse, on the island's southernmost point, was rather short and squat, and flanked on either side by white-painted cottages that were no longer in use. Perhaps they could be converted into holiday accommodation – *she could suggest the idea to Sister Monica*. It would be lovely to sit at a writing desk before one of those windows, gazing out at the ever-changing sea and sky. She would never be short of inspiration.

She walked right up to the cliff's edge, looking out across the Celtic Sea – the part of the Atlantic Ocean that nestled between Pembrokeshire, the southern coast of Ireland and the Bay of Biscay. The wind brought tears to her eyes and sent her hair dancing, and she breathed in deeply, inhaling the salty tang of the ocean. She had always loved the sea and found her mind immediately fizzing with ideas.

What about a story pitting Brother Aidan against a bunch of cut-throat pirates? Eifion the boatman would make a perfect buccaneer. Characters and plot were just beginning to take shape in her mind when a noise startled her.

She spun around and saw a figure standing in front of the lighthouse, watching her in silence.

Samir Khan, the so-called tech worker.

Rosalind still didn't know what Samir really did for a living and was in no mood to be fobbed off by more evasion. Brother Aidan wouldn't put up with it, and nor would she. She stepped away from the cliff edge, remembering that she had promised to keep to the paths, and approached him across the long grass.

'Morning, Samir.'

The young man stood with his hands wedged into his jeans pockets. Dark rings circled his eyes and she guessed he hadn't slept much. Probably no one at St Philomena's had.

'Hi, Rosalind. What are you up to?'

She narrowed her eyes. 'I might ask you the same question. Did you follow me here?'

'Of course not. I just needed to get outside for a while. I felt like a prisoner in the guest house.'

She softened her voice. 'Me too. I fancied a walk. Would you like to join me?'

He nodded and they set off together, taking the path that led around the eastern half of the island. Was this one of the "main paths" she had promised to stick to? It was little more than a grassy track winding its way between clumps of blackberries, gorse and honeysuckle. But on Caldey Island, paths didn't come much better than this. At least she was no longer so close to the cliff edge.

Samir fell into step at her side, his head bowed as if concentrating on where he was placing his feet on the rough track. 'I can't get used to not having proper streets and buildings everywhere,' he told her. 'How much longer do you think they're going to keep us here?'

'I really couldn't say,' said Rosalind. 'But I can't imagine it will be much longer.' She cast a sideways glance at him. 'I expect you need to get back to work. With an important job like yours.' *Whatever it is.*

'Yeah,' he said, although he didn't sound very keen about the prospect.

Has he lost his job? Is that his secret?

'You said it was in tech?' she prompted. 'What exactly do you do?'

He hesitated before answering. 'It's a bit complicated

to explain.'

'I'm sure you must get asked all the time,' said Rosalind, determined not to be deflected.

'Well, our firm builds digital infrastructure for blockchain payments.'

'Right,' said Rosalind, still not much wiser. The world of finance didn't greatly interest her. But at least he had given her a straight answer. 'I heard a sound last night, just after midnight. Someone left their room and went downstairs. Was that you?'

He turned to her, eyes wide. 'Yes, but… I just went out for some fresh air.' His hand darted compulsively to his jacket pocket.

'Have you lost something?' she asked.

'Lost it? No.' He sounded horrified by the suggestion.

Rosalind continued walking, smiling softly to herself. *Brother Aidan would be proud of me.* She had finally fooled Samir into confirming that he was hiding *something*. Now she just needed to find out what.

*

Nia stared out of the post office window, searching the village green in vain for any movement. After all the recent activity, nothing was happening today. The SOCO team had departed the previous afternoon, taking their gear with them, and there was no sign of the three detectives on the island this morning. The two police officers stationed at St Philomena's were still in residence, but had failed to divulge any useful information, despite Nia dropping in and questioning them under the pretext of delivering a letter for Sister Monica.

The door to the gift shop opened and Bethan Rees emerged, shooting a quick glance in Nia's direction before ducking her head and scuttling over to the café. Nia had no sympathy for Bethan. The woman had brought all her problems on herself.

Two more figures appeared, walking along the path

that led from the lighthouse. It was the novelist, Rosalind Grieves, in the company of the mysterious tech worker, Samir Khan. Nia was disappointed to see Samir heading into the gift shop, but delighted when Rosalind turned and came her way. At least here was one person who was always happy to chat.

Nia quickly stepped back from the window and busied herself behind the counter.

The bell rang as the door opened, and Nia looked up, a smile fixed to her face. 'Good morning. It's windy out there today!'

'Isn't it?' said Rosalind, pushing the door closed behind her. She went to the display of postcards near the window and began browsing through them.

'Anything in particular you're looking for?' asked Nia.

'I think I'll have this one.' Rosalind selected a card and brought it to the counter to pay. The card had a photo of the fish window in St David's church – one of the post office's bestsellers. 'What time does the post leave today?'

'It depends,' said Nia. 'Eifion delivers the incoming post each morning. And at the end of the day he takes any outgoing post to the mainland. But the exact time depends on when the last boat leaves.'

'So the post is daily,' said Rosalind. 'That's no worse than the village where I live.'

Nia nodded. 'We're lucky to have Eifion. He makes the crossing in almost all weathers. Only a real howler of a storm would keep him away. Would you like a first- or second-class stamp for that?'

'Second-class will do. It's just a postcard.'

Nia affixed a stamp to the card and rang up the amount on the till.

'Do you have a lot of post to deal with?' Rosalind asked.

'You'd be surprised. Something arrives with every boat. And then there are the letters that people on the island send to each other.'

Rosalind sounded surprised at that. 'Why would people who live on such a small island write to each other?

Wouldn't it be easier just to call round and speak face to face?'

Nia bit her lip and hesitated. 'Well, I suppose that's just how some people like to communicate.'

Rosalind frowned, but Nia said nothing more, annoyed with herself for revealing so much. Normally, she was the one extracting information from visitors to the post office, but there was something about the novelist that made people open up and say more than they intended. Nia chided herself for dropping her guard. All novelists were professional nosey parkers and trusting them was foolish.

'Well, nice chatting,' said Rosalind. 'Have a good day.'

'Same to you.' Nia waved Rosalind farewell, then waited until she had turned the corner and disappeared from view. Samir had not yet emerged from the gift shop, and Bethan was still in her café. Confident that she was not being observed, Nia turned her attention to the items of outgoing post that Novice Thomas had dropped off that morning.

There weren't many and she thumbed through them quickly. Letters with the official abbey stamp, addressed to the Abbot General and other ecclesiastical-sounding recipients. Some correspondence to a supplier in Tenby, probably relating to the running of the abbey kitchen or some such matter. She came to the last letter in the pile, addressed in familiar handwriting that she recognised immediately.

To Mrs Bethan Rees, St Samson's Cottage, Caldey Island.

Well, well. This letter was the answer to Rosalind's question – why would people who live on such a small island write to each other? The reason should have been obvious – so that someone who lived within the abbey walls could communicate in private with someone outside the cloister.

Nia turned the sign on the door of the post office to "closed" and took the letter into the back office. There, she filled the kettle and flicked the switch.

When the water was just coming to the boil, she held

the flap of the envelope over the steam. Not for too long or the paper would start to crinkle – she knew that from experience. Then, with practised care, she eased open the envelope with a fine-bladed paperknife. She extracted the letter, read the contents through twice, then returned it to the envelope and resealed it with a glue stick, kept to hand for the purpose.

She would deliver the letter to its intended recipient later.

But she had already memorised it word for word.

CHAPTER 25

'The injuries sustained by the victims point to a controlled attack,' Carys told her team as soon as she was back at the police station. 'Far from losing control, the person responsible carried out deliberate, purposeful killings. They were willing to hack Veronica repeatedly until landing a fatal blow, and hold Rick underwater by force until he drowned. Whoever carried out these murders was determined to ensure that their victims didn't survive.'

The journey from the mortuary to the incident room had taken just ten minutes, door to door. There were advantages in living in such a quiet part of the world. And she'd been pleased to find Rhodri, Elen and Hugh all busy at their desks. Her team was small – she needed each member to pull their weight.

And they needed to hear the pathologist's grim findings.

'So someone physically strong?' said Rhodri. He cast a sideways glance at Elen. 'Are we thinking it's a man?'

'Women can be just as strong as men,' said Elen.

'The killer was strong enough to lift Veronica's body

onto the altar,' said Carys. 'But that scythe would have done plenty of damage in anyone's hands. And remember that Rick had been struck on the back of the head before being held underwater, so he probably didn't put up much resistance. He may even have been unconscious. So we're looking for someone reasonably fit and capable rather than strong. What we can deduce for certain is that Veronica's killer will have got a lot of blood on their clothes. According to Dr Fowler, the fatal blow severed both carotid arteries. What I want to know is where those clothes are now.'

'I'd have popped them straight on a ninety-degree wash,' said Elen.

'A hot wash might remove visible staining,' said Carys, 'but it wouldn't reliably eliminate all traces of blood and DNA. A forensic examination could potentially recover enough evidence to secure a conviction. Let's make finding those clothes a priority. Any progress on the murder weapons?'

'I took them to forensics last night,' said Elen. 'They're running DNA checks, but there were no clear fingerprints on either the scythe or the spade. No hairs or fibres either. And Rick's phone looks like it's permanently dead.'

That was hardly a surprise, given that it had been fished out of the pond. But the lack of forensic evidence was seriously hampering progress and Carys desperately needed *something*. 'What about the Bibles?'

Elen studied her notes. 'They found blood on the Bible that was placed on Veronica's body, and that's gone for DNA testing. The guy at the lab says they're leather-bound 1966 editions of the Jerusalem Bible, if that means anything to you.'

Carys nodded. 'The Jerusalem Bible became the official Catholic edition after the Second Vatican Council mandated vernacular scripture in the liturgy. It's been revised twice since the 1966 edition, but it's possible that the abbey retained its copies of the original version.'

Rhodri and Elen exchanged a glance, and Carys knew

exactly what they were thinking – how on earth could she know a fact like that?

'If you say so, boss,' said Elen, 'but how does that help us?'

'Brother Cadoc said that the first Bible was from the abbey church,' chipped in Rhodri. 'So presumably the second one was too.'

'That means anyone could have got hold of them,' said Elen.

Carys turned to Hugh, who had so far remained silent. 'How did you get on with the background checks?'

Hugh pushed his glasses up his nose. 'I've got quite a lot to report actually.'

At last, thought Carys. 'Go ahead.'

Hugh cleared his throat. 'First of all, I checked whether anyone living on the island has a police record, and they're all clear.'

'What about the monks?'

A smile tugged at Hugh's mouth. 'Glad you asked. The tricky thing about monks is that they take on a new religious name when they make their vows, so the first step is to find out their true legal identity.'

Rhodri let out a theatrical sigh. 'I expect you're going to tell us exactly how you did that.'

'Sure,' said Hugh. 'Although it was really very straightforward. I just contacted the diocese and they gave me all the information I needed. For instance, Brother Gregory's legal name is Roger Moreton and Brother Cadoc's is Ignatius Okonkwo.'

'Okay,' said Carys, 'and what did you find out about them?'

'Nothing. The monks are squeaky clean, just like you'd expect. Now, moving on to the retreatants, Samir Khan has no police record. He grew up in Bradford and studied computer science at the university there. He now works for a startup located in the Tech City district of East London. It's something to do with digital payments. I called Samir's boss, who didn't have a bad word to say about him. He explained that Samir was taking a few days off after working really hard to deliver a project. Apparently he's been putting in sixteen-hour days for the last three months.'

Rhodri whistled through his teeth. 'No wonder the guy needed a break. But I'm not sure he's getting quite the relaxing time he was hoping for.'

'Next,' continued Hugh, 'I called Rosalind Grieves's publisher and spoke to her editor. She was less fulsome in her praise. Apparently Rosalind's been with them for years, but her sales have been in decline and her last book failed to earn back its advance. The publisher is thinking of dropping her. They're still in negotiations with her agent but the future's not looking good for her.'

'Okay,' said Carys. 'But I don't see a motive for murder, either for Rosalind or Samir. What about Paul Roberts?'

'This is where it gets interesting,' said Hugh. 'Paul works as a geography teacher at a secondary school in Monmouth. However, he's currently suspended while an allegation of sexual abuse is investigated. No charges have been brought.'

'What exactly has he been accused of?' asked Carys.

'Inappropriate contact with children.'

'The guy's a paedo,' said Elen, her mouth set in a thin line.

'Allegedly,' Rhodri corrected. 'But does that give him a motive for murdering two complete strangers?'

Carys reached for her coat and scarf. 'Let's go and find out.'

*

Carys found Paul Roberts in the sitting room of St Philomena's, a book open on his lap. He didn't look up as she entered, but his finger moved slowly down the page.

She approached, uninvited, to find out what he was reading. The text was familiar to her. *St Augustine's*

Confessions. 'St Augustine wrote that sin is not primarily about breaking rules,' she said aloud. 'It's knowing that an act is wrong yet doing it anyway.'

Paul looked up, startled. 'A police detective who reads St Augustine?'

'And a geography teacher, too.'

He chuckled and closed the book. 'Not like these other so-called retreatants. Intellectual and spiritual lightweights, the lot of them. Some aren't even Christian.'

'You're referring to Samir Khan?'

He waved a hand dismissively. 'And that author woman, Rosalind. She visits churches and writes about monks, but she doesn't believe in God.'

'Is that a problem for you, Paul?'

He narrowed his eyes. 'I'd say that hypocrisy is a problem, yes.'

Carys regarded him levelly. Even though the man was on a religious retreat, she sensed no hint of repentance in his words, only pride. 'St Augustine wrote that what others think of us is unimportant. What matters is the truth we tell ourselves.'

Paul nodded slowly, unsure whether she was agreeing with him or rebuking him. 'Exactly. God is the only moral authority. We need not fear the judgement of our peers.'

'No? St Augustine confessed everything, publicly and painfully. No excuses, no evasions. He knew that to receive forgiveness, he had to bring self-deception to an end.'

Paul's lip curled in annoyance. 'Confession shouldn't be a public spectacle.'

'No,' said Carys. 'It should be a complete surrender to the truth. Absolution isn't granted to us until we face up to what we've done and accept the consequences.'

He gave her an unpleasant scowl. 'Why have you come to speak to me? Is this about the lies people have been spreading about me at school?'

'I'm here because two people on this island have been murdered. Had you met Veronica Emmett or Rick Styles before coming here?'

'Of course not.'

'You were seen speaking to Rick after Compline the night he died. What did you talk about?'

Paul closed his eyes for a moment, as if recalling the conversation. 'Rick was the only one here who was genuinely devout. He had done wrong in the past, but he wanted to make amends for his mistakes. He talked about repentance.'

'What did he say precisely?'

'He said he was glad he had confessed his crimes. The act of repentance gave him back his freedom, even while he was in prison.' Paul hesitated. 'He encouraged me to confess to anything I might have done wrong.'

'And have you done anything wrong, Paul?'

'No!'

And yet here the man was, on a religious retreat, speaking of repentance and with his head buried in *Confessions*. Carys had rarely seen such a blatant display of unacknowledged guilt. Perhaps his experiences on the island would nudge him in the direction of admitting his crimes.

'Tell me, what did you do after returning from Compline the night Rick was murdered?'

'I spent some time here, reading. Then I went up to my room.'

'What about the night of Veronica's death?'

'The same.'

'You didn't leave St Philomena's?'

'No.'

'Can anyone vouch for that?'

He shrugged. 'Not for the whole night. None of us can!'

Carys tried to picture this unpleasant man creeping out after dark to the church, wielding an agricultural scythe to devastating effect, then arranging Veronica's body on the altar in a position of prayer. It didn't take much effort to imagine it.

'Would you agree to a search of your room for evidence?' she asked. If Paul was the killer, then it was quite possible that blood-stained clothes were stuffed in a bag at the back of his wardrobe or under his bed. A simple search might bring this investigation to a conclusion.

'No!' He shook his head in anger. 'I will not allow myself to be treated as a criminal!'

'Very well.' Carys would need a warrant to conduct a search without his permission, and that would only be granted if she had sufficient means to suspect him. 'That's all for now. But don't go anywhere. I'll want to speak to you again.'

She was about to leave when Rhodri appeared at the door. 'Boss? Sorry to interrupt, but I think you should know about this. Nia Armitage has gone missing.'

CHAPTER 26

'Who reported Nia missing?' asked Carys when they were back in the hallway of the guest house.

'Sister Monica,' said Rhodri. 'The post office is locked up and no one knows where she is. Elen knocked on the door of her cottage, but there's no one home. And given what happened to Veronica and Rick...' He tailed off. There was no need to elaborate further.

Sister Monica was waiting outside St Philomena's. As soon as Carys stepped outside, the nun came up to her, agitation evident in her manner. 'Inspector, I'm very concerned. It's completely out of character for Nia to leave the post office unattended during opening hours. She never misses a day at work. And she's not answering her phone either.'

'What do you want to do, boss?' asked Rhodri. 'Shall I call a search team from the mainland?'

Carys considered her options. Given the current spate of murders, Nia's disappearance had to be taken seriously. But a search team would take ages to get organised and travel out to the island. A few more hours and they would lose the daylight. If Nia was in danger, there was no time to lose. 'Inform Pritchard that we have a missing person report, but let's not wait for backup. Find as many volunteers as you can, and you, Elen and I will each lead a team.'

'Got it,' said Rhodri.

Soon, a total of nine volunteers were assembled on the village green. Carys divided them into three groups. In her own team she had Paul Roberts – she wanted him where she could keep an eye on him – Brother Cadoc and Bethan Rees. To Rhodri she assigned Rosalind Grieves, Novice Thomas and Dafydd Rees – another man who needed close supervision. Elen's group consisted of Samir Khan, Brother Gregory, and Eifion, who had gladly left his boat to help with the search. Sister Monica volunteered to stay at the post office in case Nia returned. Father Anselm and the other monks were too infirm to join the search but offered to pray for Nia's safe return. Carys was grateful for all the help she could get – whether human or divine.

After a brief discussion, it was agreed that Rhodri's team would head west as far as Sandtop Bay and then circle back via the lighthouse. Elen's group would go in the opposite direction, over to Bullum's Bay and Drinkim Sand. Carys's team would conduct a search of the central part of the island and then head south. If Nia hadn't been found after one hour they would regroup on the village green and Carys would summon the helicopter search and rescue.

'Everyone clear?'

Her question was met with a chorus of agreement.

*

'She won't have come this way,' said Dafydd as Rhodri and his team headed west from Priory Bay. 'Not of her own free will, at any rate.'

'Why wouldn't she?' Rhodri wasn't inclined to trust anything the surly woodsman said. Not after he'd been so uncooperative during the previous day's interview. Especially considering that he was the one who had discovered Rick's body and was responsible for the gardening tools. It was entirely possible that Dafydd knew where Nia was now and was trying to throw them off the scent.

The woodsman glanced up from behind his bushy eyebrows. 'This side of the island is too wild for a gentle stroll. Nia wasn't the sort to go off on a hike. Besides, why would she leave the post office and go for a walk in the middle of the day?'

'That's what we're trying to find out, mate. So let's keep going, shall we?' Rhodri kept in close step behind Dafydd, keeping one eye on his surroundings and one eye on the man in front. Yet for all his misgivings, there was no denying that the woodsman knew the island and all its paths and hidden places. He led them on a narrow track along the rugged coastline, punctuated by secluded beaches and rocky cliffs. Above them, gulls wheeled and turned, their unearthly shrieks forming an eerie soundtrack to the search.

The going was muddy and Novice Thomas lifted his habit above his ankles, revealing a pair of good quality trainers that Rhodri would have been pleased to own. He had pictured the monks wearing leather sandals beneath their long habits, and now he found himself speculating what else they might be wearing. Calvin Kleins? It wasn't an avenue he wanted to explore.

'Nia looks fit enough to come this way,' offered Rosalind who was struggling to keep up with the men, but seemed determined not to be left behind. 'I'm sure she could manage it if she wanted to.'

Dafydd's only response was a soft grunt.

They pressed on over the rough ground. Ominous clouds gathered overhead and the gulls swooped and circled, their cries carrying on the wind.

At the island's most westerly point they turned south and before long a sheltered bay of golden sand appeared before them, edged on the landward side by steep rocky cliffs.

'Sandtop Bay,' said Dafydd. 'She's not here.'

'How can you be so sure?' said Rhodri in irritation.

Dafydd gestured with his strong arm. 'No one's been here. Look at the sand.'

After a moment, Rhodri nodded. The beach was pristine. No litter, no footprints, no disturbance of any kind. Only a family of grey seals, dark heads bobbing in the surf.

'We need to press on,' said Dafydd. 'There's a lot more ground to cover.'

Reluctantly, Rhodri turned away from the beach and surveyed the undulating hillocks and dips of the land ahead. The coast was almost violent in its features – rocky outcrops covered in short tufts of spiky grass, with steep and narrow clefts plunging down to the sea. Dafydd was right. Nia almost certainly hadn't come this way.

'All right,' he said, recalling Carys's instructions. 'We'll continue south and follow the path round to the lighthouse.'

*

'Keep your eyes peeled and shout if you spot anything,' called Elen, hoping to engender the kind of rousing team spirit she enjoyed at Crymych Women's Rugby Football Club. She was pleased that Carys had put her in charge of a search team, but less thrilled by who she'd been given. If she'd had a choice, she wouldn't have picked a boatman who seemed more at home at sea than on land, an overweight monk, and the sulky Samir Khan who, despite being much younger than the other two, brought up the rear as if the search was too much effort and he was more bothered about spoiling his smart shoes than finding the missing woman.

'We're looking for items of clothing, personal possessions, anything that might indicate Nia came this way,' continued Elen, refusing to be put off by the lack of enthusiasm. 'If you find something, don't touch it.'

Brother Gregory seemed agitated. 'Why do you think Nia might have come this way? Isn't it more likely that she's back in her cottage? Perhaps she slipped and fell and is in need of assistance?'

Elen shook her head impatiently. 'The door to Nia's cottage was unlocked, so I went in and had a look around. She wasn't there, and she wasn't in the post office either. Brother Cadoc fetched a key and checked.'

Samir stared out across the sea, no doubt wishing he could be back on the mainland. 'She might be anywhere on the island. This is pointless.'

Only Eifion showed any enthusiasm for the search. 'Do you have something better to be doing, young man? Playing with your phone, perhaps?'

His only answer was a short-tempered scowl.

Eifion fell into step beside Elen. 'Dry land is more to your liking than choppy water, I sense, girl. How did you find today's crossing?'

'Not as bad as before,' said Elen grudgingly. 'At least I didn't throw up this time.' She eyed the old boatman with his salt-weathered skin and furrowed brow. 'Do you ever get seasick, Eifion? When the sea is really rough?'

His eyes twinkled with amusement. 'Can't say I do. Sailing's in my blood, I reckon. My dad used to say that the sea doesn't trouble its own.'

'I'll take your word for it,' said Elen. She hoped the assignment on Caldey Island would come to an end soon, but she would never admit to Carys that she couldn't handle the boat crossings. Elen had never quit at anything, and seasickness wasn't going to get the better of her.

The eastern half of the island was more open than the area around the monastery – more farmland than woodland – but the coast itself was dangerous, with broken cliffs and precipitous drops into the sea. It wasn't safe to venture close to the edge, and Elen knew that if Nia had fallen over a clifftop they would need to wait for the helicopter to have any chance of finding her. She peered gingerly over a cliff at the waves crashing onto the rocks below and shuddered. This was a wild place, largely untouched by humans, and it was hard to shift a nagging feeling that the island itself resented their presence.

*

'That's the last of the monastery buildings,' Brother Cadoc told Carys as they completed their search of St David's church and returned to the village centre. 'The abbey itself is sealed to visitors, as you well know.'

'Indeed.' Carys kept her voice neutral, choosing not to start an argument with him. This was no time for a debate about women being excluded from the cloister. They had conducted a thorough sweep of all the buildings in and around the village, including the abbey church and tower, and were now heading south towards the ruins of the old priory at the centre of the island. Carys had never ventured this far before.

'This reminds me of field trips to the Preseli Hills,' said Paul Roberts as they left the village behind and set off up an inclined track.

'Really?' Carys had expected the geography teacher to resent being called upon to help in the search for Nia, but he was proving surprisingly enthusiastic.

'Yes. I used to take the kids there. We studied the geology and the use of marginal land – sheep farming and so on. Do you know the area?'

'A bit.' Carys knew the Preselis well but was more interested in its ancient stone circles than its sheep farms. The bluestones of Stonehenge had been brought from the Preseli Hills, and the area was full of sites of pagan worship. She was also familiar with the folklore of the area, such as the story of a shepherd who travelled to the Otherworld and married a faerie. But she didn't think Paul would be interested in hearing such tales.

She was wary of Paul and needed to keep him firmly

under control. He had a long stride and was in danger of pulling too far ahead. They might miss something important if they went too fast. If he was the killer, he could easily lead them astray in their hunt for Nia. She told him to wait while Bethan, who had fallen behind, caught up.

She glanced at Brother Cadoc. 'Tell me about this part of the island.'

The monk seemed happy to oblige. 'We're approaching the site of the original priory. The old priory and St Illtyd's church are the oldest buildings on Caldey Island and were built in the twelfth century on the site of an earlier Celtic monastery. In medieval times, the priory was home to Benedictine monks. It's largely in ruins now, but St Illtyd's is still a consecrated Roman Catholic church.'

They inspected the priory buildings, which consisted of a gatehouse and a two-storey dormitory with a tower arranged around a courtyard. Carys noted the medieval fisheries and hoped she wouldn't have to bring in a team to search the pond. The rubble stone walls of the priory had partly collapsed, and the only intact structure was St Illtyd's itself. But even though the church was still in use, its leaning tower had seen better days and Carys wondered how much longer it would endure.

They searched inside the church, but there was no sign of Nia.

Their next stop was the lighthouse.

As they walked, Paul and Brother Cadoc pulled ahead, apparently keen to discuss the history of St Illtyd's church and its famous Ogham Stone. Carys used the opportunity to engage Bethan in conversation.

'When we talked before, you called Nia a busybody.'

'Did I?' The café proprietor had fallen unusually quiet, not at all her normal chatty self. She bowed her head against the wind and didn't look at Carys as she spoke. 'I must have been cross with her about something.'

Bethan rubbed her thumb against her wedding ring and Carys wondered what she was hiding. Could Nia somehow be involved with Dafydd? It would explain Bethan's deep-seated antipathy to the postmistress. And also the apparent distance between Bethan and her husband. Carys had expected Dafydd to ask if he could join the same search team as his wife, but he'd been happy to go with Rhodri instead.

'Is there anything you want to tell me about Nia?' probed Carys. 'Anything that might be relevant to her disappearance?'

Bethan shook her head vigorously. 'No. I don't know anything.'

The lighthouse rose into view ahead of them, a squat limestone tower looking out to sea, guarding the western entrance to Carmarthen Bay. This was the bleakest part of the island, and the lighthouse, oil store and two attached cottages were the only buildings here.

'Is the lighthouse manned?' Carys asked Cadoc.

'Not any longer. When it was first built, the keepers and their families lived in the cottages, but in the twentieth century it was automated and converted to run on electricity. No one lives there now.'

They fell into an uneasy silence as they neared the lighthouse. The only sound was the whistle of the wind and the washing of the waves against the shore. A wooden sign in both English and Welsh informed them that this part of the island was called Chapel Point. It was the summit of Caldey. To the east, the coast of the Gower Peninsula was just visible across the sea as a hazy blue line, and to the west was St Govan's Head. Due south, beyond view, lay Lundy, one of those semi-mythical places from Carys's childhood when her nan had tuned in to Radio Four longwave to listen to the shipping forecast. She sensed the loneliness of the spot. And then another sound rose above the wind.

The cawing of crows.

Carys ordered the others to wait, then went on alone.

The crows took flight as she approached the base of the lighthouse, black wings flapping as their voices rose in noisy complaint at the interruption to their feast.

Seated in the long grass at the foot of the lighthouse was a woman. Carys kept her distance, not wanting to disturb the scene, but even at twenty feet she recognised Nia the postmistress. It was obvious from her slumped attitude that she was dead, her body propped against the building for support. Her skin was grey and waxen, her lips tinged with blue.

The crows had already plucked out her eyes.

CHAPTER 27

It was dusk by the time SOCO finished setting up their tent. The lighthouse had switched on automatically, casting its cold, white light over the scene of death. The sight of Nia's eyeless sockets was as gruesome as anything Carys had witnessed during her years as a police detective, but she had no intention of leaving Caldey Island until she had answers.

She sent Elen to fetch food and a flask of tea from the café while she waited patiently, shivering in the white paper suit that one of the SOCO team had given her to put on over her clothes, but which had necessitated removing her coat, scarf and beret. The islanders who had joined in the search for Nia had been sent back to their homes, and Rhodri was dealing with them, offering as much reassurance as it was possible to give under the circumstances. Meanwhile, a small team of uniformed officers was scouring the clifftop, searching for anything that might have been missed.

Anthony Davies poked his head out of the tent and invited Carys inside. 'The cause of death appears to be strangulation with this,' he said, indicating a length of white rope flecked with blue that was still wrapped around Nia's bruised neck.

Carys knelt for a closer inspection. The rope was roughly half an inch in diameter. 'Polyester?' she asked, feeling the smooth surface as it slithered through her gloved fingers.

'That's correct. It's a low-stretch double-braid rope often used for mooring small boats, but I've seen tree surgeons use it to rig branches. It's very tough and durable.'

'It doesn't look new.'

'Right,' agreed Anthony. 'The lab ought to be able to tell us what it's been used for previously. There's something else. This was placed beside the body.' He held up an evidence bag, the pages of an open book clearly visible inside.

Carys took it from him, knowing even before her eyes confirmed it that the book was another leather-bound Jerusalem Bible from the abbey church. It was open at a passage from the Gospel of St John and she read the verse aloud. '"I am the light of the world; anyone who follows me will not be walking in the dark; he will have the light of life."'

She returned the evidence bag to him and stepped outside the tent, wanting to be alone to think things through. Night had closed in fully now, and standing on the clifftop she looked out across the black expanse of the sea. Nothing was visible out there, except for three flashes of light every twenty seconds from the lighthouse itself.

The light of the world. Three flashes of white light. Three murders.

The number three cropped up everywhere in the world's religions. The Holy Trinity – Father, Son and Holy Spirit. The Three Wise Men at the birth of Jesus – guided by a light in the sky just as Carys was now hoping for inspiration. The three points of the Celtic Knot, symbolising life, death and rebirth, and the triple goddess of Wicca – maiden, mother, crone.

Another, more sinister, threesome sprang to mind. The three fates of Greek mythology – Clotho, who spun the thread of life onto her spindle, Lachesis, who measured the length of the thread, and Atropos, who cut the thread at death.

Three deaths had now taken place on this holy island, and Carys felt powerless. She was reminded of the rule of three which cropped up in so many of the stories her nan had read to her as a child. Stories in which the hero had to complete three tasks to gain the prize. In none of those stories had the hero ever given up, and neither would she.

She brought her attention back to the known facts. Each murder victim had been found with a Bible verse. For Veronica Emmett, it had been from Ecclesiastes: *The living know at least that they will die, the dead know nothing; no more reward for them; their memory has passed out of mind.* Rick Styles had drowned with a verse from the Book of Acts: *And now why delay? It is time you were baptised and had your sins washed away while invoking his name.* And Nia Armitage had been found strangled at the lighthouse with the words of St John for company: *I am the light of the world; anyone who follows me will not be walking in the dark; he will have the light of life.*

These were no random choices. Dr Graham Fowler had been clear about the deliberate nature of the killings, and Nia's death by strangulation confirmed the pattern. There was meaning here, if only Carys could perceive it.

A shout roused her from her musings. She turned to see Anthony beckoning to her and ran to him.

'My team has found something,' he said. 'It could be significant.'

'Show me.' She followed him around a low stone wall to the back of the lighthouse where the door of one of the cottages swung gently in the breeze.

'It's been broken deliberately.' He showed her where the wood had been splintered and the lock knocked out. He pushed the door wide open and handed her a torch. 'After you.'

Carys switched on the torch and shone the light inside. The interior of the cottage had the deep stone chill of a church and smelled of damp and mildew. Its walls were of white plaster, green in places where water had gained entry, with bare wooden floors. All the furniture had been removed, but the room wasn't empty. A sleeping bag occupied one corner, together with a plastic carrier bag stuffed full of clothing. A camping stove stood beneath the window next to a stack of tinned food and a bowl of apples. Carys swept the beam of the torch around all four walls, but there was no sign of any occupant. Whoever was sleeping rough here was gone, no doubt frightened away by the police activity.

'All right,' she told Anthony. 'Get the team in here at once. I want it photographed and checked for prints and DNA. List all personal items and anything that could help identify whoever's been living here.'

She heard a sound and turned to find Rhodri with Elen, sandwiches and drinks in hand. Rhodri stared into the cottage open-mouthed. 'Bloody hell, boss! Have we been looking in the wrong place all along?'

Carys had no answer. Since the start of the investigation, she had assumed that the murderer had to belong to one of three groups on the island: retreatants, locals, and – unlikely as it seemed – monks. But now an unknown person had entered the mix – someone who could have been present the whole time. But who were they? Were they the killer? And if so, what was their motive?

'It's too late to carry out a search now,' she told him. 'We'll get the sniffer dogs in at first light tomorrow. In the meantime, let's make sure no one goes out tonight.'

*

It was nearly midnight when Carys parked Izzy in the deserted street in Manorbier and let herself into the cottage.

She sprinkled salt at the threshold, hung her coat, scarf and beret in the hall, then rummaged in the kitchen cupboard for some zero-effort food.

'No time to cook tonight, Nan.'

She peeled back the lid of a tin of sardines in tomato sauce and forked the fish straight into her mouth, leaning over the sink by the kitchen window. Outside, a harvest moon hung low above the trees, illuminating the cottage garden with a cold, bright light. Ghostly skeletons of hollyhocks stood bone-white against the yew, casting long shadows across the narrow lawn. Traditionally, the full moon nearest to the autumn equinox marked the completion of harvest and was a time to express gratitude for nature's bounty. But it was also a time to prepare for hardship, when those whose crops had failed had to face the reality of a hungry winter ahead. It was a time for reckoning and the settling of debts.

Carys's own harvest since beginning this investigation had not been bountiful, unless you counted results in terms of blood and corpses. The cold moon seemed ominous. Was worse still to come – or could she somehow turn the tide before another life was taken? It wasn't as if she had any real leads. No one on the island had an alibi for the time of the murders. And yet no one had a compelling motive.

She shivered in the cold kitchen, still chilled after the hours spent at the lighthouse. And the boat ride back to Tenby had been miserable and wet. Tomorrow would be an early start, back on the island.

What you need, my girl, is a hot toddy.

Her nan's voice was so clear, she might have been standing there in her quilted dressing gown and slippers, a glint in her eye, as warm as the moon was cold.

'You know what, Nan? You're right as always.'

Carys dropped the empty sardine tin into the bin and reached for the bottle of whisky her nan had kept in the top cupboard for emergencies. *In case of sore throats, coughs and sneezes. Or simply on a cold, wet night.* She poured a finger into a mug, topped it up with another for luck, then added hot water from the kettle, a squeeze of juice from a lemon, and a teaspoon of local honey.

She took the concoction through to the lounge and curled up on the sofa, cupping the warm mug in both hands. The aroma reminded her of happier days and she started to unwind as the first sip warmed her insides.

She closed her eyes and saw her sister standing before her. Long black hair, generous lips and that dark steady gaze that saw everything.

Esme reached out her hands. *I need you, Carys. I'm so scared.*

Carys's head jerked up and her eyes blinked wide open. She must have nodded off. But her sister's last words rang in her ears as loudly as if they had been screamed, not sent in a text.

She fumbled for her phone and scrolled until she found that final message. There it was in black and white.

I need you, Carys. I'm so scared.
I got involved with some bad people. Now they're coming after me.

Carys didn't yet know what Esme had done or who had come after her, but she had returned to Manorbier to find out.

She had been too late to save her sister. And too late to save Nia. But she wasn't too late to find out who was responsible.

She tipped her head back and swallowed the rest of the whisky in one. It burned her throat but that was no more than she deserved.

'I'm going to find them, Nan, I promise. And when I do, I'm going to make them pay.'

CHAPTER 28

Father Anselm sat facing Carys in the freezing tower room, his gnarled hands resting on his walking stick. 'You may search the island, yes. The abbey, however, is absolutely out of the question.'

It was the response she had been expecting to her request to conduct a search of the island and monastery, but it still came as a blow. Carys took a deep breath before continuing. 'Three people have now lost their lives, and we have reason to believe there is a fugitive on the island. It's vital we find this person as quickly as possible.'

She had already informed the abbot of the discovery of Nia Armitage's body at the lighthouse, although no doubt he had already heard Brother Cadoc's version of events, since the monk had been part of the search team that found the body. She had also revealed some details about what had been found in the lighthouse cottage.

'Three deaths! How can this have been allowed to happen?' The abbot might not be far from death himself, but he still had enough force to make Carys feel the sting of his words.

'That is precisely why we must look everywhere,' she

insisted.

Father Anselm shook his head slowly but firmly. 'Inspector, you must understand that the abbey is consecrated ground, protected by vows of enclosure and centuries of tradition. The brothers lead a life of prayer and contemplation which would be severely disrupted by officers searching cells and workspaces.'

Carys had come prepared for just such a debate. 'Father, I recognise the sanctity of the monastery – I really do. But the killer doesn't respect boundaries or sacred ground. They have killed in the abbey church and laid their victim on the altar itself.' The abbot winced at the reminder. 'In such circumstances, I cannot guarantee the safety of anyone. If one of your brothers were in danger, wouldn't you rather we prevented that instead of facing the possibility of a fourth death?'

Father Anselm seemed to consider her words for a moment, but then he shook his head. 'The Rule of St Benedict calls for stability and order. If the police were given access to the abbey, their presence would shatter the rhythm of prayer and work that is essential to our vocation. And what about the reputation of the monastic community? All we need is one headline – *Police search monastery in murder probe* – and the scandal would cause irreparable damage. We rely on goodwill from pilgrims, tourists, and donors. Have you thought of that?'

So they had arrived at the crux of the matter. This wasn't about sanctity and the spiritual welfare of the monks – it was about a threat to their livelihood. Yet Carys knew she would have to appeal to the abbot's better side in order to persuade him. 'Father, the murderer knows full well that the cloister is off limits. That makes it the safest place on the island for them to hide.'

Her hope that her reasoning might overcome his defensive instincts was quickly dashed. He leaned forward in his chair, his hands gripping his walking stick with fury. 'How dare you imply that the killer might be found within these walls! There has been no murder inside the cloister and I will not permit you to make this search.' The force of his outburst caused his shoulders to shake.

The abbot was a formidable opponent. Carys had to give him that. 'Very well, we'll confine our search to the public areas of the island. But if we fail to find the fugitive, then I warn you now – I shall seek a warrant to obtain access to the abbey.'

'So be it. My laws are those of God, but I cannot stand against the law of the land.' The abbot looked exhausted by their altercation, fatigue etched in every line of his face.

'Thank you, Father. Your life is built on truth, but so is mine – the truth of how these people died, and why.'

Carys held the tower door open as the abbot rose wearily to his feet and made his unsteady way back to the cloister from which she and her team were still barred.

*

'All right, boss. They're just arriving now.' Rhodri looked out over the bay as a police launch sped across the water, cutting its power just before it docked at the jetty. He ended the call from Carys, hoping she hadn't been too hard on the poor old abbot. Then he caught the rope that was thrown to him and tied it securely to the bollard next to Eifion's boat. A moment later, two officers in uniforms marked POLICE DOG HANDLER jumped ashore with their four-legged partners.

PC Rob "Bricks" Brickenham was in his late thirties, a former infantry soldier who had joined the police seven years earlier. He was a quiet, heavy-set man who was known for being unshakeable, hence his nickname. PC Lisa Harding, a few years younger than Rob, had grown up on a sheep farm near Carmarthen and was a natural with dogs.

The animals themselves – muscular German shepherds with pricked ears and bristling flanks – were also wearing blue police vests and reflected the personalities of their handlers. Rob's dog stood still, ears and eyes alert, while

Lisa's danced lightly on its paws, nose twitching as if it couldn't wait to get started.

'Sit, Rocky!' commanded Lisa.

The dog obeyed her instantly and Rhodri was impressed. One of Amy's many brothers had a pet dog which was very excitable and badly behaved. But that was a reflection of its owner, not the dog. Rhodri didn't hold a very high opinion of his in-laws. Outlaws, the lot of them.

He welcomed the newcomers, and set off in the direction of the lighthouse, explaining the job as they walked.

'People are calling it the monastery murders,' said Lisa. 'It's all over social media.'

Rhodri nodded miserably. He had read some of the online chatter himself, and Amy had been pestering him for gory details she could tell her friends and clients, but he had refused to give her any. The last thing the police needed was too much publicity.

'Apparently Eifion has been offered cash to bring tourists to the island,' said Lisa.

'He didn't accept, did he?' asked Rhodri, horrified at the idea of visitors showing up and making the situation even more confusing.

'Course not. You can depend on Eifion to do the right thing.'

'A hundred percent.'

'So, who are we searching for?' asked Rob.

'An unknown person, probably a male judging from the clothing we found. He's been sleeping rough in a cottage by the lighthouse.'

'You think this man is the murderer?'

'Seems like the most likely explanation.'

'He's dangerous, then?'

'He's already killed three people.' Rhodri's imagination supplied him with an image of Veronica Emmett, her torso striped with blood-red gashes from the scythe. It was quickly followed by Rick Styles's waterlogged corpse and Nia's ashen face, her body propped against the lighthouse like a rag doll.

Rob nodded grimly, his heavy jaw set. 'We'll be ready for him.'

The lighthouse cottage was under guard by one windswept officer whose nose and cheeks burned red in the cold wind. Rhodri told him to take a break and the poor bloke hurried off in the direction of the village.

'So what have we got to work with?' asked Rob.

'There's a sleeping bag. Is that any good to you?'

'Perfect. That'll do the job.'

Rob passed Kester's harness to Rhodri, then knelt down and presented the dirty sleeping bag to the dog's nose. 'He's got the scent,' he said after a minute, taking back the harness. He let out the dog's lead and the animal pressed its muzzle to the floor, working in a zig-zag pattern around the room.

'Easy, boy,' said Lisa to her own dog. 'Your turn text.'

Rhodri held Rocky's harness while Lisa held the sleeping bag for the dog to sniff. Rhodri could feel the strength and power coursing through the animal's taut body. Once it had got the scent, it was so keen to get going, it almost pulled him along too.

Rhodri gratefully handed the animal back to Lisa and watched as the team of two officers and their dogs set off. Then he settled in to await the return of the uniformed officer, wishing he'd thought to ask the bloke to pick up a coffee and doughnut.

A low throbbing sound caught his attention, at first so soft it might have been the waves battering the cliff face. It faded before returning with a dull insistence, growing in intensity. What had started as a pulse became a rhythm, the beat deepening as it drew louder. Rhodri put his face to the window and scanned the horizon. The noise resolved itself into a deafening roar, a series of distinct chops, no longer ambient but directional. It was coming from the sea.

And then he saw it. A search and rescue helicopter, sweeping low above the water, following the shore. It swept past the lighthouse and continued along the coast, heading in the direction Rhodri's search team had come the previous day. Carys was leaving no stone unturned in her hunt for the mysterious stranger.

*

Carys left the tower room feeling despondent. She had hoped, although not really expected, for greater cooperation from Father Anselm. Now she would have to call DCI Pritchard and ask him to seek a search warrant for the abbey and its cloistered interior. Could she have managed the situation better and obtained permission from the abbot to search the premises? Possibly. However, she wasn't simply dealing with an individual, but an institution that had stood for two millennia.

Carys had no time for the rigid doctrine of the established church. Her religious journey was a personal voyage, her faith born of self-discovery. She had little respect for self-proclaimed gatekeepers to the eternal.

Her phone buzzed with an incoming call and she welcomed the interruption to her brooding. It was Rhodri.

Yet when she answered, she could barely understand a word he was saying. It wasn't surprising, being stuck on an island away from the mainland. The mobile reception here was dire.

'Can you say that again?' she asked. 'I've hardly got any signal.'

'I said the dog handlers are searching the island right now. If there's anyone hiding here, those dogs will find them – they're keen.'

The news cheered her up. 'Good. Meet me in the village in half an hour.'

'Will do.'

While she waited for him to arrive, she made her way to St David's church for a moment of quiet contemplation. St David's was the parish church of Caldey Island, dating from Norman times and therefore far older than the present-day abbey. Its graveyard, dotted with simple wooden crosses, was the resting place of both islanders and monks and occupied the site of a pre-Christian burial ground. The Celts had believed that islands linked the earth to the afterlife and had sometimes ferried their dead across the sea for burial. This site had been sacred since before recorded history, was holy now, and would remain hallowed for long after she perished.

She was reminded once again of the importance of the number three.

Past, present, future. Gods, spirits, humans. Birth, life, death.

The building itself was simple in construction, built of plain grey stone with a red tiled roof. An open belltower stood above the entrance porch, its cast iron bell framed by the sky. The only remarkable feature was the church's spectacular stained-glass window depicting the early Christian symbol of a fish. The window's design had become an emblem of Caldey Island, depicted on countless postcards, mugs and souvenir tea towels.

She pushed open the heavy door, paused at the threshold, then stepped inside, savouring the layered scent that hit her of cold stone, old wood, wax and dust. There was nothing quite like the smell of an old church and she breathed it in, finding strength in the centuries of tradition it embodied.

The monks were now using St David's for their daily services while the abbey church remained out of bounds, and the air was heavy with candle wax. Small candles burned on an iron frame, even though the church was presently unoccupied. Carys proceeded down the aisle, admiring the colours of the glass in the windows. She placed one hand on the cold slab of the altar, then returned to the entrance where a stack of Bibles had been left for the use of the congregation. They were the same edition as the ones left with the victims, and she picked one up and began thumbing through it.

The leather was worn smooth by decades of handling,

the pages thin and crisp, their colour dulled to a warm cream. The spine crackled as she turned the pages, looking for the chapter and verse that had been left with Veronica's body.

The living know at least that they will die, the dead know nothing; no more reward for them; their memory has passed out of mind.

She couldn't shake the feeling that the killer was sending a message with those words from Ecclesiastes. *The dead know nothing.* In that case, the opposite was true – *the living know something.* Sometimes, they knew too much. And that could be a dangerous thing. Some people would kill to keep certain information secret.

Veronica Emmett knew that Rick Styles had driven the car that killed her brother.

What else had she known?

Carys recalled the video that Veronica had recorded on her laptop, in which she had confidently outlined her thinking and intentions. *I stalk him online, I know where he works, where he hangs out, who his mates are. I've even followed him in real life once or twice.*

Rick had become the number-one suspect for Veronica's death, but then he too had been brutally murdered – struck on the head, then held until his lungs filled with water. Carys turned the pages until she found the relevant passage in the Book of Acts.

And now why delay? It is time you were baptised and had your sins washed away while invoking his name.

Rick's sins had been well and truly washed away in the fishpond, but not by Veronica. So who else might have wanted him punished? Neither Samir Khan nor Rosalind Grieves had any known connection to him, and nor did anyone else on the island, as far as the police knew.

The final passage was from the Gospel of St John.

I am the light of the world; anyone who follows me will not be walking in the dark; he will have the light of life.

The words seemed deliberately cruel. The light of Nia's life had been extinguished in a place where light always shone in the dark. Who was the murderer taunting with these passages? The police? One thing was abundantly clear – whoever was doing this was very familiar with scripture. Unfortunately, on a holy island like Caldey, that didn't rule out many suspects.

Father Anselm had refused to countenance the idea that one of the monks was responsible for the murders. And perhaps he was right. But the fact remained that anyone – monks, retreatants, and islanders – would have had easy access to these Bibles and to the locations where the crimes had been committed. The same was true of the stranger sleeping rough in the lighthouse, whoever that person was.

Carys closed the Bible and replaced it on the shelf with the others. She would not find the answers she sought in this church.

CHAPTER 29

'Found anything yet, boys?' called Elen. She had been tasked by Carys to supervise the search of the post office for anything that might shed light on why Nia had been targeted by the murderer. So far, she and the two uniforms under her charge had found nothing out of the ordinary. They had already worked through Nia's cottage from top to bottom and found no clues to why the postmistress had met her brutal end. But Elen couldn't believe there was nothing to be found. And if there was, she was damn well going to find it.

She stuck her head through into the back office and asked again, louder this time. 'Found anything?'

'Bloody hell, Elen,' moaned PC Josh Edwards, who was rifling through the drawers of a desk. 'No need to shout. There's nothing here apart from random stationery. A paperknife, some glue sticks… exactly what you'd expect to find in a post office.'

Josh's partner, PC Nathan James, was studying a metal safe with a puzzled frown on his forehead. 'I can't work out how to open it. It's locked.'

'Safes usually are,' said Elen. She reached for a bunch

of keys hanging from a hook on the door and tossed it to Nathan. 'Try these.'

'Oh, thanks.' He fumbled his way through the keys until he found one that fitted. 'Bingo.'

The door swung open and they all gathered round to peer inside.

'Just a pile of letters,' said Nathan in disappointment.

'What did you expect?' asked Josh. 'A massive stash of cash?'

'Well, it is a post office.'

'Only a tiny one, though.'

'Shut up, you two,' snapped Elen. Honestly, who had assigned her this pair of muppets? *Rhodri*, she recalled, making a mental note to repay the favour one day. She pulled on a pair of blue nitrile gloves and reached for the letters.

She thumbed through them, one by one. When she realised what she was looking at, her breath caught in her throat.

'What is it?' asked Josh, who was now attempting to fire up the clunky old desktop computer that, together with an inkjet printer, occupied half the desk.

'Photocopies,' said Elen. There were at least fifty copies of letters – some handwritten, some typed. 'You're not going to believe this.'

Unable to restrain his curiosity, Josh stood up to look over her shoulder.

'"Dearest Bethan",' he read. '"The heat of your touch still lingers on my skin." Ooh-er. I'm guessing this isn't from her husband.' His gaze drifted to the name at the bottom of the page. 'Who's Ignatius?'

'He goes by the name of Cadoc now,' said Elen. 'Or more commonly, *Brother* Cadoc.'

'One of the monks?'

'You're having a laugh,' chipped in Nathan. But his expression soon turned to shock. 'You're not, are you?'

'Don't monks take a vow of chastity?' asked Josh. 'I thought that meant–'

'Yeah, it does,' said Elen. 'But in Brother Cadoc's case the meaning seems to be open to interpretation. The interesting question is why Nia has photocopies of private letters between Cadoc and Bethan Rees in her safe. Have you managed to get into that computer yet?'

'Piece of cake,' said Josh, leaning back in his chair and stretching his arms behind his head. 'It's not even password protected.' The screen – an old-fashioned CRT monitor – had come to life, displaying an outdated version of Windows. 'You want to watch these old operating systems – they're easy for hackers to break into.'

'Never mind that,' said Elen. 'Let's see what's on it.'

She stood behind Josh, studying the screen. Nia had placed shortcuts on the startup page, and Elen singled out a folder named *Bethan*.

'Open that one.'

The folder contained a number of documents and Josh clicked on one of them.

You think your secret is safe within the cloister, but I hold the truth in my hands. What would your husband do if he found out about you and the monk?

I can keep your secret, but it will cost you.

How much is it worth?

Place what you can afford in a sealed envelope and bring it to the post office.

You have until the end of the week.

It was undated and unsigned, but only Nia had access to this computer.

'When was this document created?' Elen asked.

Josh checked the date stamp on the file. 'Just over a year ago.'

He clicked on a second document.

You bought my silence… for a while. Now I want more.

Bring another envelope. Don't tell anyone, or everyone on the island will hear what you did.

You have until the end of the week.

'This one's dated nine months ago,' said Josh, 'and there are more, every few months. The most recent was this Monday.'

'So Nia was blackmailing Bethan,' said Elen. 'And she wasn't going to stop.'

She pulled out her phone. One bar of signal. She called Carys, hoping the call would get through. Carys answered on the second ring.

'Boss?' said Elen. 'I've found something.'

★

There was a knock at the door and Father Anselm sat up straighter, determined not to reveal how weak and frail he had become.

'Come in.'

The door opened and Novice Thomas entered bearing a plain brown envelope. To a man as young and vigorous as Thomas, Father Anselm knew he must appear truly ancient. As always, the novice had a spring in his step and his cheeks glowed from having been outside in the fresh air. Father Anselm smiled. Once he was gone from this world, and Cadoc and Gregory had finally ceased their feuding, men like Thomas would continue the traditions of the monastery. Within a year, the novice would take his final vows and become a brother. The future belonged to men like him.

'Father, a letter for you.'

'Thank you, Thomas.' Father Anselm took the letter and laid it face down on his desk. 'Tell me, how is the post being managed now that our dear sister, Nia, has been taken from us?'

Thomas bowed his head. 'A solution has been found, Father. The women in the gift shop have agreed to receive and distribute the mail from Eifion. I go to the gift shop now to collect mail for the abbey.'

'That is good news.' It was reassuring to hear that others were willing to step up and do the jobs that needed doing. It boded well for the future of the island.

'Is there anything else I can do for you, Father?'

'No, that's all. Thank you. And bless you, my child.' The abbot held up a shaky, veined hand and made the sign of the cross.

Thomas retreated, closing the door quietly behind him.

Father Anselm gave a weary sigh. He picked up the letter and turned it over but didn't open it. The envelope fluttered like a leaf in his fingers and he wondered exactly when his hands had begun to tremble like this. The police detective had noticed it immediately. Yet he did not ask for her sympathy, only her understanding.

Born just after the Second World War, the son of a miner, he had been raised in a world where men were expected to be strong. But he had never been physically strong like his brothers, who had followed their father to the pit. At grammar school, he had preferred the library to the rugby pitch. He had tried to live an ordinary life, training as a schoolteacher, but the monastic life had called to him, even when his father told him he was running away from the real world. He had found all the world he needed inside the abbey. At various times he had taken on different roles – guest master, choirmaster, novice master. The latter role had been his favourite. He was not an ambitious man and had never sought the abbotship. Rather, he had accepted it as his duty. In truth, the ring had felt heavy from the moment it had been placed on his finger.

Yet his brothers had trusted him, and the island had become his whole world: the sea, the rhythms of daily life, the visitors.

Now it was almost time for that ring to be placed on another hand. Lately he tired easily. The brothers noticed, though they pretended not to.

He turned the envelope again, then reached for his letter opener and sliced cleanly through the seal.

Dear Father Anselm,

Further to your recent attendance at Withybush General Hospital for abdominal imaging and blood tests, I am writing to confirm that...

His eyes flicked over the contents. He didn't need to read every word... *advanced pancreatic malignancy... spread beyond the pancreas... curative treatment is not possible...*

He folded the letter and placed it on his desk. Outside the window, a blackbird landed on the ledge and cocked its head in his direction before flying away again. Very soon, his own soul would depart from his body. But where would it fly?

Just because he had been an abbot, a place in heaven wasn't assured. But neither did he expect eternal damnation in hell. All men were sinners, but through the blood of Christ they were redeemed.

As for his mortal remains, they would be laid to rest in the island churchyard at St David's, marked by a wooden cross.

But first there was work to do.

In the short time left to him, he must secure the future of the abbey.

CHAPTER 30

The tower room was as cold and inhospitable as ever, and even Brother Cadoc's natural confidence seemed to falter as he stepped inside and saw the look on Carys's face. She had no intention of making the monk feel welcome in what was now firmly her domain.

'Is something wrong?' he asked anxiously.

'Take a seat,' she told him, indicating the chair that had been occupied earlier by Father Anselm. 'We have questions for you.'

She had invited Rhodri to join her for this interview, and her sergeant sat solemnly by her side, notebook at the ready. Elen's discovery of the affair between Cadoc and Bethan had shed a whole new light on the monk who was, potentially, destined to become the next abbot, and this might just be the most important interview of the investigation so far.

She waited while Cadoc took a seat, glancing uneasily around the bare room, as if there might be something on display that could explain why he had been summoned to the tower and was being treated with such hostility.

He doesn't know that Nia was blackmailing Bethan, Carys

realised. Or at least he was giving a very good impression of being unaware.

'Tell me,' she said, seeking to put him at ease. 'Why did you become a monk?'

He gave her an anxious smile, unsure of the question's purpose. 'Growing up, I attended a missionary school in Lagos. It was one of the few options for a boy like me. My parents couldn't afford other schools. A priest there encouraged me to consider a spiritual vocation.'

'You believe in vocation?'

He nodded earnestly. 'This is my calling.'

'What brought you to Britain?'

'I won a scholarship to study here.'

'In what subject?'

'Theology.'

Carys smiled to herself. She and Cadoc were more similar than he realised. And her strategy was working – he was visibly relaxing as he spoke about himself.

He continued unprompted. 'I did well at my studies, and my tutors encouraged me to continue. They said I had a gift. But the academic world felt... small to me. Too temporary. I yearned to return to the Church.'

'And so you decided to become a monk.'

His smile returned, a broad and captivating grin that revealed well-spaced, even teeth. 'I visited Caldey and was immediately struck by its beauty. The silence. The sea. The order of the days. And the kindness of the brethren. A monk needs a community, not just walls and prayers.'

'Your own role requires you to reach beyond the monastic community. To act as a bridge to the secular world.'

He nodded modestly. 'Not all are suited to that kind of service. But the monastery must have purpose beyond its walls and build links with the wider community. That is a role I am content to fill.'

Carys regarded him carefully. Cadoc was clearly an ambitious man, who believed he felt called to something great. Perhaps he would have been better suited to a life without the constraint of vows. He had been overly keen to build links with the community, and with one person in particular.

'Brother Cadoc, I am going to conduct the rest of this interview under caution. You do not have to say anything. But, it may harm your defence if you do not mention when questioned something which you later rely on in court. Anything you do say may be given in evidence. I've asked you here because evidence has come to light of a relationship between you and a resident of this island.'

She watched as his body language changed abruptly, his shoulders drawing in, his fingers tightening against his thighs. He dropped his gaze to the floor before slowly raising it again to meet Carys's.

'I don't know what you're–'

'Bethan Rees,' she interjected, her appetite for evasion exhausted. 'An inappropriate relationship between you and Bethan Rees.'

She nodded to Rhodri, who produced one of the letters that had been found in Nia's safe. '"Dearest Bethan,"' he began to read. '"The heat of your touch still lingers on my skin."'

Carys stopped him before he went any further and waited to see how Cadoc would respond. Adultery wasn't a crime, but it was a betrayal – a broken promise and a breach of trust. For a monk, it was a breaking of a solemn vow.

Cadoc looked stricken. 'I... the spirit is willing but the flesh is weak.' He stopped, then bowed his head in shame. 'It is my weakness, not Bethan's. She is not to blame. Please don't think that we intended to cause harm. We only meet when Dafydd goes to the mainland to fetch supplies.'

Carys gave him a minute to come to terms with his failings. 'We're not here to judge, nor to expose your actions. But this evidence is relevant to the murder investigation.'

He lifted his chin again. 'I don't understand. How?'

She leaned forward. 'Brother Cadoc, these copies of your letters were found in the possession of Nia Armitage, along with blackmail notes that Nia had sent to Bethan.'

His sharp intake of breath confirmed that this was news to him. 'I didn't... Bethan didn't say anything...' he fumbled. 'I knew nothing about blackmail. I swear it.'

Carys studied him for a moment longer before dismissing him. 'Then you're free to go.'

He sat for a moment longer, his hands clasped in his lap in contrition. 'Thank you. I will go at once to the abbot and confess my sins.' He stood, then left.

Rhodri let out a long sigh. 'You believed him when he said he had no idea about the blackmail?'

'Yes, I did.'

'What next, then?'

Carys rose to her feet. 'We speak to Bethan Rees.'

CHAPTER 31

Rosalind turned to a fresh page in her notebook and rested it on her lap, her fountain pen poised to write. Working with pen on paper was always so much more stimulating than sitting in front of a keyboard with a blank screen staring back at her. And since coming to Caldey, her creativity had enjoyed a renaissance. Ideas for her next book were flowing thick and fast, and a plot was quickly taking shape. Brother Aidan would travel to Caldey Island after receiving a mysterious letter. There, he would investigate a string of bizarre and brutal murders and would come very close to being killed himself. She felt the creative buzz and longed to make a start, feeling sure that this book would relaunch her career. She pictured herself signing copies and meeting delighted readers at the Hay Festival.

'Mind if I join you?' Paul appeared in the doorway with a mug of tea cradled in his hands. He didn't wait for an answer but trudged wearily to the nearest chair and flopped down heavily with a grunt.

Rosalind closed her notebook and screwed the top back on her pen. A religious retreat was a retreat from the world at large, but it seemed that it was impossible to escape the company of your fellow retreatants – whether it was wanted or not. She could have gone upstairs to her room, but after the events of recent days, she preferred to remain in a public space, even if she had to endure Paul's presence.

From his ruddy cheeks, she guessed he had been out walking. 'Have you heard any news this morning?' she asked. 'What are the police saying?'

Paul took a loud slurp of his tea. 'Nothing. They have no clue about anything.'

'I thought that detective acted very decisively yesterday in searching for Nia.'

Paul gave a hollow laugh. 'It didn't stop her from becoming the next victim though, did it?' He turned his gaze to a stain on the rug. '"The soul that sinneth, it shall die."'

The door opened again and to Rosalind's relief, Samir entered. Samir might not have been much of a talker, but anything would be better than Paul's fire and brimstone pronouncements and she immediately felt more comfortable with another person present. Samir walked to the window and peered up at the sky where a helicopter was buzzing overhead. It had been circling the island most of the morning.

'What's going on out there?' Rosalind asked.

'Police search,' he said, tersely. 'They've brought the sniffer dogs in too.'

'What are they looking for?' she asked, but it was Paul who answered.

'The killer, I would have thought.'

Samir took a seat on the sofa. 'Do they know who it is, then?' The question was directed at Paul.

'How should I know?' said Paul. 'And why are you looking at me like that?'

'Like what?'

'Like I might have something to do with it.'

Samir narrowed his eyes. 'Do you, Paul? Do you know

who killed Nia?'

Paul jabbed his finger in Samir's direction. 'That sounds like an accusation. "A false witness shall not be unpunished, and he that speaketh lies shall perish."'

It seemed that Paul had a Bible quote for every occasion.

'Come on now,' pleaded Rosalind. 'Let's not turn against each other.'

But Paul hadn't finished. 'You are the one with secrets to hide,' he said to Samir. 'What are you really doing on this island? What are you hiding?'

'Nothing,' said Samir, but he turned away, unwilling to look Paul in the eye.

'Enough!' said Rosalind in frustration. 'Let the police do their job and let us try to be civil to one another.' She stood up to leave and only then did she notice Sister Monica standing in the doorway watching them all in silence.

*

'I've been expecting you,' said Bethan as Carys and Rhodri entered the café.

'You know what this is about, then?' asked Carys.

'I watched the post office being searched this morning, and then I saw Cadoc going to the tower. I knew it was only a matter of time before you came for me.' Bethan turned the key to lock the café door, then flipped the sign to closed. 'Why don't you have a seat?'

They took a table with a view across the village green. The post office was sealed up now, crime scene tape across its entrance fluttering in the breeze like bunting. Beyond it, the square tower that served as a makeshift interview room rose solidly above the abbey's walls. Carys's world had become very small these past days, narrowed to a handful of faces and a square mile of land bounded by rugged coastline. Somewhere within that tight circle, the truth was hiding, watching, waiting to be found.

'How long has the affair been going on?' she asked.

Bethan clasped her hands together and hung her head. 'A few years now. It feels longer. Time moves more slowly on Caldey than it does on the mainland.'

'How did it start?'

She leaned back and gazed out of the window. 'Cadoc has always been friendlier than the other monks. Some of them never even leave the cloister, but he sees it as his duty to engage with the islanders and ensure that visitors are welcomed. He takes an interest in the running of the gift shop and he persuaded the abbot to invest more money in the café. He and I just hit it off right from the beginning. Neither of us meant for anything to happen, but a monk's life is difficult, and Dafydd and I... well, he's not an easy man to live with. We haven't been intimate for a long time.' A blush suffused her cheeks.

'Does Dafydd know about you and Cadoc?'

Bethan shook her head vigorously. 'Oh God, no, and I'd hate for him to find out. He's a good man. I would never want to hurt him. A thing like this... Dafydd would take it very badly.'

Rhodri placed a hand on the table. 'How badly would he take it? Would he hit you?'

Bethan's hands went to her face. 'Of course not.'

'Are you afraid of him?'

'No.'

'Then in what way would he take it badly?'

'It would kill him,' she murmured. 'Dafydd may look like a strong man, but he's terribly fragile. I've seen him crying his eyes out after finding a dead bird in its nest. And I've heard him whispering to the trees at night. He's a gentle, sensitive soul.'

Rhodri looked unconvinced, and Carys recalled the stern woodsman with his brooding presence. Could that man be squared with the emotionally vulnerable individual that Bethan described?

'It would seem that you and Brother Cadoc weren't quite discreet enough,' Carys said.

A look of thunder stole across Bethan's face. 'Bloody Nia! She had no right to go poking her nose into our business. Reading private correspondence! How dare she? And how dare she demand money from me! It's not like I had any to spare.'

'You didn't consider reporting what she was doing?'

'How could I? I couldn't accuse her without revealing my secret. In condemning her I would have condemned myself.'

'So you kept quiet. You didn't even tell Brother Cadoc what was happening?'

'He didn't need to know,' said Bethan quickly. 'Nia wasn't blackmailing him. Monks have no money of their own, do they?'

'Not if they've kept their vows of poverty and obedience,' said Carys.

Bethan blushed again. Cadoc had clearly broken one of his monastic vows. But perhaps two out of three wasn't too bad.

'So I had no choice,' continued Bethan. 'I had to pay Nia to keep her quiet. And I had to keep paying her. I knew she would never stop asking, but what choice did I have?'

'You had a simple choice,' suggested Rhodri. 'Pay her. Or silence her.'

Bethan's mouth dropped open in horror. 'Silence her? You mean, murder her? That wasn't me!'

Carys said nothing, waiting for more.

Bethan turned from one detective to the other, desperate for one of them to assure her she had done nothing wrong. But she was met by silence. Eventually she broke.

'I don't know anything about Nia's death,' she sobbed. 'Really, I don't. I can't say I'm sorry she's dead. But I didn't kill her. You have to believe me!' She shook her head, tears falling onto the tabletop. She reached her hand across the table, then drew it back. 'Dafydd doesn't need to know about any of this, does he?'

'I can't promise that,' said Carys. 'One final question.

Where were you on Sunday evening and on Monday evening after Compline?'

'At home, watching TV.'

'With Dafydd?'

'No. Alone.' Bethan hid her face in her hands.

It was the same answer that Dafydd had given. Bethan couldn't provide an alibi for her husband, and he couldn't vouch for her.

Two people under the same roof yet living separate lives.

*

Carys and Rhodri left the café and headed over to the village green. A wooden bench stood in the shelter of the gift shop and Carys suggested they sit for a moment to consider their next move. After the breakthrough of finding Nia's blackmail letters, the investigation had stalled once again.

To their right rose the abbey, seemingly impregnable. Carys had not yet been allowed to view its hidden cloister and felt her exclusion from the all-male domain keenly. She was waiting for DCI Pritchard to authorise her request for a search warrant. Until that happened, the abbey would continue to guard its secrets.

'Thoughts?'

'About Bethan?' said Rhodri. 'If you're asking if she killed Nia, I just can't see it. She doesn't seem the type. But what about Dafydd, if he somehow found out about the affair? I can easily picture him strangling a woman, whatever Bethan says about him being a gentle giant.'

'But what would be his motive? If Dafydd was going to take his anger out on anyone, then Bethan or Cadoc would be his natural targets.'

'True.'

'And why Veronica and Rick?'

The search and rescue helicopter swept overhead, the rapid thrum of its rotors cutting through the air as it continued its search for whoever had been sleeping rough at the lighthouse. It circled over the monastery buildings before heading off in the direction of Priory Bay.

'Any news from the dog unit?' Carys asked.

'So far nothing.'

She sighed. How many places could there be for someone to hide on an island this size?

'What I think,' said Rhodri, 'is that since Nia was blackmailing Bethan, perhaps she also attempted to blackmail the murderer. The fishpond where Rick was drowned is right opposite the post office and Nia's cottage. What if she saw something and tried to use it to her own advantage?'

'"I am the light of the world,"' recited Carys. '"Anyone who follows me will not be walking in the dark; he will have the light of life."' 'What message is the killer trying to send?'

'Search me, boss. You're the Bible expert.' Rhodri gestured at the Celtic cross she wore around her neck. 'You're a Christian, right?'

Carys chuckled. 'It's complicated.'

She rose to her feet, drawing her coat close around her and reaching into her pocket to touch the iron key for luck. 'Come on, Rhodri. We can't sit here all day. Let's go and catch up with Elen.'

CHAPTER 32

The boat's engine still wasn't running right, but Eifion had been so busy ferrying the police back and forth that he hadn't had time to pop over to Pembroke Dock to buy parts. If he kept putting it off, then sooner or later the engine might conk out completely, leaving him stranded on the island, or worse, adrift at sea as a storm blew up.

A sailor could only afford to push his luck so far. He might have told Elen that the sea doesn't trouble its own, but the truth was that if a mariner failed to do his job right, the sea could be unforgiving in its wrath. So after dropping Carys and the other detectives at Priory Bay and arranging to return when required, he took the boat back to Tenby for some urgently needed maintenance.

The problem was the cooling pump. Eifion had patched it as best he could, but it really wanted a new impeller, and his supplier hadn't had one in stock. But he'd placed an order over the phone and they'd delivered it to him that morning, so this was his chance to fix the problem once and for all. Half an hour's work and it would be good as new. After checking there were no messages from Carys, he opened the pump housing, removed the old impeller, cleaned out the pump and fitted the replacement. Job done.

He was just refitting the cover plate when he became aware of a man standing on the jetty, looking down at him. The stranger was smartly dressed in a suit and long dark overcoat. Eifion could tell immediately from the man's bearing that he wasn't from these parts. A Londoner perhaps. He had that smug look about him that spoke of money.

'Do you sail to Caldey?'

As Eifion had expected, the stranger's accent was posh. Could have been London, could have been Oxford or Cambridge – it was all the same to Eifion.

'Normally, I do, but the island's closed to tourists at the moment.'

'Why is that?'

'There's a police investigation. Strictly no visitors allowed.' Eifion recalled the tourists who had tried to persuade him to sail over the other day so they could gawp at the comings and goings. He'd heard about dark tourists on a podcast he listened to. Voyeurs of other people's tragedies, they were. He'd been proud to refuse their dirty money and had told the dog handlers all about it.

The man in the suit reached inside his breast pocket. 'I'm willing to pay cash if you'll take me there now.'

A small smile of regret played at Eifion's lips. 'I'm sorry, but it's not worth my while to get in trouble with the police.'

The man withdrew a fat leather wallet. 'I'll make it worth your while.'

Eifion's smile faltered. This was the trouble with being a boatman. In the summer, life was good and the tourist season lucrative. In winter, times were lean. The boat repairs had cost him a pretty penny too. It was easy to be tempted, under such circumstances.

That wasn't Eifion's fault. It was simply a fact.

The man began counting out a wad of twenties and

Eifion's resolve wavered with each crisp note that emerged from the wallet. By the time the stranger was holding out two hundred quid, Eifion knew there could only be one outcome to the negotiations.

'Hop on board,' he told the man. 'I'll take you right away.'

*

The dogs had picked up the scent at last, and PC Lisa Harding felt that familiar tug of the harness – Rocky had found the trail. Beside her, Rob Brickenham's arm straightened too as Kester began to strain at his leash.

'We've found him,' she said, excitement building in her chest. They had been scouring the island for hours and had hit that sense of despondency that set in when a job seemed impossible. For all they knew, the homeless man might have left the island days ago and would never be found.

Now, all that had changed in the blink of an eye.

The dogs quivered with contained energy, noses to the ground as they drew in the scent that clung to the damp undergrowth. They hurried forward and it took all of Lisa's skill to keep Rocky from tearing off on his own. She had to hurry to keep pace with Rob and Kester.

Rocky strained at his harness, pulling her deeper into the trees. The fugitive had chosen a good hiding place, far from open ground, away from buildings, concealing himself in the thicket at the heart of the island. The dog leapt over fallen tree trunks, and Lisa dashed behind at full speed.

She caught a blur of movement as their quarry hurried through dense woodland, crushing bracken underfoot. Branches snagged at her face as she ducked between trees, her boots crunching over autumn leaves. The fresh tang of pine sap and the loamy smell of mulch filled the air.

'Police!' bellowed Rob, panting with exertion. 'Stop!'

But their target paid no heed to his shouts.

The dogs weaved around obstacles, and Rob crashed

through the undergrowth using momentum to snap the slender branches that snagged at him like spiders' webs. But Lisa lacked her partner's bulk and preferred not to have her face cut to pieces by the whiplike saplings that filled the forest floor. She pulled to the left, leading Kester towards a clearer path. There, she put on more speed, catching up with Rob and then overtaking him. She could no longer see the man they were chasing, but she knew he must be just ahead.

She emerged suddenly into daylight as the trees came to an end, and now she could see everything. A man was fleeing before her, dashing full pelt across open grass. The monastery rose up before her, the gift shop and café standing incongruously to either side. After so many hours of searching, they had flushed their target out of dense woodland into the heart of the island in a few short yards.

He continued desperately in a straight line across the village green. There was only one place he could go.

*

A man emerged from the trees at the edge of the village, half running, half stumbling, a look of sheer panic on his face. He turned to look over his shoulder at the two large German shepherds that were chasing him, followed by their handlers.

Carys sprang to her feet. 'Is that the rough sleeper?'

'Looks like it,' said Rhodri. 'The dogs certainly think so.'

The man was heading straight for the monastery.

Carys followed him up the steps to the abbey tower, the dogs and handlers in hot pursuit. Rhodri followed, close behind.

At the top of the steps he lunged to the right, vaulted over a five-bar gate, ignoring the sign that read *Private Monastery Enclosure* and sprinted across the terrace to a wooden door at the side of the main abbey building.

By the time Carys caught up with him, he was

hammering against the door, calling to be let inside. There was nowhere left for him to run, and Carys and Rhodri slowed to a halt. The dog handlers stayed back, the dogs panting from the exertion of the chase, their pink tongues hanging out.

The iron handle of the monastery door turned with a grating sound, and the heavy door swung open. Brother Gregory stood in the doorway. He looked shocked to see the man, but the fugitive was clearly no stranger to the monk. 'Gregory!' he pleaded breathlessly, 'grant me sanctuary, I beg you!'

The monk stepped out and caught the man in his arms, supporting him as he staggered forward, exhausted. 'It's going to be all right,' he assured him. 'Don't worry.'

Behind him, Father Anselm appeared from the monastery's dark interior, a deep frown furrowing his forehead as he shuffled forward, leaning on his stick. He stood in the doorway, barring entry to the building. A quiet anger blazed in his eyes. The abbot glared first at the stranger and then at Carys and she wasn't sure whose presence he objected to more.

'We'll take it from here, Father Anselm.' Carys nodded for Rhodri to arrest the stranger, but Brother Gregory moved to intercept him.

'No.' The monk held up one large hand, palm open but firm enough to make Rhodri stop in his tracks. 'This man has asked for sanctuary. You cannot enter holy ground.'

Carys shook her head. 'Brother Gregory, the law of sanctuary was abolished five hundred years ago. Release this man into police custody, or we will have no choice but to arrest you.'

'No,' the stranger begged. 'Don't give me up, I beg you!' He clutched at Gregory in desperation. His clothes were filthy, his hair and beard long and matted. He wore the expression of an animal caught in a trap.

Rhodri took another step forward but Carys raised a hand to stop him. 'There's no need to be frightened,' she said. 'I'm DI Carys Morgan and this is my sergeant DS

Rhodri Evans. Can you tell me your name?'

The man's eyes darted wildly from the abbot to Rhodri and then to Carys. 'It's Patrick. Patrick Mulholland. But everyone calls me Pat.'

'Okay, good. Pat, can you tell me what you are doing on the island? It looks like you've been sleeping rough at the lighthouse. Is that right?'

He nodded but said nothing.

Instead, Gregory answered for him. 'Pat's been going through some difficulties. He needed a place to stay while he took time out to think about his future.'

'I see,' said Carys. 'So you two are friends?'

'That's right.'

Father Anselm, meanwhile, had turned red in the face. He looked ready to explode. 'And you allowed him to sleep at the lighthouse?' he bellowed at Brother Gregory.

'I did, Father,' said Gregory in a firm voice. 'The principle of *hospitalitas* exhorts us to welcome every stranger as if he is Christ himself. Didn't Jesus say to his disciples, "I was hungry and you gave me food, I was thirsty and you gave me something to drink, I was a stranger and you invited me in?"'

'Yes,' Anselm conceded, though his tone suggested that such sentiments weren't necessarily to be taken at face value. 'But you should have come to me first, Gregory. We have rules regarding visitors.'

'I was obeying the rules laid down by Christ and St Benedict,' Gregory retorted, standing his ground. He and the rough sleeper, Pat, were clearly very close.

'How exactly do you know each other?' asked Carys.

'I've known Pat for longer than I've been a monk – from a time when I lived in Ireland. Pat became a novice in a monastery in County Limerick, but he fell out with the abbot there. He's tried to build a life for himself in the secular world, but it's not easy going it alone. When he reached out for my help, I couldn't turn him away.'

Gregory's gentle authority appealed to Carys. His reasons for defying the abbot were clear – he wanted to support a friend in need. Her own failure to help Esme when her sister had begged for help compared unfavourably with the monk's selfless actions. But however much Gregory trusted his old friend, Carys was not obliged to do the same. Right now, Pat was a suspect in a triple murder inquiry, and she urgently needed to interview him. Was there a way to do that without arresting both him and Gregory?

'Pat, I need to ask you some questions. Were you at the lighthouse yesterday afternoon?'

Pat nodded miserably and began to sob.

'Tell me what happened,' said Carys.

Pat swiped at his eyes with the back of his hand. 'I was in the cottage when I heard voices outside. I crept to the window and peered out. Two people were standing beneath the lighthouse.'

'Did you see who they were?'

Pat shook his head. 'The daylight was failing and I didn't want to be seen, so I stayed well hidden.'

'Go on.'

'I heard voices, but not what was said. I was inside the cottage and the wind was making too much noise.' He glanced at Gregory as if seeking permission to continue, and the monk nodded his head. 'I heard a woman scream, but I couldn't see what was happening.'

Gregory frowned. 'You didn't go to help?'

'Forgive me,' said Pat. 'It was wrong, but I was too scared.'

'What happened next?' asked Carys.

'It went quiet. I waited, and then I ran. I hid in the woods and waited. Then the dogs found me.'

'You were sleeping in the open all night?' queried Carys.

Pat shrugged. 'I'm used to rough sleeping.'

'Pat, three people have been murdered in the last few days. Have you seen or heard anything that might help us find whoever is responsible?'

'No.' The answer was clear and definitive, and for once

Pat seemed in no doubt.

'And can anyone vouch for your whereabouts at the times of the murders?' She glanced sidelong at Gregory, but the monk shook his head.

'Brother Gregory brought food to me each day,' said Pat, 'but once night fell, I stayed in the cottage and didn't see anyone.'

On the face of it, Carys had no reason to arrest him. 'Thank you,' she said, before turning to Father Anselm. 'Perhaps you could offer Pat a bed in the monastery?' She glanced up at the rows of windows. 'You must have a spare room in a building this size. A bath wouldn't go amiss either.'

The abbot bowed his head. Under the gaze of so many onlookers, he had little choice other than to accede to her demands.

Carys savoured the small victory in their ongoing battle of wills. Besides, if Pat was in the monastery, she would know exactly where to find him.

CHAPTER 33

Giles Levington was glad to finally step off the boat at Caldey Island. The crossing had been rough as hell. Diesel fumes from the engine exhaust had filled his nostrils and no doubt permeated his cashmere coat. He would have to get it dry-cleaned when he returned to London, which he intended to do as soon as possible. He had never understood the point of Wales, and this tiny island, located somewhere off the arse-end of an insignificant peninsula was as far from civilisation as he could imagine. Who would want to live in such a rural backwater? It had taken him over five hours to drive from central London to Tenby, and the traffic around Newport had been even worse than the M25.

'Mind your step,' said the taciturn boatman as Giles disembarked. 'It gets slippery when it's wet.' But he didn't offer a helping hand.

Given that Giles had forked out two hundred pounds to make this crossing, he thought the boatman could have shown him a little more courtesy. Instead, he'd said virtually nothing during the entire journey, and had left Giles to sit outside getting covered in sea spray while he steered the boat from the shelter of the cabin.

But Giles was determined to get value for money. 'Wait here,' he commanded. 'Don't leave without me.' He stepped ashore, almost losing his footing as the boat rocked in the water.

The seafaring life held zero appeal for Giles, and his legs were still jelly as he walked along the dirt path leading away from the jetty. He much preferred the city, with all the conveniences of modern living – Uber, Starbucks, a reliable phone network – he checked his phone and found only a single bar of signal.

Seriously?

Never mind, he would soon be driving back to London.

Presumably, it was the isolation of Caldey Island that had given Samir Khan the idea of coming here. Giles's employee evidently believed he could evade attention by lying low on a distant lump of rock in the middle of the Atlantic – or wherever the hell this place was. And he might have done, if the police hadn't contacted Giles requesting background information about Samir. Giles had been very happy to help the police with their inquiries, giving them a glowing reference for Samir, in return for learning that his employee was hiding out on an island called Caldey. Giles had never heard of the place but had wasted no time formulating a plan before jumping into his car and heading west.

He'd never been to Wales before and had no intention of ever returning. Whose bright idea was it to write all the road signs in Welsh? The unpronounceable word *Gwasanaethau* had flashed past numerous times before he'd realised it meant *Motorway Services*. But at least that idiot boatman was capable of understanding English.

He trudged on through the wood, wondering if this place was inhabited at all, when he came to a sign pointing to St Philomena's guest house. He took a right turn and soon found himself standing before a grey stone house. It wasn't the sort of place he would have chosen to go into hiding. No, Giles would have chosen somewhere with better weather and no extradition treaty with the United Kingdom.

No doubt Samir imagined that Giles would never find him here. But that had been a big mistake. Samir's biggest mistake, however, had been stealing data proving that Giles's company was merely a front for illegal money laundering for wealthy foreign clients. Data that would send Giles to prison for a long time if it ever found its way into the hands of the authorities.

Giles had a simple plan to recover the stolen data – he would ask Samir nicely to hand it over. Then he would fire him from his job and make sure the bastard never worked in finance again.

And if Samir refused? Giles had a backup plan, and it was also very simple. He reached inside his coat pocket and checked that the gun was ready and loaded. Then he walked up to the house, whistling as he went.

The door was answered by an elderly nun. She eyed him suspiciously.

'Perhaps you could help me,' said Giles. 'I'm looking for Samir Khan.'

'And who might you be?'

He fixed the suggestion of a smile to his face. 'If you could just tell him I'm here? I need to speak to him urgently.'

To his dismay, the nun produced a cordless phone from her habit and began to dial a number. 'I'll let DI Morgan know you're here. She'll know what to do.'

The police? No part of Giles's plan involved the police. The police were precisely what he had come here to avoid.

He had never hit a nun before, but there was a first time for everything.

'Listen…' he began, but to his great relief, Samir Khan appeared from the trees just beyond the guest house, strolling along the path. He held a vape in his hand and was breathing out a long white plume.

Giles couldn't believe his luck.

He took a step towards him.

Samir looked up. As soon as he saw Giles, his mouth fell open and the vape fell from his hand.

Then he turned. And ran.

*

The call from Sister Monica was breathless and slightly garbled. At first Carys feared there had been another murder but then she understood that a stranger had arrived on the island, asking for Samir.

'Can you describe him?' asked Carys.

'Tall, about forty years old, and dressed in a cashmere coat and a dark suit.'

'And where is he now?'

'He's chasing Samir!' cried Sister Monica. 'Oh, do come quickly.'

'We're on our way,' said Carys. 'Go inside and lock the door.'

She ended the call and broke into a run, Rhodri and Elen at her side.

CHAPTER 34

Samir sprinted through the woodland, heart pounding in his chest. How the hell had Giles Levington tracked him down to Caldey Island? He'd gone to great lengths to cover his tracks and had thought he would be safe from his boss here.

'Samir!' shouted Giles behind him. 'We need to talk.'

Samir had no intention of talking, especially not to Giles. He wished now that he'd gone straight to the police and told them all he knew. But he'd been too scared. Giles's business partners weren't the kind of people who would wait for the police to come looking for them. If they felt threatened in any way, they would act ruthlessly to remove the threat.

But how could he shake off his pursuer on an island as small as Caldey? There simply weren't that many places to hide. His only advantage was that he knew his way around, while Giles was clueless. Where could he hide – the lighthouse? The monastery? The old priory? He just couldn't think!

One thing he did know: Giles was gaining on him, and he could already hear the other man's panting as he closed the distance between them.

Samir veered off the main path, hurling himself into the undergrowth. A tree root tripped him, and he tumbled into brambles. With a cry of pain, he tore himself free and stumbled forwards.

Giles was crashing through the woods, spitting a stream of profanities. Perhaps he would abandon his pursuit, not wanting to ruin his expensive coat.

Samir risked a backwards glance, but he had underestimated his opponent. Giles was tearing through the thicket like a madman, oblivious to the state of his clothes. Samir had never seen him so angry.

He stumbled out of the woods and found himself in the clearing at the foot of the huge cross with the life-size statue of Jesus nailed to it. *Calvary Cross*, Paul had called it, before delivering a lecture about Christ's suffering at the hands of the Romans.

Never mind that – Samir felt a growing sense of certainty that he was about to suffer at the hands of Giles Levington. Sure enough, he wheeled around to see Giles crashing through the trees. His boss had caught up with him and there was nowhere left to run.

'Okay,' Samir called, raising his hands in a gesture of submission. 'Let's talk.' If he could keep the other man occupied for long enough, surely the police detectives would come to his rescue. Then he could confess everything to them and Giles would be arrested.

Giles brushed stray twigs and leaves off his coat as he strode towards Samir. 'All right, Samir. Hand it over.' He held out a hand expectantly.

'Hand what over?' Samir knew that his only hope was to play for time.

'Don't play dumb with me,' snarled Giles.

Samir's hand went instinctively to his pocket where he kept the memory stick. He had kept it safe all this time, sleeping with it beneath his pillow, returning it to his pocket as soon as he got dressed. It contained a complete record of the financial fraud that Giles had been committing for years. While the company's stated goal was to ensure transparency in online transactions, its true purpose was to illegally channel millions of pounds through offshore bank accounts. And Samir had gathered enough data to expose the entire operation. The evidence on this memory stick would put Giles Levington and his fellow directors behind bars.

But his unconscious hand movement was not lost on Giles. His eyes flicked to Samir's right trouser pocket and then back to his face. An ugly smile spread across his lips. He reached into his breast pocket and pulled out a gun.

'Let's not waste time, Samir. The game's up. Give me the memory stick. Now!'

The sight of the gun should have scared Samir to death, but he was already as scared as he could be. Perhaps it was the presence of the crucified man standing over him that gave him courage. Or else he had lost all sense of self-preservation. Whatever the reason, he felt strangely calm – as if destiny, or God, or the universe itself, had led him to this point.

'Or what?' he demanded.

'Or what?!' Giles's eyes bulged in fury. He raised the gun and aimed it at Samir. 'Or I'll shoot, you idiot!'

Samir shook his head. His whole body was quivering with fear, but the sight of Giles with his mud-splattered suit and his unchecked arrogance filled him with the resolve he needed. 'Go on then!' he said.

Giles's knuckles turned white as his fingers tightened around the grip.

The gun went off.

*

The gunshot ricocheted through the trees, and a group of woodpigeons took fright, flying into the air, their wings clapping loudly.

'This way!' yelled Carys. A thread of fabric caught on a bramble marked the place where Samir and the other man had left the path. Beyond it, the undergrowth was trampled, the ferns and nettles flattened.

'Boss.' It was Elen. 'I've got this.'

Before Carys could overrule her, Elen dashed ahead, her head down, arms pumping at her sides.

'Elen!' Rhodri dived into the brambles after her and disappeared.

All Carys could do was follow.

She soon reached a clearing and took in the scene at a glance. She was standing at the foot of the Calvary Cross. Samir lay on the ground, his face pressed to the grass. But he was still alive – the shot had missed.

The man was advancing towards him, a gun in his outstretched hand. He'd missed once. He wouldn't miss twice.

He had his back to the detectives.

Elen charged across the clearing and launched herself at him, flying through the air and wrapping both arms around his legs. He cried out in surprise, lost his balance and toppled to the ground. The gun fell from his hand, landing a few feet away. Rhodri ran and picked it up. By the time Carys reached them, Elen had the shooter flat on the ground with his hands cuffed behind him.

'Elen plays prop for Crymych women's rugby team,' said Rhodri.

'The A team, I assume. You took a risk there,' Carys told Elen.

'Sorry, boss.'

Carys walked over to Samir and knelt at his side. 'Are you all right?'

'I'm fine.'

'You have Elen to thank for that.'

He nodded.

Elen hauled her captive to his feet.

'Who is this?' Carys asked Samir.

'His name is Giles Levington. He's my boss. And he's guilty of financial fraud and money laundering.' Samir took an object from his pocket and held it out to her. 'He wanted this.'

It fitted comfortably into Carys's palm. A memory stick, little more than an inch in length, but probably capable of holding gigabytes of data.

'Scotland Yard will be interested in that,' said Samir.

Carys turned to the man who stood snivelling in his muddy clothes. 'Giles Levington, I am arresting you on suspicion of attempted murder and possession of a firearm with intent to endanger life.'

She would see about the accusations Samir had made later and would probably hand Giles over to the National Crime Agency, who would be better equipped to investigate financial fraud.

'Take him to Haverfordwest and get him processed,' she told Rhodri. To Elen she said quietly, 'Good work.' The younger detective beamed as if she'd just won the rugby world cup.

Carys was left alone with Samir. She held up the memory stick. 'If this contains evidence of a crime, why didn't you hand it over to the police earlier?'

'Because I'm too much of a coward. I thought I could do the right thing, but when it came to it, I couldn't handle the pressure. I kept telling myself I had come to Caldey Island to get my head straight, but really I was just avoiding a decision.' He breathed out a sigh of relief. 'Such a small object, yet it's been weighing me down like the heaviest of burdens.'

'You did the right thing in the end.'

'Only when Giles pointed a gun at my head.' He cast a glance up at the figure of Jesus on the cross. 'You know, I don't believe everything the monks do, but I'm starting to see the appeal of a quiet life far from the city.'

Carys gave him a smile. 'A quiet life is greatly underrated.'

CHAPTER 35

Rhodri closed the book he had been reading from
aloud, kissed his sleeping son on his forehead, and
tiptoed from the room, closing the door softly
behind him. Amy had already put Lila in her cot, and he
checked that she was sleeping soundly.

Like a baby.

For once, both children had settled without fuss.

He wasn't about to waste the opportunity.

He found his wife in the kitchen scraping the remains
of their takeaway meal into the food bin. He walked up
behind her and wrapped his arms around her waist,
inhaling the coconut smell of her shampoo. He loved every
inch of her – her generous curves, her soft hair, her
dimpled cheeks when she smiled.

'Leave that,' he whispered in her ear. 'Let's go
upstairs.'

'Rhodri Evans!' She turned around to face him.
'What's got into you?'

What had got into him? Maybe it was the murder
investigation, which was like no other he had worked on.
So much death – yet so much excitement. Chasing Rick

Styles and handcuffing him before he could make his escape by boat. The sheer physicality of those sniffer dogs today, their lean, muscular bodies running after the vagrant. Not to mention, the danger of facing down an armed assailant, although admittedly it was Elen who had done most of the facing down. Seeing her take that gunman down with a spectacular rugby tackle had made him want to cheer just as he and his mates had done when Wales won the Six Nations in 2019 with a decisive victory over Ireland on the final day. In short, work had never been so thrilling. It had given him a buzz of energy that now transformed itself into a passionate desire for his wife.

She placed her hands on his chest and pushed him gently but firmly away. 'It's Thursday.'

'So?'

'So we've got to be up early for work tomorrow and I need to get Billy's games kit ready. And if I don't put the dishwasher on, we won't have enough dishes for breakfast. Besides, I've been on my feet all day at the salon and I need an early night.' She turned back to the sink.

He crept up behind her again. 'What about spontaneity?'

'What about you coming home late from the Five Arches on Tuesday night?'

Rhodri groaned. 'I thought I'd explained about that...'

'You *explained* that it was all the fault of Jon Jenkins and the other lads.'

If there was one thing his wife did well, it was sarcasm. Rhodri felt his hopes of a romantic evening quickly draining away. He couldn't believe Amy was still punishing him for one small transgression. 'I said I was sorry.'

She must have sensed his disappointment because she smiled at him and said, 'Never mind, I've booked a restaurant for next Tuesday evening. Mum said she'll babysit.'

'Tuesday?' Rhodri was confused. Why was his wife happy to go out for dinner on a Tuesday but not have sex on a Thursday? He felt he was playing a game with rules that had never been explained.

A worrying thought came to him. Perhaps there were no rules.

'*Tuesday*,' Amy repeated as if the date held special significance.

'Tuesday.' Rhodri racked his brains but came up blank.

'It's our first date anniversary,' she said with a sigh.

'Oh, yes, of course.'

Their *first date* anniversary! How was he supposed to remember that? There were so many dates to remember – their wedding anniversary, their birthdays, the children's birthdays, all the birthdays of Amy's extensive family network. It was *someone's* birthday every bloody week. He smiled. 'Where have you booked?'

'That new place over in Saundersfoot. Everyone's raving about it. I had a customer in today who said she'd had the best fish she's ever tasted.'

'Isn't it very expensive?'

He knew he'd said the wrong thing as soon as the words were out of his mouth.

Amy shot him a reproachful look. 'It's our *first date* anniversary, Rod. That should be special. I want to go somewhere lush, not just down the pub.'

Rhodri would have been more than happy with a beer and a burger. Why did they have to go to some fancy restaurant? They'd have to get a taxi too, if they both wanted a drink, and that would only add to the cost. But he didn't want to disappoint her. And he certainly didn't want to mention money – that would only start an argument. Anyway, he'd be getting paid overtime at the end of the month after all the hours he'd spent on Caldey Island.

'Fair play,' he said. 'That will be lovely.'

Later in bed, Rhodri checked the latest posts on a Facebook surfing group he followed, while Amy scrolled through aspirational home interiors on Instagram, interrupting him every minute to show him yet another kitchen island, set of bi-fold doors, or walk-in wardrobe.

'Very nice,' he told her, knowing they would never be able to afford any of those things. He didn't know why she bothered looking.

At half past ten, they kissed and turned the light out.

Rhodri could tell from her breathing that she had fallen asleep almost immediately, while he lay awake, unable to settle. Eventually he fell into a fitful sleep, punctuated by dreams of sleek surfboards, fretful children and massive kitchen islands.

*

The old man and his dog approached Carys as she turned the key in Izzy's lock and began the short walk up the hill to her cottage. He was tall but stooped, his thin frame angular beneath the light of the single streetlamp. Even in half shadow, she recognised his gaunt features before he spoke.

'Good evening.' It was an old man's voice, but it carried the same ring of arrogance as when he had preached from the pulpit all those years ago.

The Reverend Michael Morrow. Retired now. *Father Michael,* to his congregation, including Nan, though even she had cooled towards him over the years. But to Carys he would always be *that man.*

'Good evening, Reverend Morrow.'

He glanced at her in surprise, a sharp look that quickly took in her face. Recognition spread across his features and his lips pursed into sullen disapproval. 'Carys Morgan. I heard you were back.'

'Did you, now?' She wondered who had told the old priest she had returned to Manorbier, and what else they had said about her. But it was no surprise that tongues were wagging. In a small Welsh village, everyone knew everyone's business.

The dog, a little Scottie, raised its leg at a telegraph pole and then came to sniff Carys's boots. Its owner made no attempt to move it along.

'Back for good, are you?'

Was she? "For good" sounded like a very long time indeed. She had returned to Pembrokeshire for one reason alone – to investigate what had happened to her sister, Esme. She'd thought she would miss the bright lights of Cardiff and the anonymity of the city where you could be yourself and no one would question the lifestyle you chose. But already she was finding she didn't miss it much. Instead, she was quickly falling back in love with Manorbier – with the small, quiet things she had taken for granted as a child. The water, the stone, the trees, the beach. Changing constantly, yet always the same.

But was she back for good? Carys had learned not to plan that far ahead. You never knew what was around the corner.

'We'll see.'

He paused a beat before nodding. 'Well, I expect I'll see you again.'

'I expect so.' Carys waited for him to set off, dragging his dog with him along the shadowy lane. Then she hurried home, sensing the eyes of the priest, her old adversary, on her back.

Once inside, she locked and bolted the door, leaning back against the solid timber, her heartbeat so fast she could feel the blood surging in her veins.

He's just an old man. A harmless old man with a dog. He has no power over me.

But he hadn't been harmless twenty years ago.

He had lied, and deceived, and ruined lives.

Let it go now, Carys.

She slowed her breath with a short mantra, watching her anger come and go like the breeze, until it thinned to nothing. Then she hung her outer garments in the hall and went through to the kitchen. There was just enough heat from the range to take the chill off the room, but it was far from warm and she was glad of her thick jumper.

'It's a good evening for a hearty stew, Nan.'

She gathered ingredients from the cupboard and the

fridge. Neck of lamb, rosy-skinned potatoes, onions, carrots and swede. She placed the lamb into a large copper pan and poured over stock, chopping the vegetables as she brought it to the boil. When everything was added to the stew, she turned down the heat and covered it, leaving it to simmer.

'You can't rush good food, eh, Nan?'

She boiled the kettle and brewed a mug of chamomile tea. Then she checked the pan and gave the ingredients a quick stir. The stew would take a good hour on the stove. There was time.

She carried the mug upstairs and sat down on the bed. From the top drawer of her bedside locker she drew out a polished wooden box, five inches by three, its lid carved with a Celtic cross.

Inside were the things she held most precious. A shell Dan had given her on their first date; a photo of Carys aged two with baby Esme cradled in her mother's arms on the beach at Manorbier; a raven's feather; a friendship bracelet Esme had once made for her; a carved lovespoon; a locket with a long strand of jet-black hair, which according to Nan had belonged to a mermaid; a deck of Tarot cards; a silver cross on a chain; and a short handwritten note.

She held the cross up to the light, letting the fine chain run through her fingers. It had tarnished over the years and was in need of a clean. Nan had sworn by baking soda for restoring silver, but the cross was too precious for Carys to risk it. She set it aside and unfolded the yellowed paper of the note. It was dated October 1989. Eight months before she was born.

Dearest Dawn,

I have to leave. The Church is sending me to Africa for a short while but don't worry. I'll be back. Then we can be together. Always.

All my love,

R.

Carys had discovered the cross and note at the age of sixteen while rummaging through the few items her mother had left behind, searching for something unusual and vintage – an item of jewellery or a scarf – to wear to a party. She knew straightaway that they were important – clues that could lead to her father's identity. She took them to her nan, not caring if she got in trouble for going through her mother's things. Nan should have hidden them better if she didn't want them to be found.

'Who's R?' she asked.

Nan didn't even look up from the *bara brith* mixture she was stirring in a big porcelain bowl. 'Rowan Harris.'

'Is he…?' The sixteen-year-old Carys couldn't say the word.

But her nan gave her the answer she sought, 'Yes, Carys. He's your father.'

And with that, she forgot all about the party. 'Tell me about him.'

Nan sat her down at the kitchen table, continuing with her baking as she told her everything. Rowan Harris had been a curate in the village, just twenty-one years old, under the wing of the parish priest, Father Michael. Everyone had liked him, especially Dawn, who had shown little interest in going to church until Rowan showed up.

'So they started going out together?' It sounded incredibly romantic to teenage Carys.

'He and your mother became very close,' Nan agreed. 'But then he went to Africa and never returned.'

'Why not?' asked Carys indignantly. 'He promised Mum he would come back soon.' It seemed like the ultimate betrayal and she found herself suddenly hating her father. Was this the reason Nan had never spoken of him? 'Didn't he know she was pregnant?'

Nan began to spoon the *bara brith* into a baking tin. 'Not even your mother realised it then. By the time she knew, Rowan was gone.'

'But couldn't she have written to him? Told him he was going to become a father?'

Nan sighed. 'She tried to, Carys. She went to Father Michael and asked for Rowan's address in Africa. Remember, there were no mobile phones in those days. No email.'

'So what happened?'

'Father Michael told her Rowan didn't want anything more to do with her. He had found something more important – his true vocation.'

'And that was it? She just dropped the whole thing?'

'What else was she supposed to do?'

The conversation with Nan turned Carys's world upside down. That very day, she marched straight to the vicarage and demanded to speak to the priest. She asked him directly about Rowan Harris. He told her that it was Rowan's decision to go to Africa.

'That's not what it says here,' Carys told him, brandishing the note. 'It says *The Church is sending me to Africa*. That's not the same thing at all.'

Father Michael shrugged and muttered about the necessity, when one had a religious calling, of accepting the will of God. Just because Rowan hadn't made the decision to go to Africa himself, didn't mean it wasn't what he *wanted*.

Carys might only have been sixteen but she knew a lie when she heard it. 'You sent him, didn't you?'

The question caught the priest off guard, and he hesitated just a fraction too long. In that moment Carys guessed the full truth.

'You sent him away to stop him being with my mother!'

Anger flashed in Father Michael's eyes. 'I sent him away for his own good, and for the good of the Church! Rowan was a young man with his whole life ahead of him. He didn't need to throw all that away for the sake of some...'

'For the sake of some what? What were you going to call my mother?'

'Never mind,' said the priest. 'It doesn't matter.'

'It matters to me.'

Father Michael shot her a dark, hateful look. 'Your mother wasn't cut out to be the wife of a priest. She was a wild thing. I think her subsequent actions prove the point, don't you?'

If the parish priest was referring to the fact that Carys's mother had a second child with another man and then walked out on her children when Carys was two and Esme just a baby, then she had a response ready for him.

'Have you considered that Mum behaved the way she did because you tricked her into believing that my father abandoned her?'

Father Michael had no answer to that. Carys stormed out.

She hadn't spoken to him again in twenty years. Not until tonight.

It had taken her two years of painstaking research to establish that Rowan Harris had travelled to Sierra Leone in 1989, aged just twenty-one. He had been caught up in the fighting that broke out two years later when that country erupted into civil war. He was one of the fifty thousand civilian casualties to have died in the conflict.

Reverend Morrow's betrayal had shattered her trust in organised religion but strengthened her faith in God. Not a fiery god of vengeance and retribution, but one who walked alongside the broken and the lost; who could be found not only in churches, but in the leaves of a tree and the ripples on a lake.

She carefully put the silver cross and note back into the box and returned the box to the drawer.

Then she wiped a tear from her eye and stood up. 'The stew will be ready now, Nan.'

CHAPTER 36

The damp grey weather the following morning was mirrored by the sombre mood in the incident room. After the previous day's highs, with the success of the dog unit and Elen's tackle of Giles Levington coming in for special praise from DCI Gareth Pritchard, Carys had to face the fact that three people had died in violent circumstances and they were not much closer to solving the crimes than at the start. The only concrete achievements were that Giles was being investigated by the National Crime Agency for fraud and Samir had been allowed to return to the mainland to help them with their inquiries. Neither man was now Carys's concern.

What else had they uncovered? Apart from approximate times of death for each victim, the recovery of probable murder weapons, and the Biblical quotations found with each body, not much. Now that Samir had gone, the two remaining retreatants would doubtless be asking once again if they could leave the island and, without good reason, Carys couldn't justify another refusal.

She did have one new item for the whiteboard,

however. She pinned a photograph of the rough sleeper to the board, and wrote his name, Patrick Mulholland, beneath it. Then she addressed her team.

'Three victims.' She pointed to the photographs of Veronica Emmett, Rick Styles, and Nia Armitage. 'Veronica was killed with a scythe, Rick was struck with a spade then held underwater until he drowned, and Nia was strangled with a rope. All three were found with Bible verses. Thoughts, anyone? We need a new angle.'

'We've established a connection between Rick and Veronica,' said Rhodri. 'She was stalking him because he was responsible for her brother's death. And it's possible that Nia was blackmailing the murderer.'

'More than possible,' said Elen excitedly. 'I searched the rest of Nia's computer and found this.' She was holding a printed sheet of paper and read from it now. '"*I know what you did at the pond. Meet me at the lighthouse this afternoon. If you're not there, I'll go straight to the police.*" This document proves that Nia was killed because she was blackmailing the murderer. It was timestamped the morning of her death.'

'Excellent, Elen,' said Carys. 'Is there anything in the document or on the computer that indicates who Nia's target might have been?'

'Nothing,' said Elen. 'But at least it confirms our working theory.'

'Yes.' The blackmail hypothesis had been the most likely explanation for Nia's death ever since they'd discovered that she'd been blackmailing Bethan Rees. Blackmailing a café owner over an extramarital affair was one thing, but Nia had as good as signed her own death warrant when she decided to blackmail the murderer. That person had shown themselves to be utterly cold-blooded when it came to disposing of their victims.

'It still doesn't explain why Veronica and Rick were murdered,' said Carys. 'Let's consider the Bible verses. There's obviously some symbolism intended. In Nia's case, I think we can understand now what the words meant. "I am the light of the world; anyone who follows me will not be walking in the dark; he will have the light of life." The lighthouse shone a metaphorical light onto Nia's activities, exposing her wrongdoing to the world.'

At least, that was one way of interpreting the words. Carys was reminded of essays she had written during her theology degree. Her study of the world's religions had taught her to look for hidden meanings and never take anything at face value.

Rhodri shrugged. 'Boss, all this religious stuff might just be a smokescreen.'

Elen took up the thread. 'Like someone's trying to frame one of the monks. Or one of the retreatants.'

'Never mind *framing* one of the monks,' said Carys. 'It could *be* one of the monks. In my experience, pious people are just as capable of doing harm as anyone. Sometimes more.'

'Seriously?' scoffed Rhodri. 'I don't see poor old Father Anselm shuffling around with his stick to commit murder.'

'He might be more capable than you think,' countered Carys.

'Actually, boss,' said Elen, 'I don't think he is. I went through all the copies of letters I found in Nia's safe. Some of them were sent by the hospital to Father Anselm. He's been undergoing tests for a pancreatic tumour. Judging from the symptoms he's been experiencing, he's even weaker than he appears. I don't think he's got long to live.'

Carys nodded slowly. Perhaps she had been too hard on Father Anselm during their encounters in the tower room. The abbot was frail and was simply trying to defend the institution he had devoted his life to. 'Then what about the others? Cadoc or Gregory, for instance? Cadoc was having an affair with Bethan. Gregory was hiding someone in the lighthouse. They both had secrets.'

Hugh had been sitting quietly listening to the others, but now he raised a hand. 'Actually, I have something to report too. The sniffer dogs found more than just the rough sleeper yesterday. While they were searching, they came across a recent bonfire in the woods. Among the ashes, they recovered the charred remains of a phone and some burnt fragments of clothing. They've been sent to the lab for analysis.'

Carys seized on the lead. 'Fragments of clothing? We've been wondering what happened to the clothing the murderer wore when they killed Veronica. It would almost certainly have had blood spatter on it.'

Rhodri was also sitting up straighter. 'The woodsman, Dafydd Rees, was burning leaves the day we arrived.'

'Good observation,' said Carys. 'We'll talk to him.'

'I've had my eye on him,' said Rhodri. 'There's something off about that bloke.'

Hugh cleared his throat. 'Actually, there's one more thing you should know. I was checking Veronica Emmett's bank statement and I found a payment to an account in Sister Monica's name. Payments for guests staying at St Philomena's are supposed to go to the official monastery account. Why would Veronica have sent money to Sister Monica?'

'Why indeed?' Carys was feeling brighter than she had at the start of the meeting. 'Good work, Hugh. Nia's postmortem is scheduled for later today. In the meantime, Rhodri, you and I will head back to the island.'

*

'You were under strict instructions not to bring anyone to Caldey Island, and to inform the police of any suspicious activity,' said Carys. 'What was it about a man offering you two hundred quid in cash that didn't strike you as suspicious?'

Eifion hung his head in shame. 'I knew it was wrong, but the money was too much for me to refuse. I've lost business with the island being closed to tourists this past week, and I needed to buy new parts for the boat.'

'The police are paying you a generous rate for use of your boat,' Carys pointed out. 'So you're not out of pocket. In fact, you're probably doing better than you normally do at the end of the season.'

'Fair point,' admitted Eifion. 'I'm sorry.'

'Eifion, mate,' said Rhodri, 'that bloke nearly killed someone. If he hadn't been such a useless shot, we'd be looking at four murders now, not three.'

'I know.'

'All right,' said Carys, 'let's say no more about it.' The boatman looked chastened and she was satisfied he wouldn't make the same mistake twice.

The sea was calmer that morning and they made the crossing in record time. The boat's engine was sounding a lot healthier too. Eifion had obviously put the money he'd earned to good use.

They left him at the jetty and headed up the path leading from Priory Bay. Dafydd Rees wasn't hard to track down. They found him feeding branches into a woodchipper. Carys waved to get his attention over the thrum of the engine and the whirring of the blades as they chewed through wood. When he noticed the presence of the detectives, he turned the machine off and removed his ear protectors.

'What do you want with me, now? I need to get this done before the weather turns too wet.' He indicated a large mound of waste twigs and branches.

'It's about a discovery that was made on the island yesterday,' said Carys.

'I don't know what you mean.'

'Some items of interest were found in the ashes of a bonfire you were seen attending on Monday morning.'

Dafydd planted his feet wide and folded his arms across his broad chest. 'I often build bonfires at this time of year. Some of the trees have honey fungus growing on them, so I burn the wood to stop it spreading.'

'Do your trees grow mobile phones too?' asked Rhodri. 'Or items of clothing?'

Dafydd curled his lip. 'What are you talking about? All I burned was logs.'

Carys showed him a photo of the burnt phone and the charred fragments of cloth. 'Do you recognise these?'

He shook his head. 'Like I said, nothing to do with me.'

Rhodri stepped forward. 'Did you supervise the bonfire the whole time it was burning?'

'What's this now – health and safety?'

'Just answer the question, mate.'

'Not every minute,' growled Dafydd. 'It takes a long time for that much wood to burn, especially when it's damp. I don't have time to stand around supervising a bonfire. I just make sure it gets started properly, then check back from time to time.'

'So what time did you start the fire?'

He narrowed his eyes. 'This was on Monday morning? I started that fire on Sunday, mid-afternoon.'

'And it was still smouldering the next day?' asked Rhodri.

'Like I said, it takes a long time to burn.'

Carys nodded. She remembered the bonfires Nan used to make every autumn. Even with a small amount of garden waste, the leftover ashes would still be too hot to touch the following day.

'Is that all?' asked Dafydd impatiently. 'Because I really need to get back to this chipping.'

'It's not all,' said Carys. 'When we interviewed you before, you said something interesting about Brother Cadoc. You told us he wasn't a true monk. What exactly did you mean by that?'

Dafydd dipped his head, averting his gaze. 'He encourages the tourists. He doesn't respect nature.'

'Is there more to it than that?'

'I don't know what you mean.'

Carys softened her voice, not wishing to cause any more pain than was necessary. 'Dafydd, is everything all right between you and your wife?'

'Me and Bethan? Of course it is.'

'Have you ever suspected her of being unfaithful to you?'

Suddenly, all the fight went out of him. His arms dropped limply to his sides and he hung his head. 'You're talking about her affair with Cadoc. Yes, I know about that.'

'You do? Were you aware that Nia Armitage was blackmailing her?'

He looked up. 'Nia? No, I didn't know that. But I'm not that surprised. Nia was a nasty woman. I kept my distance from her, and so did Bethan.'

'I'm sorry to tell you that Bethan made regular payments to Nia in return for her silence.'

His fists clenched at his sides, but Carys sensed more regret than anger. 'Bethan didn't need to do that. She could simply have told me. I wouldn't have blamed her.'

'You wouldn't?'

'No.' He shook his head, and a tear formed in the corner of one eye. 'I know I'm not an easy man to live with. I'm not much of a talker, not like Bethan. I love my wife, but she should have found a better man to marry.'

Rhodri leaned in again. 'Have you ever hit her, Dafydd? Did things ever turn violent between you?'

The tear trickled down Dafydd's cheek. His fists uncurled and he held his palms out in an open gesture. 'I've never hit anyone in my life. And I would certainly never hurt Bethan.'

★

Novice Thomas followed Brother Gregory around the monastery garden as the older monk pointed out the various herbs. In his former life, he'd known little about plants and cared less. There had hardly been any in the streets where he'd grown up, only a few dandelions pushing up between broken paving slabs, or brambles growing wild on derelict plots where warehouses had once stood. Now, under Gregory's careful instruction, he was discovering a whole new world.

'This one is feverfew,' said Gregory, running his fingers

through a low-growing bushy plant with tiny daisy-like flowers which were now dying back. 'It's very easy to grow and good for migraines. It's also supposed to reduce fever and inflammation.'

'Feverfew,' repeated Thomas, liking the evocative name immediately.

'And this one is rosemary,' said Gregory, stopping by a woody shrub with dark green spiky leaves. 'Rub your fingers on that and then smell them.'

Thomas did as he was instructed. The rosemary had a strong, aromatic fragrance that reminded him of a soap one of his foster mothers had used. He held his fingers close to his nostrils, breathing in the heady fragrance.

'Rosemary is good for memory and concentration,' said Gregory. 'And for getting the circulation going. I told Father Anselm he should massage his legs with a dilution of rosemary oil but I don't think he took my advice.'

'He should have done,' said Thomas immediately. Gregory was wise, and Thomas hoped he would be elected abbot when Father Anselm died. From the abbot's recent decline, Thomas doubted he had long left in this world.

They moved on to lemon balm (anxiety and poor sleep), St John's wort (low mood and nerve pain), and angelica (digestion and coughs). Thomas knew he wasn't going to remember all of these names. He'd never been able to learn long words at school. But he also knew that this wasn't the last time Gregory would show him the plants. The older monk was a patient teacher, rather like the father Thomas had always longed for growing up.

Gregory stopped by a plant with feathery green leaves and tall spikes of flowers, long past their best. 'I know you won't remember everything I've taught you today, Thomas, not at first. It takes time to become familiar with the natural world. But there's one plant in this garden you should remember. Do you know what this is?'

Thomas shook his head.

'It's called *aconitum*. Another name for it is monkshood.'

'That's a good plant for a monastery garden.'

'Perhaps,' said Gregory. 'Aconitum was traditionally used to treat fevers and as a sedative. But even small doses can be lethal if ingested or absorbed through the skin.'

Thomas took this in. 'Why grow it in the garden then?'

'As a reminder. Every garden, just like every human soul, has its shadow side.'

Before Thomas could ask what he meant, another monk entered the garden. Brother Cadoc strode up looking angrier than Thomas had ever seen him. He was like an avenging angel and Thomas took a step back in alarm.

Cadoc stopped just short of Brother Gregory, glaring at his fellow monk in fury. 'What were you thinking of, Gregory? Sheltering a vagabond on the island in defiance of the abbot?'

Gregory squared up to him. He was broader than Cadoc, though not as tall. 'Pat is no vagabond, but a man of God. I did the right thing, providing him with food and shelter. Father Anselm has given Pat his blessing and allowed him to move into the monastery.'

Cadoc leaned closer to Gregory, dropping his voice to a hoarse whisper. 'Father Anselm may not be around to protect you and this man for much longer.'

'What's that supposed to mean?' demanded Gregory.

But even Thomas understood Cadoc's meaning plainly. Father Anselm was very seriously ill. All the monks knew that.

'Soon,' declared Cadoc, 'a new abbot will be elected, and he may not be sympathetic to your wayward behaviour.'

His words drove Gregory into a state of fury. '*My* wayward behaviour? What about *yours*?'

Cadoc's eyes narrowed and he took a step back. 'I don't know what you mean.'

Thomas looked on with fascination. He didn't know what Brother Gregory meant either, but he hoped he was about to find out.

Yet to Thomas's disappointment, Gregory quickly recovered from his outburst. 'It is not my place to judge you, Brother,' he said evenly to Cadoc. 'Come, Thomas, there's work to do in the kitchen.'

CHAPTER 37

'**D**o you think he's telling the truth?' Rhodri asked Carys as they left Dafydd to his noisy wood chipping. 'About Bethan and Cadoc, I mean.'

'I think there's something he still hasn't – or can't – tell us.'

'Do you want to take him into the station for questioning?'

'No,' said Carys. 'I want to hear what Sister Monica has to say about this discrepancy with payments to St Philomena's. But first I want to find out what Brother Cadoc knows about it.'

Brother Cadoc wasn't his usual affable self when Carys eventually managed to track him down as he left St David's church following the canonical hour of Sext. Something had clearly rattled him, although he pretended otherwise.

'I would like you to come with me to the tower room,' said Carys. 'I have something to show you.'

When they reached the privacy of the tower, she showed him the bank statement that Hugh had obtained.

'Were you aware that the payment Veronica Emmett

made for her stay at St Philomena's was paid into a private bank account?'

Brother Cadoc studied the statement in puzzlement. 'That is not a monastery account. How can this have happened?'

'That's what we need to find out,' said Carys. 'I'm going to speak to Sister Monica about it now.'

'Do you have any objection if I accompany you?'

Carys couldn't think of a good reason to refuse Cadoc's request – in fact he might prove useful – and so the three of them walked over to St Philomena's together. Sister Monica was busy in her study, seeing to paperwork. Her eyes betrayed surprise at the arrival of two detectives in the company of a monk, but she covered it quickly with a welcoming smile.

'Brother Cadoc, Detectives, would you like a cup of tea?'

'That won't be necessary,' said Carys.

'Then how can I help you?' asked the nun.

A thin wash of grey light pressed against the tall window behind the desk, flattening the colours in the room.

'Sister Monica,' said Carys, 'I need to ask you about Veronica Emmett.'

'What about her?'

'When Veronica arrived on the island pretending to be Sarah Black, you already knew her true identity.'

'I did.'

'And the reason you said you knew was because she booked her place on the retreat under a different name.'

'That is correct.' The nun sat very still, hands clasped in front of her. She must have known what was coming.

'But that wasn't strictly true, was it?' said Carys. 'Veronica didn't use her own name for the booking, but she did make a payment from her bank account in her real name. You didn't tell us about the bank transfer.'

Sister Monica blinked. A muscle tightened in her jaw. 'I didn't think it mattered.'

'No? Or was it because you were afraid of what we'd

find?' Carys let the silence lengthen. Somewhere deeper in the guesthouse a door closed.

'I really don't know what you mean, Inspector,' said the nun eventually.

Carys sighed. 'You were afraid to reveal this information to the police because it would have meant admitting that the payment was made to your own personal account.'

No one spoke. The ticking of an old-fashioned clock on the mantelpiece was the only sound. Carys waited.

'Brother Cadoc,' said Sister Monica, 'may I speak with you in confidence?'

The monk answered softly. 'It would be better if you said what is on your mind while DI Morgan is with us.'

'Yes, I suppose there is no point trying to avoid it any longer.' Sister Monica regarded Carys, her face filled with sorrow and regret. 'The bank account is not mine. At least, I never touch the money in there. It goes to help a sick relative of mine in Latvia.'

'Latvia?' Carys had noticed the nun's accent but had never asked where she was from. Perhaps she should have.

'You may find this hard to understand,' said Sister Monica sadly, 'but in Latvia, the public healthcare system is not as good as in the UK. Many people must make contributions towards their treatment, and for complex illnesses it can be expensive, especially for those on low incomes. My aunt is retired and cannot afford to pay. And so I decided to help her in the only way I could.'

She appealed to Cadoc. 'The amounts I diverted were not large. I only took what I needed from a handful of the retreatants.'

'All the same, Sister,' the monk replied sternly, 'you have broken your vow of obedience, not to mention the law of the land.' He cast a sideways glance at Carys.

'I think we'll leave you to sort this out,' said Carys, standing up. 'Thank you, Sister Monica. Thank you, Brother Cadoc.'

Rhodri followed her out of the study, throwing a

puzzled look her way.

'Is something the matter?' she asked him.

'Well, it's just that... shouldn't we arrest her or something?'

'And waste valuable time when we have a triple murderer to catch?' Carys regarded her sergeant with amusement. 'Rhodri, did you join the police to lock up nuns?'

'No, boss, but she broke the law.'

'You're right. It's our job to enforce the law. But it's also our job to do the right thing. Sometimes those goals are in opposition.'

'I don't get it.'

'Rhodri, you can report my behaviour to DCI Pritchard if you like. I get the impression he's a big fan of doing things by the books.'

'I'm not going to report you, boss,' said Rhodri, aghast.

'I didn't think so.' Carys gave him a mischievous grin. 'That's because you know I'm right.'

★

An essential part of plotting a mystery was holding something back from the reader – a revelation or surprise deferred until close to the end of the book. Perhaps even on the final page. Rosalind Grieves had learned this lesson early in her career when her editor had pointed out that she was giving away too much too soon, enabling her readers to guess the solution halfway through. She'd had to rewrite that first manuscript extensively. In future books she took care to keep the "big twist" for later.

At the same time, it was important to play fair with the reader, giving them all the information they needed to solve the mystery themselves, and not to lie to them. Misdirection, however – the subtle art of distraction or withholding information and encouraging readers to make false assumptions – was all part of the game. In fact, it was a necessary ingredient for setting up that final twist.

Rick Styles had understood this as well as any mystery writer.

Roguish Rick. The nickname conjured up a character who was rough and ready on the outside but with a heart of gold. He'd asked her to ghost-write his memoir but she had politely declined, explaining that she was a writer of fiction, not fact. But that was before his mysterious death in the fishpond. Now Rosalind was rethinking her decision. Maybe she would write his story posthumously, once things had settled down. She could fictionalise it or include herself in the book and make it semi-autobiographical.

She was pleased to find the lounge at St Philomena's empty for once. Samir had gone, and there was no sign of Paul, so she settled herself into her favourite chair, put her mug of tea on a side table, and turned to the page in her notebook where she had jotted down the details of Rick's story. She re-read her notes, tapping her pen against the page.

Rick had told her a lot of background material about his early life – the kind of details that were essential for any memoir – but of course it was the jewellery theft that was of most interest, and he had divulged a key piece of information that he had never revealed to the police.

He had entrusted this to her as bait, hoping it would persuade her to write his story. It must have been her disarming manner that encouraged him to tell all. She had cultivated that manner precisely so she could learn secrets that other people never would.

Rick had told her about the jewellery robbery, and that he'd been driving a stolen getaway car when he accidentally hit and killed Jack Emmett, Veronica's brother. That much was public knowledge. What the police didn't know was that Rick had been helped by an accomplice who had been a passenger in the car when it crashed and who had made off with the diamonds.

That accomplice was now on Caldey Island.

Rosalind hadn't said anything about this to the police. If challenged, she would have argued that Rick revealed it to her in confidence, and hadn't told her who his accomplice was, in order to protect their identity. All of which was true. But that hadn't stopped her from trying to work out who it was.

She considered the island's women first for the simple reason that they were too easily overlooked as suspects. And while she knew better than to make assumptions, she felt that Sister Monica was unlikely to have taken part in a jewellery theft. Having said that, the nun played her cards close to her chest and Rosalind sensed she guarded secrets. She couldn't be completely ruled out as a suspect.

There were two other women worth considering. Nia Armitage (now deceased) and Bethan Rees were close in age to Rick. What had they done with their lives prior to coming to Caldey? Rosalind wrote a note to herself to find out. Between the two of them, she thought Nia far more likely to have a criminal past. Bethan was just too... nice!

She turned next to the male names on her list. It couldn't have been any of the older monks because they'd lived in the monastery for many years. Rosalind had established that from speaking to Sister Monica. But what about Brothers Cadoc and Gregory? Cadoc had come from Nigeria to study. That meant he'd been living in the UK for most of his adult life. Gregory had been a farmer before joining the monastery, so he too, couldn't be ruled out. Nor could the novice, Thomas, although Rosalind's impression of the young man was that he was far too timid to have been Rick's accomplice. She recalled how he had been sick when Rick's body was hauled from the pond. Cadoc and Gregory, by contrast, were highly capable men who, like Rick, might now be atoning for a dark past.

And what about this stranger who had been found sleeping rough at the lighthouse? If anyone deserved to be treated as a suspect, it was him. Unfortunately, Rosalind had been unable to find out much about him, except for his name, Patrick Mulholland.

She sighed at her lack of progress. Brother Aidan would have done a far better job, interviewing each of the suspects in depth and gaining entrance to the abbey to snoop around inside. She, on the other hand, had barely scratched the surface.

But she had to work with what she had. She returned to her list, considering the next name. Dafydd Rees. The gruff woodsman was a distinct possibility. As was Paul Roberts. Why was Paul always going on about sin and retribution? He was guilty of something, for sure. She underlined his name twice. Samir Khan was also a key suspect, especially since Rosalind had confirmed he was hiding something in his pocket – *a diamond?* But he was now working with the police and was beyond her reach.

Who did that leave? Rosalind had exhausted her list of islanders, but as a consummate plotter of mysteries, she knew better than to stop there. Rick had told her that his accomplice was on the island but had been careful not to reveal whether they lived on the island or were staying at St Philomena's.

And perhaps that was because there was one other person who had been on the island at the time who had, quite literally, sailed beneath suspicion.

The boatman, Eifion.

She tried to think back to that first day when the retreatants had met at Tenby harbour and boarded the boat to travel to Caldey. Had Rick and Eifion recognised each other? Rosalind had an excellent memory, but she couldn't recall whether there had been any flicker of recognition between the two men.

Eifion was older than Rick, but that made him the perfect age to mastermind a robbery. The impressionable and vulnerable Rick Styles might easily have fallen under the sway of this older man. Yes, she could see it now – the relationship between the two men would make a compelling backstory, helping to explain Rick's character. In her mind's eye, Rick was transforming from criminal to victim, as indeed he had done when he was drowned in the fishpond. And there was a symbolic link too – the pond, the sea, the boatman. It made perfect sense.

It was the sort of moment that often occurred near the end of her writing day when she'd been battling a scene for hours, getting nowhere, ready to throw her laptop out of the window. An idea would suddenly occur to her and she would dash off a thousand words as if the story was writing itself.

She snapped her notebook shut and jumped to her feet, filled with a sense that providence had led her to the island and that it was her destiny to identify Rick's accomplice.

Perhaps, even, to locate the diamonds. Now *that* would be a story worth writing.

CHAPTER 38

A sea mist was rolling in as Carys and Rhodri left St Philomena's, leaving Sister Monica and Brother Cadoc to sort out the embezzlement of guest house funds. Carys suspected it would involve a great deal of confession on Sister Monica's part, and a fair amount of forgiveness on Brother Cadoc's part, but they would eventually come to an arrangement that suited them both. The nun's misdemeanours would be swept under the carpet so as not to draw attention to the monk's lax oversight.

The mist was gradually shrouding the island in white, and Carys hoped the weather would not hinder the investigation. Although they had made some progress that morning, speaking first to Dafydd and then to Sister Monica, they had not moved significantly closer to understanding who was responsible for the three murders, nor establishing a clear motive. At present, Carys couldn't definitively rule out any of the islanders or retreatants. Nor did any of them stand out as suspects.

Rhodri's phone rang and he answered it on speakerphone.

It was Hugh. 'Word just in from forensics. They've analysed the length of rope that was used to strangle Nia.'

'And?' said Rhodri.

'It seems the rope has spent some time in contact with the sea. They identified salt crust, grains of sand and traces of algae.'

'Okay. Thanks, Hugh.' Rhodri ended the call.

'So the rope is most likely from a boat, then?' said Carys.

'Possibly,' said Rhodri. But he seemed unwilling to make eye contact with her.

'What are you worried about?'

'Nothing. It's just that...'

Carys knew precisely what was bothering him. 'The only boat on this island is Eifion's. You and he are close, aren't you?'

Rhodri nodded. 'I've known him for years. He's almost like a father to me. There's no way Eifion could have anything to do with the murders.'

'Then you have nothing to worry about,' said Carys. 'But we have to keep an open mind. Are you up to this?'

He gave a reluctant nod.

'Right then, we need to establish whether the rope really did come from Eifion's boat. Even if it did, there's no reason to jump to the conclusion that Eifion had anything to do with Nia's death. We just have to follow the facts and see where they lead.'

Rhodri brightened at her words. 'Okay, then. Let's talk to him.'

They found the boatman where he always was – on his boat. This morning, the vessel was obscured by mist, not appearing until they were almost close enough to jump aboard. It was secured to a bollard by a rope that looked, to Carys's untrained eye, identical to the one used to strangle Nia.

Except that this one was brand new.

'Eifion?' Her voice was swallowed by the swirling dampness.

The boatman stepped forward, looking grim. 'Ready to go back to Tenby, are you? I'm afraid you'll have to wait. My engine's playing up.'

'I thought you'd fixed it,' said Rhodri.

'So did I. Bloody thing let me down the other day too.'

Carys took hold of the railing at the boat's prow and lowered herself onto the deck. 'We don't need to return to the mainland yet. We wanted to talk to you.'

'Oh, yes?' Eifion's gaze flitted anxiously between them as Rhodri stepped onto the boat at Carys's side. 'What about?'

'Nothing to worry about, Eifion,' said Rhodri. 'Just a few questions.'

But if his words were intended to be reassuring, they had the opposite effect. 'Well now you're making me nervous.'

'You were here on the island when Nia went missing, weren't you?' said Carys.

Eifion gave a firm nod. 'You know I was. I took part in the search, in Elen's team.'

'And you were here the evening that Rick was murdered.'

'I was. I wanted to pay my respects to the poor girl who died, so I stayed late and went to Compline in St David's. I like to hear the monks chanting. Soothes the soul, it does. Everyone went. It would have looked odd if I hadn't.'

'And where were you on the evening that Veronica was murdered?'

'On Sunday? Well, I'll have to think.'

'Come on, Eifion,' encouraged Rhodri. 'You must have been back in Tenby before nightfall, surely?'

Carys shot her sergeant a warning look before turning back to the boatman. 'You said just now that the engine let you down the other day. Which day was that?'

Eifion scratched his head. 'It would've been Sunday. It's the cooling pump, see, it was–'

'You're saying that your boat broke down on Sunday evening?' interrupted Carys. 'Here on the island?'

'That's right.'

'Tell us exactly what happened.'

He shrugged. 'Damn thing wouldn't start. I borrowed some tools from the shed that Dafydd uses, and I managed to get it going again. But it took a while. I probably didn't get away until after nine. Wasn't sure if I was going to make it back to harbour, to be honest.'

Carys glanced at Rhodri, who had paled. They both knew the timeline – Veronica Emmett had gone to her room in St Philomena's at eight o'clock and recorded her final video at 8:15pm. No one had seen her alive after that.

'Let's talk about the mooring rope next.' Carys gestured to the rope that tethered the boat to the jetty. White, flecked with blue. Approximately half an inch thick.

Eifion's brow wrinkled in confusion. 'The rope? What do you want to know about it?'

'How would you describe it?'

'Standard double-braid polyester. It does a decent job.'

Carys bent down to touch it. 'It looks new.' The rope was clean and slithered smoothly between her fingers.

'Rope doesn't last forever.'

'When did you replace it?'

'Last week.'

'And what did you do with the old rope?'

'I haven't had a chance to dispose of it yet. It's still in here.' He pointed towards the cabin.

'Show us.'

Eifion went to the cabin and lifted the lid on a wooden storage box. He started to rummage through the contents – an old life jacket, a pair of waders, assorted snorkels and flippers.

But it came as no surprise to Carys that there was no rope.

'I swear it was here,' said Eifion. He looked from Carys to Rhodri in bewilderment. 'I don't understand.'

'Who else has access to the boat?' asked Rhodri.

'When she's moored here, anyone on the island could

come aboard. I'm not on the boat every minute of the day. I have to take the post ashore. I pop into the café for food and drink. Sometimes I stop for a chat.'

'So anyone could have stolen the rope?' prompted Rhodri.

Eifion nodded in response. 'But who would do that?'

CHAPTER 39

Dafydd Rees lifted the heavy branch in his gloved hands and tossed it easily into the woodchipper. The powerful machine chewed it up, spitting out flecks of wood and spraying him with fine sawdust. Talking to that detective earlier had delayed his work. Now he'd be hard pushed to get through this pile of deadwood before dark. He bent to pick up another branch and heard the snap of a twig behind him. He turned, expecting to see the detectives back to hassle him again.

But it wasn't the DI or her sidekick. It was the man he'd been trying to avoid ever since he'd set eyes on him, stepping off the boat from Tenby with the other retreatants. A man Dafydd had believed – and desperately hoped – he would never see again.

The branch slipped from Dafydd's grasp and his stomach turned over. He thought he might throw up. For a moment he was twelve years old again – a skinny, underfed kid from the Rhondda Valley – and the geography teacher was beckoning him into the classroom. For a bit of extra tuition.

For some special attention.

'Come and sit next to me, Dafydd. It's just the two of us here. The other children have all gone home.'

He'd been too young and too frightened to protest.

He removed his ear defenders but kept his protective visor in place. Every instinct told him to hide from this man. To run like the wind. But his legs felt like lead, rooting him to the spot.

'That's an impressive machine you've got there,' said the man, indicating the woodchipper. Its drum was still spinning even though it had long finished devouring its meal of dead wood. The machine was hungry for more.

Was it possible, wondered Dafydd, that Paul Roberts didn't recognise him? He'd changed a lot since those distant school days. Filled out, grown taller, lost some hair. He was a man, not a boy. *Mr Roberts*, as Dafydd had known him, had moved on to another school when Dafydd was fourteen, taking his perverted sexual activities with him.

Guilt still gnawed at Dafydd's insides when he thought about that. How many other boys had Paul Roberts gone on to abuse? Could he have been stopped if Dafydd had spoken up? But he'd only been a kid. Who would have listened to him? Not his dad, who hadn't listened to anyone since he'd lost his job when the pit closed. Not his mam, who struggled to make ends meet and had no time for other problems.

Besides, nobody talked about those things back then. Especially not Dafydd, who had learned not to talk much about anything.

'You won't breathe a word of this, now will you, Dafydd? It's our little secret.'

He had kept that secret all these years, refusing even to tell his wife when he woke in the night, bathed in sweat and bawling his eyes out like a little boy.

But Dafydd wasn't a little boy anymore. And Paul Roberts was no longer a young man. He was older, and greyer, and weaker, although he still had that same look in his eyes, a look that said he could do as he pleased. That he was untouchable.

Are you? Dafydd wondered. *Are you still untouchable?*

Paul Roberts stepped closer, peering into the jaws of the machine, completely oblivious to the danger.

He has no idea who I am. The realisation was both liberating and sickening. All those times the geography teacher had touched him. All those disgusting things he had done. Had they meant nothing to him?

'You're special, Dafydd. You're a very special boy.'

All it would take was one swift movement, one single act of strength and courage, and Paul Roberts would disappear into that chipper head-first. The spinning drum with its sharp blades would make mincemeat of him. It wouldn't be instantaneous. Dafydd would have to hold him there, as the machine went about its business, pulling him in and carving him up. Piece by piece. Limb by limb. But then it would be over, and he would be free.

Yet something held him back.

Paul Roberts straightened up and stepped away from the roar of the machine. 'You could have killed me, just now, Dafydd. I'm sure it entered your mind.'

Dafydd gasped. So the man *did* recognise him after all. 'Why are you here?' he rasped. His voice felt as if it had turned to sawdust.

Paul regarded him with a look of contempt. 'I've been doing a lot of thinking recently, Dafydd. About the past. About *our* past. About what we did together.'

Dafydd took a step backwards, his skin crawling. *Our past?* He felt sick. Paul Roberts had destroyed his childhood and left terrible wounds that would never heal. How dare he talk about his actions as if Dafydd were complicit! Yet he seemed to have lost his ability to speak. His mouth opened, but no words emerged.

Paul spoke instead. 'You know that I meant no harm, don't you, Dafydd? If I ever caused you trouble, I want you to know that I'm sorry.'

Dafydd's eyes were locked on Paul's. 'You're sorry?'

'If I caused you any distress.'

'Distress?' Dafydd's jaw began to work. 'Distress?'

Paul nodded. 'You never told anyone, did you? That's good. This should stay between the two of us. Nobody would understand.'

It was precisely what he had said all those years ago.

'You won't tell anyone, will you, Dafydd? This should stay between the two of us. Nobody would understand.'

Dafydd stared at the man who had ruined his life. He had kept that secret, never breathing a word of it to a living soul. It was why Bethan had turned away from him, seeking comfort with Cadoc. And he had been helpless to stop her.

'Nobody would understand,' Dafydd murmured. He had believed those words his entire life. But what if they were a lie? What if every single word that Paul Roberts had ever told him was a lie?

'That's good, Dafydd. You always were a good boy.'

Paul reached to touch his shoulder, and Dafydd seized his hand and twisted it. Paul cried out, but Dafydd didn't flinch. He had pictured this scene for more than twenty years and knew the script by heart. He dragged Paul closer to the woodchipper.

'What are you doing?' Paul yelled. 'Let go of me!'

Dafydd wrenched his arm behind his back, making him scream in agony. He shoved Paul's head up to the gaping mouth of the machine, where the noise was loudest. The engine roared. The drum span relentlessly.

'You came to say sorry?' Dafydd's voice was back now, stronger than ever before.

'Yes!' cried Paul. 'I'm sorry for what I did.'

'And you want my forgiveness? Is that it?' The blades of the chipper shrieked as they sliced the air.

'Yes!'

The man was weak, and Dafydd felt strong. He forced the man's head even closer to the hungry jaws of the machine. 'You shall never have my forgiveness! Nothing you can say will ever make up for what you did!'

Paul was crying now, his shoulders shaking. A grown man reduced to tears. 'Please,' he begged, 'I know that what I did was wrong, but I swear I've changed. I'll never do anything like it again.'

'No, you won't.' Dafydd held him there a little longer, relishing the feeling of turning the tables on his persecutor at last. 'You will never touch another person in that way. And you will pay for what you did. I will make sure of it!'

He shoved the man to the ground, watching him sprawl helplessly before him. Paul looked up, his eyes wide with fear.

'Going to the police, I am. And I'm going to tell them everything.' Dafydd picked up a fallen branch and Paul cringed with terror. 'Now, go! If you're still here when the machine has finished with this, I swear I'll feed you into it!'

He dropped the branch into the mouth of the chipper and waited while it chomped its way through the wood. When he turned around, Paul Roberts was gone.

CHAPTER 40

'So can we remove Eifion from our list of suspects now?' said Rhodri. 'Anyone could have taken the rope.'

Carys strode along the jetty, her sergeant at her side. They had left Eifion on the boat, with permission to do whatever he needed to nurse the engine back to life, but instructions not to leave the island.

'Eifion isn't off the hook yet,' she warned Rhodri. 'In fact, he's still very much on the list. The problem is, we haven't been able to eliminate anyone from our inquiries.'

The situation was beyond frustrating. Despite the small number of people on the island, not a single one had an alibi, and there was still no clear motive for the murder of Veronica and Rick.

Carys's phone rang and she answered on speaker without breaking her stride. 'What have you got for me, Hugh?'

'More results from forensics, boss.'

Hugh sounded excited. She could picture the eager detective pushing his glasses up his nose and shuffling the papers on his desk. 'Don't keep us in suspense.'

'The charred fabric found in the bonfire – it's been identified as undyed wool.'

Carys frowned. 'Do we know what it was used for?'

'Historically, undyed wool was used to make all kinds of garments. In modern times, some people choose it because of its ecological credentials. It's free from synthetic dyes and so on. But in view of your present location on Caldey Island… we can't ignore the fact that it's used to make monks' habits.'

Carys thanked him and ended the call.

'How did a monk's habit end up in the bonfire?' Rhodri asked. 'Unless a monk put it there himself. And why would one of the monks do that, unless…'

'Unless the murderer is a monk,' concluded Carys.

Their footsteps had brought them back to the village green. It seemed impossible to roam far on the island without returning to this central point. The mist was thinner here than at the jetty and the monastery loomed ahead, as imposing and impregnable as ever. Well, that was about to change. Carys would speak to Father Anselm again and if he didn't grant her access to the inner sanctum of the monastery, she'd bring down the full weight of the law. Finally, with the forensic identification of the burnt fabric, she had the evidence she needed to get a search warrant.

'All right,' she told Rhodri. 'It's time we searched the cloister.'

*

Brother Gregory was very keen on greens. Lightly sautéed and mixed with grated beetroot and a mustard dressing, curly kale was an excellent source of vitamins for the monks during the winter months. Heaven knows, the monks needed to keep their strength up. They were dwindling in number and half of them, the abbot included, were now very frail.

He cracked a dozen eggs into a bowl and whisked them,

ready to go into the flan. Then he grated a block of cheddar and sliced an onion. All he needed now was the curly kale. But where had Novice Thomas got to? He was supposed to be helping with food preparation in the kitchen. Lunch was served at one-thirty precisely, otherwise they would be late for the canonical hour of *None* at two-twenty.

Sometimes it was difficult for novices to adjust to the rigid monastic discipline of timekeeping. And Gregory knew that Thomas's life had lacked structure before entering the monastery.

Many novices fell by the wayside, returning to the secular world instead of taking their final vows, yet Gregory sensed that Thomas would not be among them. He was a keen and diligent student, and Gregory hoped that both he and Patrick would choose to remain in the monastery, one day committing themselves fully to monastic life.

In the meantime, however, they both had a great many things to learn, and reliability was top of the list.

'I will just have to pick the kale myself.' Gregory wiped his hands on a tea-towel and went outside to the vegetable garden. Thomas had taken a keen interest in the herbs during their half hour of horticultural instruction that morning, and Gregory wondered if he might be studying them now, having lost track of time. But Thomas was not among the herbs. Gregory continued on through the garden, heading for the vegetable patch.

At the far end of the garden stood the old apple tree. It had been planted well before his time and was now gnarled and sprawling. It was a pleasant place to sit in the summer, its branches providing welcome shade. Despite its age, it still produced a good crop each year and Gregory had been happy to share the apples with Patrick to keep him going. Father Anselm had been wrong to rebuke him for that. There was enough food for all.

Gregory squinted through the mist that had rolled in off the sea. There was something lying on the ground by the tree. It looked like a pile of old sacking, but something told him it wasn't.

He moved closer, gripped by a rising fear.

Please, Lord, no.

He broke into a run – something he hadn't done for nigh on thirty years. His knees protested at the exertion, but the words of St Paul came to him: *I have fought the good fight, I have finished the race, I have kept the faith,* and he found the strength to keep going.

It was a body that lay beneath the tree. The body of Novice Thomas.

Gregory dropped to his knees and felt for a pulse. There was nothing.

He bowed his head, overcome with anguish, and repeated the words Jesus had uttered at Gethsemane: 'My soul is consumed with sorrow to the point of death!'

Then he wept.

On the ground, next to the novice's head, a creamy-white grub was wriggling from a rotten apple.

CHAPTER 41

Carys finally had access to the monastery. In the end, a warrant hadn't been necessary. Father Anselm had summoned her himself, sending Brother Cadoc as his envoy to request the police's assistance. But as she stood in the abbey garden, looking down at the body of Novice Thomas, Carys wished it hadn't taken another death for the abbot to change his mind.

SOCO had been summoned back to the island, and with Eifion's boat still being repaired by its owner and visibility so poor, the team had come in the lifeboat. They had only just arrived on the scene.

Anthony Davies rose to his feet after completing his initial inspection of the body. 'No obvious signs of violence. No wounds, no strangulation marks. The only similarity with the other deaths is this.' He handed Carys a Bible which had been placed beneath the body.

Carys handled the book carefully with gloved hands. It was open at Genesis chapter three, verse six. '"And the woman saw that the tree was good to eat, and fair to the eyes, and delightful to behold: and she took of the fruit

thereof, and did eat, and gave to her husband who did eat."
And so sin entered the world,' she murmured, gazing up
at the apple tree, its branches sagging with the weight of
ripe fruit.

As the team continued their search and prepared the
body for removal to the mainland, she asked Brother
Cadoc to show her and Rhodri to Thomas's cell.

The interior of the monastery was much as she had
expected – sparsely furnished, plainly decorated with tiled
floors, white plaster walls and exposed wooden beams.

Cadoc led them up a winding staircase to a small attic
room.

'Thank you, Brother,' said Carys. 'We'll take it from
here.' She waited until the monk had retreated down the
steps before inviting Rhodri to open the door.

'It's not exactly the Ritz, is it?' he muttered, stooping
low to enter the chamber.

The cell had a sloping ceiling and tiny dormer window
that overlooked the village green. A single bed covered in
a coarse woollen blanket occupied one corner. A narrow
shelf was fixed to the wall above a wooden desk and chair.
It was a spartan way of life, yet at least the monks enjoyed
community, purpose and regular cooked meals. That was
more than could be said for some in the world outside the
monastery.

Rhodri opened a cupboard, but it contained nothing
but a few items of clothing – spare underwear, socks, a
habit.

A few books were scattered across the desk, and Carys
picked up a Bible. Beneath it was a folded letter. She
unfolded it carefully and read it aloud. '"*I know what you
did at the pond. Meet me at the lighthouse this afternoon. If
you're not there, I'll go straight to the police.*"'

Rhodri's brow creased as he tried to make sense of it.
'So Nia sent that letter to Thomas. That means she saw
Thomas drowning Rick at the fishpond. And Thomas
must have strangled Nia too. But if Thomas was the killer,
who killed him?'

On the shelf above the desk stood a glass containing a handful of herbs, now wilting. Carys reached for it, recognising the plant instantly. 'Aconitum. It goes by many names – monkshood, wolfsbane, devil's helmet. But whatever you call it, it's a deadly poison.'

Rhodri frowned. 'Are you sure, boss? Just looks like a plant to me.'

Carys nodded. Her nan had taught her well. She knew the names of all the common herbs and wildflowers – and many uncommon ones too. 'We'll need to send it to forensics for formal identification, but yes, I'm sure.'

Rhodri was struggling to keep up. 'You think Thomas might have poisoned himself?'

'The post-mortem and toxicology report will tell us for certain. Come on, let's search the rest of the room.'

There wasn't much to search. Apart from the books, a sewing kit, a rosary and a reading light, the desk was bare.

'No personal items,' said Carys. 'Let's check the bed.'

She pulled the sheets and blanket off. The mattress was old and thin and wouldn't have provided a very comfortable night's sleep. She turned it over. The mattress had a small tear in one corner that had been inexpertly mended with clumsy stitches. Carys pressed her fingers around the mended patch and felt something hard underneath.

She pulled at the thread with her fingernails, drawing open the gap in the fabric. A small velvet drawstring bag nestled inside. Carys turned it upside down and a dozen glittering gemstones fell onto the desk. Each stone was clear but dazzling, catching the dim light of the room and breaking it into a brilliant prism of colour.

'Bloody hell, boss,' said Rhodri. 'Diamonds!'

'"*The love of money is the root of all evil*,"' Carys murmured.

CHAPTER 42

' ongratulations,' said DCI Gareth Pritchard, shaking Carys warmly by the hand as she entered his office. 'You got a good result.'

'Thank you, sir. It was a team effort.'

The case against Novice Thomas had come together quickly following the discovery of his body. His full name was Thomas Fincham. As a novice, he had not yet adopted a new monastic name. Hugh had dug into Fincham's background and uncovered the troubled story of his childhood – taken from his mother by social services at the age of five and moved from one foster home to another before finally ending up in a children's home. He had grown up in the West Midlands, not far from Rick Styles, and it was reasonable to assume that the two men had first come into contact with each other there. Prison records confirmed that Thomas had visited the older man in prison on more than one occasion. If Thomas had indeed acted as Rick's accomplice in the jewellery theft, escaping from the crashed getaway car with the diamonds, that explained how the gems had come to be in Thomas's cell. The recovered diamonds matched precisely the description of those that were stolen.

The rest was conjecture. Brother Gregory described the young novice as deeply religious and committed to a monastic life. Had Thomas, perhaps after visiting Rick in prison, gone to the monastery seeking atonement for his crime? And had he recognised Veronica Emmett as the sister of the man he and Rick had inadvertently killed? If so, perhaps he had murdered her, fearing exposure, then murdered Rick, who had no doubt guessed the terrible crime Thomas had committed. Nia's death was explained by her attempt to blackmail Thomas – perhaps she had overheard the novice talking about the diamonds to Rick and had been overcome by greed.

'I hear that you have conclusive forensic evidence now,' said Pritchard, breaking through Carys's introspection.

'Yes. Hair and skin tissue recovered from the bodies of the three victims match Thomas's DNA. And the post-mortem has confirmed that he died from aconitum poisoning.'

'Suicide.'

It wasn't a question. It was now a fact. The police were certain that Thomas, in a fit of remorse, had ended his killing spree by taking his own life.

'What about that peculiar business with the Bibles?' asked Pritchard.

The Biblical verses had bothered Carys from the very beginning. It had been clear that they were dealing with someone immersed in scripture. It should have come as little surprise that a monk was behind the murders.

'Thomas turned his back on his former life,' she explained, 'embracing Christianity and throwing himself into the monastic world. He read the Bible, he prayed, he attended religious services eight times a day, starting at half past three every morning with Matins. The Bible verses were his way of explaining his actions.'

Pritchard wrinkled his nose in distaste. 'Who was he explaining to?'

'Who knows? Himself? The other monks? God? "The

living know at least that they will die, the dead know nothing,"' she quoted for Pritchard's benefit. 'Veronica died because of what she knew. "It is time you were baptised and had your sins washed away." Perhaps Thomas had never truly forgiven Rick for luring him into a life of crime. As for, "I am the light of the world; anyone who follows me will not be walking in the dark," I think he was justifying Nia's death by portraying her as a sinner.'

'And what about his own death?'

'"And the woman saw that the tree was good to eat… and she took of the fruit thereof…." I think that perhaps Thomas was excusing his actions by appealing to the idea of original sin.'

'Well, he doesn't need to excuse anymore,' said Pritchard. 'And on another topic, I understand that Dafydd Rees has come forward with allegations against Paul Roberts. Roberts has been arrested, and together with the other allegations from former pupils at his school, I've no doubt that he'll be charged.'

'That's good, sir.'

Pritchard nodded with satisfaction. 'Good work all round, Carys. Now go and celebrate. You deserve it.'

Carys left his office but didn't feel like celebrating. There had been four deaths, and three of them would have been avoided if she had been able to solve the mystery sooner. If Father Anselm had granted her full access to the monastery from the beginning, maybe Rick and Nia's murders could have been prevented and Thomas would still be alive to answer questions. Not for the first time in Carys's life, a man of God had thwarted her attempt to reach the truth.

*

She couldn't sleep.

After congratulating her team, Carys had left the station and returned to Manorbier, calling in at the supermarket in Tenby on the way to replenish her food stocks. She had then set about some serious baking.

Bara brith, another of Nan's favourites. Carys liked to make it the traditional way with fresh yeast. She mixed the flour, salt and yeast in the same porcelain mixing bowl that Nan had used, feeling that familiar sense of continuity with the past that came from placing her own hands where she had watched Nan's hands at work. 'Now rub in the butter, but make sure your hands are nice and cold,' she recited to herself. Once the mixture resembled fine breadcrumbs, she added a jug of black tea, along with the fruit and spices. She covered the bowl with a tea towel and set it aside.

After baking it in the oven, she had gone to bed.

But sleep had come only in brief snatches. It was now early morning, still pitch black, and she had been lying awake for hours.

This is hopeless.

When she was restless like this, there was only one thing to do and one place to go. She threw back the covers, slid out of bed and dressed quickly, wrapping her scarf tightly around her neck and donning her purple beret. She headed outside, taking the road that led down to the beach. The village slept, silent and still. To her right, the limestone walls of the castle rose up, sheer and impenetrable, as they had stood, unvanquished, for eight hundred years. As she neared the beach, the gentle brushing of the waves on the shore grew louder, drawing her on.

The bay was deserted. It was too early for even the keenest of dog walkers. The sky was blanketed with clouds and there was no light from the stars or moon, but the faint glow of dawn painted the land and sea in monotone shades of grey. Carys crossed the short stretch of soft sand and picked up the narrow flight of rocky steps that led up from the far end of the beach.

The coastal path wound its way gently upwards, through grass and bracken and wind-gnarled hawthorn, climbing ever higher as it rounded the gentle curve of the bay. Far beneath her, the sea washed against the rocks, and in one place, a short wooden bridge carried her over a yawning vertical chasm carved by the water.

After a few minutes, she came to a large flat slab of sandstone balanced on two smaller uprights and nestled in the ground. The stone measured thirteen feet by eight and was two feet thick. Beneath it lay a hollow chamber that the young Esme had dared Carys to crawl into.

'Come and lie down next to me, Carys, and pretend you're dead.'

The site was a cromlech, or Neolithic burial chamber, known locally as *King's Quoit*. It was a popular spot for walkers to stop and admire the horseshoe of Manorbier Bay. But it was also a reminder of the unbroken link to the past. Men and women had lived here for thousands of years.

Carys placed her hands against the stone and murmured a private prayer, one of her own devising. A prayer that was not Christian, nor pagan, nor Buddhist, but all three and more, and spoke of her own unique spiritual beliefs.

She sat down on the rock and replayed the final conversation she'd had with Rosalind Grieves as the novelist was preparing to board the boat back to the mainland.

'Did you find what you were looking for when you came to Caldey?' Carys asked her.

'I think so. I came here to research my next book, but also to find inspiration.' Rosalind gestured at the backdrop of the monastery with its white roughcast walls and red tiled roofs – a small forest of towers, spires, steeples and chimneys. 'I can't say I'm very religious myself, but I do love the architecture and the atmosphere of a place like this. It's a magical setting, don't you think?'

Carys couldn't deny it, but the magic of this island had turned several shades darker this past week, and Carys didn't know if she would ever want to return.

'Rick Styles asked you to write his memoirs, I understand?'

'That's right.'

'Are you going to?'

'I don't know. Maybe one day.'

'He told you about his life of crime and his time in prison?'

'A little.'

The writer seemed reluctant to go into more detail and Carys challenged her. 'It seems odd that he told you his life story but didn't mention that Novice Thomas was his accomplice.'

Rosalind gave an enigmatic smile. 'If Rick had mentioned an accomplice and I didn't tell the police, would I have committed a crime?' She didn't wait for Carys to reply. 'And even if I had, could you prove it? You can't prove a negative.'

Rosalind's words confirmed what Carys had already guessed. 'I'll look forward to reading your next book. And Rick's memoir, if you ever write it.'

But there was something else niggling at her. She had been lied to before by a man of the cloth and had the uneasy sensation that it had happened again.

What had Father Anselm's last words been to her before she left the island on Friday evening?

'I hope now that you will leave us in peace, DI Morgan.'

'I hope so, too, Father.'

'Novice Thomas was a bad apple. We will not allow his crimes to tarnish the reputation of the abbey. Caldey has been a monastic island for nearly fifteen hundred years, and, God-willing, will remain so long after I am gone.'

'Let's hope so,' said Carys. Yet talk of bad apples didn't sit easily with her. Three murders and a suicide could hardly be swept under the carpet as if they had never happened.

The abbot had seemed rather too keen to send her packing and erase all trace of the police investigation from the island. Carys was reminded of how the Reverend Michael Morrow had tried so desperately to usher her from his study when she was sixteen and had gone to confront him about her father. The priest had dismissed her concerns, insisting that he was too busy to talk – that he had a sermon to prepare, a sick parishioner to visit – when all along he hadn't wanted to admit that he had sent his curate to Africa to get him away from Carys's mother.

Was Father Anselm also covering something up? Or was Carys allowing her childhood experiences to cloud her judgement?

She fingered the iron key in her pocket. 'Give me a sign, Nan. Tell me what to do.'

She leaned against the stone for a while longer, listening as the morning stirred slowly to life. The calling of the birds, the lapping of the waves, the gentle breathing of the wind upon her face. There was no dramatic sign from the universe, no obvious reply to her request for guidance. Yet as the sun rose behind her, bleeding colour back into land, sea and sky, Carys knew exactly what she had to do.

CHAPTER 43

'Hurry up and finish your breakfast, Billy. We have to leave early today. Mrs Daly's coming in for her hair appointment before she goes to work and I need to pick up something for Lila's tea tonight. Come on, Lila, one more mouthful for Mummy. Good girl! Rhodri, what have you done with Billy's football boots? You didn't leave them out in the rain, did you?'

Amy was a spinning top set loose in the kitchen this morning, whirring from kids to kettle to lunchboxes without stopping. Rhodri kept out of her way for fear of knocking her off balance.

'They're in the hallway.' Thank God he'd remembered to clean the boots the previous night before it rained, otherwise his life wouldn't be worth living.

Somehow, Amy was managing to juggle childcare with Instagram, keeping one eye on her kids and one on her screen. 'Look at this, Rod. Now that's what I call a home to die for!'

'Nice,' said Rhodri, casting a careless glance over some influencer's carefully curated image of domestic perfection. Houses probably looked a lot smarter, he supposed, if you didn't fill them with kids. But he wouldn't have traded the messy reality of his own home for some clinically tidy fantasy on social media. 'I like our place, Amy. It's just right for the four of us.'

He was treated to a scornful look from his wife as Billy spilled milk over the table and Lila sprayed banana porridge from her high chair. He was relieved when his phone rang, even when he saw who was calling. 'I've got to take this, love. I won't be long.'

'Pass me the cloth, Rod. I've got to wipe this mess.'

Somehow he managed to answer the phone and pass Amy a damp cloth without botching either operation. Multi-tasking – he was really getting the hang of it.

'Hi, boss, what's up?'

Carys's voice sounded faint, dropping in and out, as if she were in a dead zone for mobile reception. *Somewhere in Pembrokeshire, then.* The rural county was known for its patchy signal. Rolling hills, wooded valleys and small, isolated communities. Three bars and you could count yourself lucky. Even the weather could knock you down to one.

'You'll have to speak up,' he said, placing one hand against his ear to block out Billy's shouts and Lila's wailing. 'I can't hear you very well.'

'The Bible found with Thomas...' Carys was saying.

'What about it, boss?'

Her voice broke into a series of random glitches and stutters.

'Say that again? You're breaking up.'

Billy charged past him, his hair a mess, taking the stairs two at a time in his eagerness to reach the top, and Rhodri sighed. It had been a long time since he'd felt that way himself about getting ready in the morning.

'... look for discrepancies...,' said Carys. He could hear the familiar sound of an engine throbbing in the background.

'What sort of discrepancies?'

More digital static ensued. Amy hurried past with Lila

in her arms and porridge on her blouse. *Help me*, she mouthed, and Rhodri knew that he had to bring this call to an end.

'Got all that?' said Carys.

'I think so, boss. You want me to search for discrepancies in the Bible found with Thomas, is that it?'

There was a final burst of static on the line, then silence. Rhodri tucked his phone into his pocket and began scouring the hallway for Billy's boots. He knew he'd put them somewhere.

He located them just as Amy descended the stairs with Lila and Billy. Miraculously, all traces of porridge had been removed, and Billy's hair was freshly combed. Rhodri marvelled at his wife's ability to bring order to chaos.

She kissed him on the cheek. 'Don't forget it's our anniversary dinner tonight. The kids are going to stay at Mum's. It'll be just the two of us.'

'Dinner. Course I won't forget. Love you.'

He kissed both kids on the forehead and waved them goodbye. Then he went into the kitchen to load the dishwasher. He was halfway through his task when he realised why the engine noise in the background of Carys's call had sounded familiar.

Eifion's boat.

That's why the phone signal had been so bad. Carys was heading back to Caldey Island.

Rhodri didn't have a good feeling about that, but he knew better than to question what she was up to.

Being married to Amy had taught him one very valuable lesson.

Follow your instructions and do as you're told, Rod.

Life was simpler that way.

*

The Bibles were the key to the puzzle. Carys was certain of it. While everyone else seemed to think that the investigation was over, she couldn't accept the solution as it currently stood. It was a feeling as much as anything. A nagging doubt that something was amiss.

Three murders. One suicide.

The pathologist had confirmed it.

Yet Carys didn't believe that explanation anymore. And so she was returning to the place it had all begun. The monastery on Caldey Island.

The crossing was relatively calm today, yet still the little boat pitched and rolled as it made its way across the sea. Carys sat at the prow, breathing in the salty air, her eyes fixed on the approaching island. The monastery was hidden from view, just as it had concealed the truth for so long. All she could see from this distance were the cliffs and bays, the trees and broad expanses of grass. And beyond it all, on the furthest tip of the island, the lighthouse standing sentinel for approaching ships.

In the cabin, Eifion stood at the wheel, steering a course through the waves. He'd been more than happy to take her back to the island – glad of the chance to earn a little more cash before winter set in.

'You don't resent me treating you as a suspect, then?' she'd asked him on arriving at Tenby harbour that morning.

'Not at all. You were just doing your job. And sailing is my job. So hop aboard.'

She hoped that Rhodri had grasped the importance of her phone call and understood the task she'd given him. She'd felt from the very beginning that the Bibles would unlock this mystery, and she was more convinced of it now than ever.

Four deaths. Four Bibles.

The fourth was the odd one out. Explaining why would finally reveal the truth.

CHAPTER 44

All was quiet when Carys stepped ashore at Priory Bay. 'You can wait for me here, Eifion,' she said, before taking the now very familiar path through the woodland up to St Philomena's.

Leaves fluttered to the ground as she walked, making a carpet of red, yellow and brown. A red squirrel darted in front of her and ran vertically up the trunk of a silver birch. A wood pigeon in the upper branches took fright and flew off. The island was returning to its natural state for the winter months, free of visitors.

The guesthouse was silent as Carys approached. The retreatants had all now departed, but she found the front door unlocked. Despite all that had happened, the islanders still abided by their old ways, and Carys felt consoled that even after the most tragic events, normality had a way of reasserting itself. One day, the Caldey Island murders would be all but forgotten.

Stepping inside, she walked through the strangely empty hall. She peered through doorways into deserted rooms until she eventually found Sister Monica in her study catching up with paperwork. Whatever had transpired between the nun and Brother Cadoc behind the closed doors of St Philomena's, an amicable solution to the misplaced funds had clearly been reached.

'DI Morgan. What a surprise. How can I help you, dear?'

'I was hoping to speak to Father Anselm, but I didn't want to enter the abbey uninvited.'

'Let me see if I can get hold of him for you.' Sister Monica picked up the phone and dialled. 'Oh, hello, Brother Cadoc, it's Sister Monica here… yes everything's fine… DI Morgan is here and she'd like to speak to Father Anselm. Is he available? Righto.' The nun smiled at Carys and indicated she should take a seat. 'He's just gone to check,' she said, cupping her hand over the mouthpiece. 'Oh, hello again, Brother Cadoc. He's gone where? I'll let her know. Thank you.' She replaced the receiver and looked at Carys. 'Apparently he's gone to St Illtud's.'

'Perfect,' said Carys.

Women weren't barred from St Illtud's church so the abbot would have no choice but to see her there. And if he didn't know that she was coming, that was all to the good. She set off to intercept him before he returned to the monastery.

★

'What exactly does she want us to look for?' asked Elen, peeling the wrapper off a toffee bar and taking a hungry bite.

'She didn't say,' said Rhodri. 'Just *discrepancies*. Then she got cut off.'

'You didn't call her back?'

'I was busy.' He glared at Elen. 'Is that your breakfast? It doesn't look very healthy.'

'Well, listen to Rhodri Evans, health guru,' mumbled Elen through a mouthful of carbs. 'What did *you* have for breakfast? Goji berries with organic almond milk? No, I thought not.'

'Did Carys mean discrepancies in the text of the verses?' interrupted Hugh. 'Or in the actual physical edition?'

Rhodri shrugged in annoyance. 'Why is no one listening to me? I already told you, she didn't say.' He'd signed the Bible out of the property office on arriving at the police station that morning. It sat on his desk now, still sealed in its protective plastic bag. The Bible found with Novice Thomas's body.

'Well, let's take a look,' said Hugh. He pulled on a pair of gloves, unwrapped the Bible and laid it carefully on the desk. 'I can see something immediately.'

'You can?' said Elen.

'Yes. It's an older copy than the others.' He opened the cover of the book and turned some pages. 'Look how the paper has dried and yellowed.'

Rhodri had to concede that Hugh was right. The pages were thin, almost like tissue-paper.

'We should compare it to the others,' said Elen.

Rhodri accepted the sense of that and returned to the property office. Ten minutes later he was back with three more Bibles.

'Okay,' said Hugh. 'Put them side by side. We'll work through methodically.'

Rhodri did as requested and Hugh turned to the first page of each.

'Well, look, we've got completely different editions. This one' – he pointed at the blood-spattered Bible found with Veronica – 'says *The Jerusalem Bible, Translated from the original languages, with introduction and notes. London; Darton, Longman & Todd, 1966.*'

'That's what the guy from the lab told me,' said Elen. 'Jerusalem edition, 1966.'

'Brother Cadoc said it came from the abbey church,' added Rhodri.

'Right,' said Hugh. 'And the ones found with Rick and Nia are the same. But the Bible found with Novice Thomas says *The Holy Bible, Translated from the Latin*

Vulgate, diligently compared with the Hebrew, Greek, and other editions in divers languages. The Douay-Rheims version; London; Burns & Oates Ltd. 1958.'

'So it's a different edition,' said Rhodri. 'Why does that matter? We'll be here all day if we're going to compare chapter and verse of every page.' He had never been much of a details person and found Hugh's painstaking approach tiresome. Rhodri preferred to think of himself as more of a big picture thinker. Unlike Hugh, who was a keen player of online games and puzzles, if there was a way of jumping straight to the end of a problem, Rhodri would gladly take it.

'Well, I can't explain exactly why it's important,' said Hugh. 'But it's an obvious discrepancy.'

'Like Carys told us to find,' said Elen pointedly.

'These things matter,' said Hugh. 'People can get very tetchy about different editions of sacred texts. Do you know what happened in the Wars of Religion that followed the Reformation?'

'I hope you're not going to tell us,' said Rhodri, fearing that Hugh was about to launch into a history lecture.

Elen interrupted. 'Guys, before you two start a theological argument, can I point something out? There's a handwritten dedication on the flyleaf of the older Bible.' She turned back the page and showed them what they'd both missed. In old-fashioned copperplate were the words:

Wilfrid Beaumont
Confirmed in Christ
St. David's, 25 May 1958
Be thou faithful until death (Rev 2:10)

Rhodri tugged at his hair. 'What does this mean? Who on earth is Wilfrid Beaumont?'

Hugh leaned back in his chair. 'Well, Rhodri, I think I can answer both of those questions for you.'

A smug, knowing look had spread over his features and Rhodri felt like punching him. 'Go on then,' he urged.

Hugh pushed his glasses up his nose and tapped the dedication with his gloved finger. 'The first clue is in the words *Confirmed in Christ*. It obviously refers to the Christian sacrament of confirmation, so Wilfrid Beaumont was confirmed on 25 May 1958 at St David's. Since confirmation usually takes place around the age of twelve to fourteen, that means he was probably born around 1945, shortly before or after the end of World War Two. Now whether St David's means the cathedral in Cardiff, or a smaller parish church, I couldn't tell you. Not without a bit of additional research.'

Rhodri glared at Hugh, his frustration reaching breaking point. 'Who. Is. He?'

But Hugh had no intention of being rushed to a conclusion. 'Well, since this Bible was found in a Reformed Cistercian monastery, it most likely belongs to one of the monks.'

'But none of the monks are called Wilfrid,' protested Rhodri.

Hugh shook his head sadly. 'You should pay more attention, Rhodri. I explained before that monks adopt a new name when they take their vows. And I told you I already contacted the diocese to find out their legal identities.'

'So which one is Wilfrid?' asked Elen.

Hugh beamed at her. 'The abbot himself – Father Anselm.'

CHAPTER 45

arys didn't encounter a single soul on her walk across the island. The café and gift shop were closed for the season, the post office still locked up following the death of the postmistress. There was no sign even of Dafydd Rees at work in the woodland. No smoke from a bonfire. No buzz of a chainsaw. Perhaps he and Bethan were at home together, catching up on years of missed conversation.

This was how Caldey Island was supposed to be. A place of prayer and solitude, completely without distraction. The original twelfth-century priory stood at the very heart of the island amid nature and was reached by an arched opening in a stone wall. As Carys stepped through the gateway, she felt as if she was being transported back in time. Thick stone walls rose up on all sides, like a castle with narrow slit windows and topped by crenellations. Tendrils of ivy clambered up the crumbling stonework while bush roses and faded wildflowers claimed the ground at its base. Even the gaping window spaces were filled by plants.

The ruins of the old priory were deserted but a faint

light flickered through a stained-glass window at the far end of the courtyard. Carys walked through a second arch and emerged in front of St Illtud's church itself. The building was an accumulation of centuries of construction, modification and repairs. Sandstone, limestone, bricks and mortar. At its far end rose the precariously leaning tower that she had noticed on her previous visit during the search for Nia. Pushing open the door, she stepped inside.

In the chancel, a single candle burned on the altar. Father Anselm was standing in front of the Ogham Stone, leaning on his walking stick. Before proceeding, Carys checked her phone. She had no signal but set the phone to record and slipped it inside her coat pocket. Slowly, she walked down the aisle.

'I knew you'd come back,' said the abbot without turning to look at her. 'It was too much to hope you were gone for good.'

'We need to talk. About the Bible.'

'What do you wish to know, my child?'

She came to a halt beside him, facing the stone. 'The fourth Bible was a different edition to the first three. Douay-Rheims. The others were all copies of the Jerusalem Bible.'

He studied her with rheumy eyes. 'You are very observant. That is a good quality for a police detective.'

'I'm sure we can agree that details matter, both in police work and theology. Tell me about the Douay-Rheims.'

The abbot coughed, a weak sound that shook his frail body. 'After the Second Vatican Council in the 1960s, monasteries like ours were forced to adopt the Jerusalem Bible. Pope John XXIII believed that the Church needed to change to meet the needs of the modern world. The Jerusalem Bible was easier to understand. It was considered to be more accessible – more inclusive, if you like.'

'But you preferred the older editions,' said Carys. 'The Douay-Rheims, for example.'

The abbot's eyes gleamed in the candlelight. 'The language of the Douay-Rheims is not merely an archaic form of English. It is English shaped by Latin – the Vulgate that ordered the Church's prayer for over a thousand years. In its verses, I hear the rhythm of the psalms as I learned them as a boy. The Jerusalem Bible, in contrast, tries to explain everything and leaves no room for interpretation.'

'For *your* interpretation,' said Carys.

The abbot set his mouth in a thin line. 'You may think me a foolish old man, too fixed in my ways to adapt to a changing world.' He raised his stick to point at the Ogham Stone. 'Do you see this stone? It may not look like much compared to the gold coins of Rievaulx or the Majesty of Sainte-Foy, but it is rightly regarded as Caldey's great treasure because it connects us to our roots. The stone dates from the sixth century, from the earliest days of Christian worship here on Caldey Island. Don't you find that remarkable? Fifteen hundred years, and I am merely the latest custodian in a long line of abbots. You see, DI Morgan, my perspective is very different to most people's.'

'I know that you are gravely ill, Father. Nia Armitage kept copies of confidential letters sent to you from the hospital.'

'Ah, yes. I heard about what Nia did. So you will know that I have few days remaining on this earth. First the doctors told me a year, but that was months past. Now they say it will be weeks. Only the Lord knows when my hour will come. In the short time left, I must do all I can to secure the future of the abbey.'

'I imagine you'd do anything to secure that future,' said Carys softly. 'Perhaps even commit murder?'

*

'So if this Bible belongs to Father Anselm,' said Rhodri, 'what was Thomas doing with it?'

'It makes no sense,' said Elen. 'Why wouldn't Thomas have used the same kind of Bible as before – the Jerusalem edition?'

There was only one good explanation, but it took Hugh to voice it aloud. 'Because Thomas didn't kill himself. Someone else killed him. And that person didn't know which edition had been placed with the first three victims.'

'Father Anselm,' murmured Rhodri. 'The abbot murdered Thomas.' He waited a moment to see if the others would pick a hole in his reasoning, but they remained silent.

Shit.

Breathing hard, he fumbled for his phone, dialling Carys's number, but the call went straight to voicemail. 'She's not answering, or she's got no signal.'

He made an executive decision.

'Elen, grab your coat. We're going back to Caldey. Hugh, you stay here in case we need backup.'

'Not another boat ride!' Elen groaned, but she picked up her coat and followed him to the door.

CHAPTER 46

The abbot levelled a long and cold stare at Carys. 'Why would you accuse me of such a dreadful crime? Thomas was the murderer, not me.'

'I know that he murdered three people.'

'Precisely.' The abbot nodded his head with vigour. 'He killed three times, then took his own life. How could you imagine that I am in some way involved? These are contradictory explanations, DI Morgan.'

'Contradictory?' Carys smiled. 'At Christmas, we celebrate the birth of Jesus, but we also mark the winter solstice. That's why we decorate trees and hang garlands of holly and mistletoe. We're honouring a much older tradition. Is that a contradiction?'

The abbot scowled. 'That is just heathen nonsense.'

'Really? My grandmother went to church every Sunday but was also what people once called a witch. Friends and neighbours came to her for cures and charms, even though they would consult their doctor about the same ailments. So you see, Father, it is quite possible to hold seemingly contradictory beliefs – for instance, that Thomas was the murderer, but that you murdered him.'

The abbot turned to her and regarded her with watery eyes. 'I knew you would return. You spot important details. And you don't let them pass. I saw that clearly at our very first encounter.'

'I'm sorry for being a thorn in your side, Father. But you see, it is my job.'

He let out a long sigh. 'DI Morgan, will you hear my confession?'

★

'Eifion's not answering,' said Rhodri in frustration as his second call to the boatman went straight to voicemail.

'He's probably still on the island,' said Elen, who had taken the wheel and was driving at considerable speed along a narrow road, much to Rhodri's admiration. Elen was a bloody good driver – not that he would ever tell her that.

'Then how are we going to get there?' he moaned. 'I can't call out the lifeboat. The crew won't appreciate being used as a water-taxi service.'

'We'll just have to commandeer another boat,' said Elen.

'Commandeer? What are we, pirates now?'

British police did have the right to requisition a vessel if there was a threat to life, but that was an extreme measure and Rhodri was sure there was a better way. And then it came to him.

He picked up his phone again and dialled a different number. This time, it was answered after a single ring.

'Rhodri, mate, how's it going?'

'All right, Jon. Listen–'

'You're not pulling out of curry night, are you? It's all arranged with the lads.'

'No, no, nothing like that,' said Rhodri quickly. 'Listen, Jon, about that new speedboat of yours. You offered to give me a ride.'

'Sure. How about tomorrow or–'

'How about today,' cut in Rhodri. 'How about you meet me at the harbour in ten minutes?'

★

'Walk with me,' said Father Anselm. He set off slowly across the cobbled floor of St Illtud's, his stick clicking on the stones as he went. At the first station of the cross near the door to the church, he stopped to catch his breath. The small bronze relief on a plain wooden cross depicted Jesus being condemned to death by Pontius Pilate. Was the abbot likening Carys to the notorious Roman governor? Or did Anselm see himself as judge and executioner of Novice Thomas? Whatever his intentions, Carys seriously doubted that the old man would ever stand trial for his crime. Besides, he clearly had no interest in justifying his actions to a secular court. He answered only to a higher authority.

'Thomas came to me after Nia's death and asked me to hear his confession,' said the abbot. 'He was very upset, yet I had no idea what he was about to tell me.'

'You hadn't suspected him of being the murderer?'

'Certainly not. Thomas was a devout novice, one of the most dedicated to the monastic life I have ever known. He wanted nothing more than to become a monk and devote his life to the abbey.' They had moved on to the second station now – Jesus struggling as he carried the cross. Anselm studied it with tired eyes. 'And yet the burden he bore was too heavy.'

It was clear, too, that the burden Father Anselm carried was also too great for his tired shoulders to bear. It had not taken much prompting to persuade him to open up.

'I'm listening,' said Carys.

'Thomas admitted to me that before he became a novice, he led a very different life. He was embroiled in crime and took part in a jewellery robbery. That ended when his getaway car killed an innocent pedestrian.' They were now standing by the third station of the cross – Jesus falls the first time. Father Anselm took a deep breath before continuing. 'His accomplice was caught and sent to prison, but Thomas fled the scene. In the years that followed, he repented of his crime, turned to God and came to the monastery. He set his heart on becoming a monk. But everything changed when the latest batch of retreatants arrived on the island last week.'

'He recognised his partner-in-crime, Rick Styles,' said Carys. 'And also Veronica Emmett, the sister of the man who was killed in the getaway.'

'You must understand that until Thomas's confession, I knew nothing of this,' said Anselm. 'Thomas kept it a secret, fearing that if it became known, he would be forbidden from taking his vows.'

Carys nodded. She could believe that Thomas, just like Rick, had been genuinely remorseful and had sought to put his past behind him. But unlike Rick, he had avoided paying the price for his actions and had therefore been unable to escape his wrongdoings. In order to receive absolution, it was first necessary to show contrition and to accept penance.

'Thomas was collecting letters from the post office when he ran into Veronica Emmett,' explained Father Anselm. 'He told me that he recognised her at once and realised that she could ruin everything. So he lured her to the church on Sunday evening and killed her there. He sought to disguise her murder as the inexplicable actions of a lunatic.'

'The laying out of her body on the altar,' said Carys. 'The presence of the bloodstained Bible.'

Anselm's lips trembled and his fingers gripped his stick tightly. 'You can understand the horror I felt when he revealed this to me.'

'Naturally.'

They continued their slow progress around the church in silence for a while, passing the fourth, fifth and sixth stations, until they were standing before the seventh station – Jesus falls the second time.

The abbot resumed his slow, deliberate telling of his

tale. 'Yet Thomas had not learned his lesson – that past sins catch up with you if they are not acknowledged. His accomplice in the robbery, Rick, realised that Thomas had killed Veronica, and sought to persuade him to go to the police. But Thomas refused to contemplate that course of action. He was fixated on joining the monastery. And so Rick was drowned in the fishpond for his efforts.'

They came to the eighth station of the cross – Jesus meets the women of Jerusalem. The abbot paused before speaking again. 'Thomas would, I believe, have stopped then. He had killed the only two people who could connect him to his past. But Nia, our postmistress, had seen him at the pond with Rick and decided to turn her knowledge to her advantage.' He shook his head sadly. 'She was a latter-day Eve if ever there was one.'

Carys pursed her lips. 'And so she had to be silenced too.' They were now by the ninth station – Jesus falls the third time.

'Thomas laid his soul bare before me,' said the abbot, contemplating the tenth station – Jesus is stripped of his garments. 'And begged for my forgiveness.'

'Your spiritual duty,' said Carys, 'which you have now broken by speaking to me, was to keep Thomas's confession a secret. But you should also have insisted that he could not be reconciled with God unless he handed himself over to the police and admitted his crimes.'

The abbot hung his head and shuffled past the eleventh station – Jesus is nailed to the cross. 'That, as you say, was my duty. Yet as abbot, it was my duty to rid the monastery of the evil that had taken root here.'

'You poisoned him,' said Carys simply. They stood now before the twelfth station – Jesus dies on the cross.

She contemplated the simple bronze image before her. It depicted the suffering of Christ in his dying moments, still putting the needs of others before his own by entrusting the care of his mother, Mary, to his disciple, John. Was that how the abbot imagined himself?

'In Paul's first letter to the Corinthians,' said Anselm,

'he writes: *Put away the evil one from among yourselves*.'

Carys turned sharply to face him. 'And in St Matthew's Gospel, the devil misquotes scripture to suit his own purposes.'

The abbot stared at her with an expression of loathing. His voice, when it came, was a hoarse whisper. 'Are you comparing me to Satan? What you think is of no consequence!'

He lifted his right arm, his teeth bared in anger, his bony fingers white around the walking stick. He was an old man, frail and unsteady, yet he swung the stick with the power of St Michael wielding the sword.

Carys raised a protective arm and stepped aside, but her foot caught on a cobble. She cried out in pain as her ankle twisted and her leg buckled under her. When the blow came, she was powerless to break its force. It struck her on the side of the head and she fell backwards, hitting her head against the hard stone floor.

The medieval roof of the church spun in her vision and the last thing she saw before everything went black was the fourteenth and final station of the cross – Jesus is laid in the tomb.

CHAPTER 47

The boat barely touched the water. Rather, it seemed to skim its surface, kissing the waves briefly before taking flight again.

It was bumpy, though. Bloody hell.

Rhodri loved it, but Elen screamed the whole way.

As arranged, Jon Jenkins had met them at Tenby harbour, keen to show off his new toy. When Rhodri had explained the need to get to Caldey Island as quickly as possible, a broad grin had stretched across Jon's face. 'Quickly, you say?'

A journey that would have taken half an hour in Eifion's slow boat was going to take about five minutes in Jon's.

The boat crested a huge wave, kicking up a spray of white foam, and Elen screamed louder than ever.

'This is epic!' shouted Rhodri over the din of the twin outboards. He dreaded to think how much a boat like this cost to buy, but it seemed churlish to ask, given how readily Jon had offered his services. Even the running costs must be enormous – those twin outboards must drink fuel faster than the lads could put away their first beer on curry night.

Jon expertly brought the boat into land at Priory Bay,

docking behind Eifion's boat at the jetty. Rhodri and Elen stepped ashore, Rhodri with a spring in his stride, Elen looking as if she were about to empty her stomach.

'You want me to wait for you, Rod?' Jon asked.

'No need, mate. We can get a lift back with Eifion.'

'See you tonight, then,' Jon called as he turned the boat around and sped away.

Rhodri put a steadying arm around Elen's shoulder. 'You all right, girl?'

Her face looked green, but she gave a brave nod. 'I'll be okay.'

'Right then, come on.' He set off at a run up the path, Elen struggling to keep up. They ran into Sister Monica crossing the village green.

'Have you seen DI Morgan?' panted Rhodri.

'Try St Illtud's,' said the nun. 'She went there to speak to the abbot.'

'The abbot?' Rhodri and Elen exchanged a glance, then set off, Rhodri cursing under his breath as they went.

★

Carys and Esme run together into the water. They are holding hands. A wave washes over their bare legs, then pulls back, sucking them with it. Their heels sink into the wet sand and they laugh. Another wave comes, stronger this time and reaching their thighs, splashing cold water over their swimming costumes. They shriek with delight.

'Carys, Esme, time for tea!' Their nan is calling to them from the beach.

They wave at her, pleading for five more minutes.

Nan holds up two fingers in compromise. Two minutes longer. They jump and splash in the water.

Soon, Nan is calling again.

'Carys! Esme!' But her voice is further away. The tide has come in, covering the sand, and the shore is a long way off now.

Carys feels the water rising. It covers her waist, her chest, her neck. Esme's hand slips out of hers. And then her feet can no longer touch the bottom. She's under the water. It's over her head. It's filling her nose. She struggles for the surface, but the weight of her body drags her down. She needs air, but now there's only water. Her lungs are burning and she opens her mouth, gasping for life.

'Carys!'

She opened her eyes with a start, the light too bright and momentarily blinding her with its intensity. Blinking, she tried again, allowing her vision to adjust slowly to her surroundings. She was still in the church, the hard, cold cobbles of the floor pressing into her back, the Ogham Stone standing tall over her like a headstone. A candle burned on the altar, and as she tilted her head, the colours from a stained-glass window filtered into view like a rainbow after a storm. She tried to sit up but her head ached like the devil.

Rhodri and Elen were leaning over her. 'Careful, boss,' said Rhodri. 'You're bleeding.'

Carys reached a hand behind her head and her palm came away slick with blood. 'I'll be all right. It's a scratch. Help me up.'

Rhodri looked doubtful but helped her to sit.

'Take it easy,' said Elen. 'You've been injured. You should stay here until we can get that head wound looked at properly.'

'No,' said Carys. 'I need to get up.' With the help of the two of them, she struggled to her feet, steadying herself against the stone wall as she tested her balance.

'What happened?' asked Elen.

'Father Anselm hit me with his stick.' Carys scanned the church for the abbot, but he had vanished. 'Where's he gone? He killed Thomas, after Thomas killed the others.'

'We know,' said Rhodri. 'But we've just come from the village, so we'd have seen him if he returned to the abbey. He must have gone in the opposite direction.'

Carys nodded. 'Towards the lighthouse.'

The abbot's intentions were clear in her mind. With

only days to live, he feared nothing except further damage to the reputation of the monastery. It was bad enough that one of the monks had been shown to be a murderer. Father Anselm would do anything to avoid being charged with murder himself.

She set off, her skull throbbing as she made her way towards the exit. 'Come on,' she urged the others. 'We have to stop him.'

★

Every aged muscle in his body protested at the effort it was being forced to make, but Father Anselm pressed onwards, hobbling along the rough track with the aid of his stick. Pain and suffering meant nothing now. Soon his agony would be at an end.

He felt as Jesus must have felt carrying the cross to Calvary. *The place of the skull.* Just a few more yards. The white tower of the lighthouse rose to meet him, beckoning him on. Its light was a beacon, warning ships of the treacherous cliffs and the rocks beneath them. And a beacon of a different kind, guiding the abbot to his final resting place.

He had made mistakes. He saw that now. Grave errors of judgement, and perhaps he was about to make another one. But he was not a well man, and the drugs that the doctors had given him had clouded his mind. Yet his heart remained true, and he had only ever acted in what he believed to be the best interests of the monastery.

Whether he had done right or wrong, that would be for God to judge. He had no intention of submitting himself before a human court of law.

'Father Anselm! Stop!' They were calling to him, but he didn't slow down, didn't even turn his head to look.

The wind gusted as he lurched past the lighthouse and approached the cliff edge. The elements were testing him. Testing his resolve. But he would not be beaten.

'Father Anselm!'

The forces of the law – the law of men – were closing on him, closing in rapidly. Yet he was close to his destination, close to the edge of the only world he had known for over forty years.

Sea and sky filled his vision – birds soaring high above, seals on the rocks far below.

'God, give me strength!' he cried aloud.

And, as if his prayer had been answered, the clouds parted and a ray of sunlight broke through.

The end of the world was nigh.

*

'Stop!' Rhodri's chest was burning, but it was down to him now. Elen was fast enough at short sprints, especially ones that ended with her hurling herself at someone and dragging them to the ground in a rugby tackle, but she wasn't built for distance, and they had long since left Carys behind – she should never even have left the church with that head injury.

The chase had begun with the tiny figure of the abbot hobbling along in the distance. Now, the old man was right at the cliff edge and he juddered to a halt, turning to face Rhodri. He held out his arms, white robes billowing in the wind, his walking stick raised in one hand like an Old Testament prophet brandishing a staff.

Rhodri stopped in his tracks, afraid to get any closer in case he spooked the abbot. 'Now, don't do anything stupid,' he called. 'Step away from the edge, please, Father Anselm.'

But the abbot showed no intention of complying.

His eyes were wild with defiance, or perhaps with the strange exultation of a man who had already crossed a threshold and wasn't coming back. His robes whipped about him like a shroud, and his mouth worked soundlessly, as if conversing with some presence Rhodri couldn't see.

The abbot staggered as the wind buffeted his frail form,

urging him closer to the edge. A loose pebble slipped and vanished into the void. The old man's shoulders rose and fell, his fragile knuckles grasping the stick. One wrong move and he'd go over.

'It doesn't have to end like this,' Rhodri managed, his breath raw in his throat.

But the abbot showed no sign of hearing him. 'By his own strength shall no man prevail!' he cried. Then he toppled backwards.

Rhodri lunged forward to grab him, but he was too slow. His hands closed on thin air as the abbot disappeared over the edge of the cliff. There was a brief, terrible emptiness, then nothing but the crash of waves far below.

CHAPTER 48

Rhodri had only just made it back to Tenby in time. He was going to have to hurry to catch the lads down the pub before they moved on to the curry house. But they would understand why he was late when they heard what a rollercoaster of a day he'd had. First, the triumph of discovering that the fourth Bible belonged to the abbot, then the high-speed crossing to the island in Jon's boat, and finally the tragic clifftop ending that he'd been unable to prevent despite his best efforts.

Boy, did he need a beer.

Arriving home, he took the stairs two at a time and burst into the bedroom to find Amy all dressed up and putting the finishing touches to her hair and makeup. He stared at her in amazement. He had no idea where she was going, but wherever it was she looked stunning.

She breathed a sigh of relief when she saw him. 'There you are, Rod! Hurry up and get changed. The table's booked for seven.'

He had the good sense to stop and think before he opened his mouth. He didn't know how he'd screwed up, only that he had. If he said anything now, it would be the wrong thing.

Amy glared at him. 'You forgot, didn't you?'

'I, er…'

'Our first date anniversary dinner, Rod! I reminded you this morning.'

The morning chaos in the kitchen felt like an age ago now. The spilt milk, the projectile porridge, the urgent call from Carys. It was hardly his fault that he'd forgotten the anniversary dinner.

It wasn't even a proper anniversary.

Still, Amy wouldn't see it that way.

The fact was, he'd double-booked. Curry with the boys. Dinner with his wife.

Shit.

'No probs,' he said. 'Just give me five minutes.'

He had no time for a shower but gave himself a quick freshen-up before changing into smart jeans and a clean shirt. In the bathroom, he surreptitiously texted Jon.

Sorry, mate. Can't do tonight. Something's come up. Boat was fantastic. I owe you one.

He hated letting his best friend down – especially after Jon had come to the rescue with the speedboat – but what else could he do? Mates were mates, but his wife would always come first.

At seven on the dot, he and Amy were sitting at their table in the restaurant. In the subdued lighting, with her dress and everything, she looked incredible. He could hardly believe he was married to such a beautiful woman. 'You look gorgeous,' he told her, making sure he stopped there and didn't add *for a mother of two.*

'Thanks, Rod. You look great too.'

Rhodri smiled. With the kids parked at his mother-in-law's tonight, he reckoned sex was definitely on the dessert menu.

When the waiter came to ask what they wanted to drink, Rhodri ordered a beer.

'Sparkling water for me, please,' said Amy.

'Water?' he queried once the waiter had gone. 'Are you

feeling all right?' Amy always had white wine when she went out.

'I'm feeling fabulous.' She reached across the table and cupped his hand with hers, her eyes glistening. 'Rhodri, I have some exciting news.'

'What?'

She gave him her prettiest smile – the one guaranteed to melt his heart. 'I'm pregnant.'

He blinked. Had he heard that right?

'Well?' she asked tentatively. 'Aren't you going to say something?'

There was only one thing to say. 'That's wonderful news, Amy! I'm just surprised, that's all.' He leaned across the table and kissed her on the lips.

Surprised didn't really begin to cover it. *Spooked, rattled, caught off-guard*. These were closer to how he felt. *Freaked-out, panicked, brain completely scrambled*. Yeah, that was more like it.

The waiter returned to take their orders.

Rhodri buried his head in the menu but the words swam before his eyes.

A third child? They could barely handle the two they already had. And where would the baby sleep? Amy would be wanting a bigger house.

Then the penny dropped. All those Instagram kitchens, all the time she'd been spending on property websites. She was already making plans to move.

But how were they going to afford it?

His own plans began to unravel before his eyes. No more surfing. No more beer and curry. Instead, he would have to put in more overtime, there would be sleepless nights and dirty nappies and endless laundry. He began scouring the menu for the cheapest item but even the fish pie was twenty-five quid.

He could have cried. Or laughed. Or both.

Three kids. God help him.

Amy squeezed his hand, her smile so bright it lifted him straight out of his doom spiral. 'I know it's a lot to take on board, Rod. I didn't plan for this to happen. But we'll work it out. We always do. And you know what? You're going to be an amazing dad. Again.'

The tightness in his chest loosened, and the sense of panic receded. Not completely, but enough for him to breathe. Amy was right. As always, she was right.

He pictured their future, the five of them together, knowing that babies didn't stay babies for long. One day, he would have his own little crew on the beach, tiny wetsuits and boards, and he would look back on this moment and smile.

Because life was a wave and the only way to live it was to ride it, and let it take you where it would.

CHAPTER 49

Two weeks later

The election of a new abbot was a significant event in the affairs of a monastery and was governed by traditions that sought to ensure a stable and orderly transition of power. Only monks who had made their solemn vows were eligible to stand and vote in the election. The process was both administrative and spiritual, and – in order to ensure fairness and propriety – was overseen by a visitor from outside the monastery. For this election, Dom Pierre had travelled to Caldey to fulfil the role. A tall, slender man, his back bent from years of prayer, he carried the quiet authority of a man long trusted to do the right thing.

A period of *sede vacante* had elapsed, allowing the monks the opportunity to give careful consideration to their choices, and on this morning, they were summoned by the bell to the Chapter House. Once all were assembled, Dom Pierre began by conducting a short Mass and then exhorted them to spend as much time as they needed in silent prayer.

Brother Gregory sat in stillness, allowing his mind to become open and his choice to be guided by God. Father Anselm had been a good abbot – until those final days when he had perhaps not been of sound mind – and it would be hard for another to take on his burden. If chosen, Gregory would do his best to act as head of the household, but if another were selected, he would gladly submit to their authority.

Eventually it was time for the votes to be cast.

Each monk wrote down the name of the one he believed God was calling to be abbot.

It didn't take long for Dom Pierre to count the votes. The result was unanimous.

Everyone had voted for Brother Gregory – except Brother Gregory, of course, who had magnanimously voted for Brother Cadoc.

Gregory rose to his feet and went to accept the blessing of Dom Pierre, who confirmed his appointment as the new abbot of Caldey. The other monks lined up and, one by one, offered Father Gregory – as he was now to be called – the kiss of peace.

As Brother Cadoc knelt before him, Father Gregory leaned forward. 'Go in peace, my brother.'

Cadoc bowed his head in obedience.

The two monks had reconciled with each other the previous day. Cadoc had confessed to his sins of the flesh and his failings in the governance of St Philomena's. Sister Monica, in turn, had confessed to the financial irregularities of which she had been guilty. Gregory had forgiven them both. Everyone deserved a second chance.

Patrick Mulholland had been so grateful for the help that Gregory had given him that he had agreed to stay on and help in the kitchen, taking over the duties of Novice Thomas. Father Gregory hoped that soon Pat would feel called to take his monastic vows and become a fully-fledged monk. He was the lost sheep welcomed back into the fold, and their hope for the future.

The monastery had been through difficult times in

recent weeks, and no doubt there would be rough waters to navigate as the community faced up to the evil that had taken root within it. Gregory was glad that Brother Cadoc would be at his side to help steer him through that storm.

For now, there was one thing the new abbot was certain of – the monastery on Caldey would endure for years to come.

*

Two weeks had passed since Father Anselm had flung himself off the cliff at Caldey Island. Or stumbled and fallen, depending on which version of events you chose to believe. His body had been washed out to sea, eventually being recovered by the lifeboat. He had escaped standing trial for his crime. Now God would have the final word.

Carys had spent those two weeks in an endless round of interviews with a senior officer from Professional Standards, going over what had happened on that final day of the investigation. Why had she confronted the abbot alone? Why hadn't she informed her colleagues of her intentions? What might she have done to ensure a different outcome?

Fortunately, she had the abbot's full confession recorded on her phone, as well as Rhodri and Elen to back her up. The inquiry had eventually concluded that there was nothing she could have done to prevent the abbot's death.

Now she finally had a day off and knew precisely what she was going to do. She woke later than usual, without an alarm, and slid out of bed, enjoying the freedom to set her own pace for once. The morning was chilly but dry and bright – perfect weather for getting jobs done. She began with small tasks. Sweeping crumbs from the kitchen floor. Kneading dough for bread and leaving it on the warm range to rise. Darning socks with needle and thread. Then she went outside.

The garden was long-neglected and past its best, but

there were still berries to gather and herbs to harvest. Carys filled a small bowl with blackberries, then picked some nettles, using gloves to protect her hands from the stinging leaves. These late-season nettles made strong, bitter tea, rich in iron and other minerals, very fortifying for the dark months ahead. She also picked some purple asters and bright pink sedum and placed them in a small wicker basket.

She returned to the kitchen, inhaling deeply and enjoying the pungent aroma of the rising dough. Then, putting aside the berries and nettles for later, she headed back out, this time leaving the cottage garden behind and striding into the village. There were few pavements – and few cars – in Manorbier and she walked down the middle of the road. The castle was open to visitors today and she went inside, passing over the wooden drawbridge and beneath the great stone entrance arch. Once inside the inner ward, she climbed the steep steps of the gatehouse tower all the way to the rooftop and looked out.

In one direction lay a lush, wooded valley. In the other, the sparkling blue of the sea. Over her head, the red dragon flag of Wales snapped in the breeze. There was a world here. Not a large one, but one familiar and safe, and Carys knew she had made the right decision to leave Cardiff. She removed her beret, shaking out her long black hair and letting it billow in the wind. Then she breathed, tasting the sharp, clean bite of sea air on her tongue.

This is what freedom tastes like.

Unable to suppress a smile, she descended the spiral staircase and set off back up the hill in the direction of St James the Great. On the way she spotted a vehicle pulling up at the side of the road and braced herself for another encounter. It was unavoidable in such a small community, and she might as well get used to it.

It was a Ford Ranger pickup with camping gas cylinders packed into its open back. The door opened and Dan stepped out, wearing shorts over lightly tanned legs. He nodded at her in greeting. 'Hi, Carys. Taking a day off, are you?'

'I've been busy recently.'

'So I heard. The mad monks of Caldey.'

She grinned. 'Something like that.'

He dipped his chin in that old familiar way and she could tell there was something on his mind. 'So,' he said at last, 'You've decided to stay?'

She shrugged her shoulders noncommittally. 'For now.'

He gave her a tentative smile and brushed an unruly lock of blond hair from his eyes. 'That's good. Then... maybe we could meet up for a coffee?'

So, that was his game. 'You know I don't drink coffee.'

'Tea, then.'

'I'll let you know, Dan.'

She set off again, leaving him behind, half of her curious and wanting to accept his offer, the other half afraid of where that might lead.

Nowhere good, Carys, keep on walking.

She carried on, the road steepening as it climbed the hill. At the end of the road, she entered the churchyard.

The autumn equinox was long past and the sun hung low in the sky, throwing long shadows of crosses across the short grass. Carys picked her way between the graves, stopping before the simple headstone she had come to visit.

Olwyn Morgan and Esme Morgan
Beloved Grandmother
Devoted Sister and Granddaughter
Rest in Peace

There was no one else around, and Carys stood alone. A familiar feeling.

Everyone leaves me, sooner or later.

First, her father had gone – even before her birth. Then she had lost her mother, then her grandmother, and now her sister.

They're all gone.

But Carys hadn't come here to mope about the past. She had come to look to the future.

She knelt to arrange the flowers she had brought in the basket.

'There you go, Nan. Flowers from your garden. These might be the last for a while, mind. Winter's on its way.'

She stood back to admire the small display of colour. Pink and purple against the grey stone. In the October sun, they seemed to glow.

'I don't know why I'm talking to you, Nan. You're not here.'

The Celts believed that when a person died, they journeyed to the Otherworld, and Carys was certain that Nan's soul no longer remained beneath this cold earth. The Celts had buried their dead with grave goods that might be useful in the afterlife, and Carys had insisted that the undertaker place one of Nan's favourite cooking pots in the coffin with her.

She smiled.

In Esme's case, Carys had not offered any items for burial. For while there were many things Carys didn't know – like where her mother had gone – there was one fact of which she was absolutely certain. Whoever was buried in this grave alongside her grandmother, it wasn't Esme.

The corpse that Carys had identified as her sister had shown enough resemblance to fool the police, but Carys had known as soon as the blue sheet was lifted from the woman's face in the mortuary that it wasn't Esme.

Esme wasn't even dead.

I need you, Carys. I'm so scared.

I got involved with some bad people. Now they're coming after me.

I'm going to disappear, but I need your help.

Carys hadn't yet tracked down those bad people. Nor

had she identified the woman who had drowned in the sea off Manorbier. But Esme's desire to vanish and the fact that she had engineered her disappearance – with Carys's help – were beyond doubt. But where was she now?

Carys didn't know. Yet.

'Nothing's ever quite as it seems, eh, Nan? But don't worry, I'm going to find her.'

Carys turned and set off back down the hill to the cottage. The dough would be ready for the oven now, and those nettles were waiting to be brewed. Later, she might turn the blackberries into jam. There was plenty for her to do.

THE HOUSE OF SILENT BONES (CARYS MORGAN #2)

The truth won't stay buried.

When a builder dismantles a crumbling wall in the cellar of a grand seafront house in Tenby, the last thing he expects to find is a human skeleton. The remains belong to a young man who vanished on Hallowe'en night, 1995.

As Detective Inspector Carys Morgan unpicks the lies woven by a tight-knit group of former schoolfriends – a lawyer, a hotelier, a football coach, a chef and a gardener – she uncovers a web of guilt, complicity, and self-preservation that has bound them together for three decades. All of them knew the victim. None of them is telling the truth.

As Hallowe'en approaches once again, Carys realises this isn't just a cold case. Someone is willing to kill to protect their secrets.

The House of Silent Bones is the second book in the gripping Pembrokeshire crime series – where ancient faith meets modern evil on the wild Welsh coast.

THANK YOU FOR READING

We hope you enjoyed this book. If you did, then we would be very grateful if you would please take a moment to leave a review online. Thank you.

CARYS MORGAN SERIES

Carys Morgan® is a registered trademark of Landmark Internet Ltd.
The Caldey Island Murders (Carys Morgan #1)
The House of Silent Bones (Carys Morgan #2)

TOM RAVEN SERIES

Tom Raven® is a registered trademark of Landmark Internet Ltd.
The Landscape of Death (Tom Raven #1)
Beneath Cold Earth (Tom Raven #2)
The Dying of the Year (Tom Raven #3)
Deep into that Darkness (Tom Raven #4)
Days Like Shadows Pass (Tom Raven #5)
Vigil for the Dead (Tom Raven #6)
Stained with Blood (Tom Raven #7)
The Foaming Deep (Tom Raven #8)
A Dying Echo (Tom Raven #9)
The Raven's Call (Tom Raven #10)

BRIDGET HART SERIES

Bridget Hart® is a registered trademark of Landmark Internet Ltd.
Aspire to Die (Bridget Hart #1)
Killing by Numbers (Bridget Hart #2)
Do No Evil (Bridget Hart #3)
In Love and Murder (Bridget Hart #4)
A Darkly Shining Star (Bridget Hart #5)
Preface to Murder (Bridget Hart #6)
Toll for the Dead (Bridget Hart #7)

ABOUT THE AUTHOR

M S Morris is the pen name of husband-and-wife writing duo Margarita and Steve Morris, authors of gripping crime fiction. Margarita comes from Yorkshire and Steve from Wales, and they met and got married at Oxford University. Now living far from their native landscapes, they often return to them through their writing, creating compelling mysteries shaped by places they know intimately and love deeply.

Find out more at msmorrisbooks.com where you can join our mailing list, or follow us on Facebook at facebook.com/msmorrisbooks.

www.ingramcontent.com/pod-product-compliance
Lightning Source LLC
Chambersburg PA
CBHW020912060726
47591CB00004B/1205